D1202879

MODERN SPACE ADVENTURES CRAFTED IN THE GRAND TRADITION

"Daring adventure, protagonists who think on their feet, and out of this world excitement! Welcome to FAR ORBIT, a fine collection of stories in the best SF tradition. Strap in and enjoy!"
   —Julie E. Czerneda, author of *Species Imperative*

"Successfully captures the kinds of stories that were the gateway drugs for many of us who have been reading science fiction for a long time. Well done!"
   —Tangent

FAR ORBIT

Speculative Space Adventures

Edited by

BASCOMB JAMES

World Weaver Press

FAR ORBIT: SPECULATIVE SPACE ADVENTURES
Copyright © 2014 Bascomb James

All rights reserved.

This is a work of fiction; characters and events are either fictitious or used fictitiously.

"Dear Speculative Fiction, I'm Glad We Had This Talk" Copyright © 2012 Elizabeth Bear. Originally published in *Clarkesworld*.
"Open for Business" Copyright © 2014 Sam S. Kepfield.
"Composition in Death Minor" Copyright © 2014 Kevin G. Jewell.
"Spaceman Barbecue" Copyright © 2014 Peter Wood.
"Obsidianite" Copyright © 2014 Kat Otis.
"Starship Down" Copyright © 2008 Tracy Canfield. Originally published in *Analog*.
"Backscatter" Copyright © 2013 Gregory Benford. Originally published in *Tor.com*.
"A Game of Hold'em" Copyright © 2014 Wendy Sparrow.
"From a Stone" Copyright © 1996 Eric Choi. Originally published in *Science Fiction Age*.
"Charnelhouse" Copyright © 2014 Jonathan Shipley.
"Bear Essentials" Copyright © 2014 Julie Frost.
"The Vringla/Racket Incident" Copyright © 2014 Jakob Nexø Drud.
"A Trip to Lagasy" Copyright © 2014 Barbara Davies.
"Saturn Slingshot" Copyright © 2014 David Wesley Hill.

Published by World Weaver Press
Alpena, Michigan
www.WorldWeaverPress.com

Cover designed by World Weaver Press
Cover image: Cepheus B, shot by Chandra X-ray Observatory, Spitzer Space Telescope, used courtesy NASA/JPL-Caltech.

First Edition: April 2014

ISBN: 978-0615959245
ISBN-13: 0615959245

Also available as an ebook.

FAR ORBIT

"We began as wanderers
and we are wanderers still…"

Carl Sagan

FAR ORBIT

Dear Speculative Fiction, I'm Glad We Had This Talk

An Open Letter to SF

Elizabeth Bear

Look.

I'm sitting down to have this conversation with you as a friend, as somebody who loves you. As somebody who's devoted thirty-odd years of her life to you.

We've all made some mistakes. We've all had moments in our lives when we got a little self-important, maybe. Where our senses of humor failed us.

I'm as guilty as anyone of taking myself too seriously.

But for you, it's become an addiction. You seem to think that nothing fun can have value; that only grimdark portentousness and dystopia mean anything. You wallow in human suffering and despair, and frankly—it makes me tired.

I remember when we were younger. You were so clever, so playful. So much fun. We had some good times. You could make me laugh and think at the same time. You made my pulse race.

But we got older and started understanding a little better how complicated the world is. How layered people's motivations are. At first, you seemed to handle the moral complexity well. You'd give me something like *The Forever War* or *The Left Hand of Darkness*, and we could talk about it for hours.

I mean, I sensed your ambivalence. But I had some ambivalence of my own. That's the thing about ambivalence—it's a kind of tension. And tension drives a narrative, right?

And I don't know if you got uncomfortable with the tension? Maybe you felt like you couldn't live in limbo anymore, but you'd seen too much to believe in happy endings anymore. I'm guessing, I admit—but I wonder if you felt like had to find some way to resolve things. Get some closure. And escapism . . . just wasn't open to you any more.

You started thinking you had to be cynical and mean to accomplish anything. You got wrapped up in your own history and your long-running arguments. You buried yourself in the seriousness of it all, and you forgot how to tell a joke. You even got—I hate to say it—kind of pretentious. Didactic, even.

The thing is, that kind of cynical pose is really just a juvenile reaction to the world not being what we hoped. We can't have everything—so we reject anything. But it's adolescent, darling, and most of us outgrow it. We realize that as much as the world can be a ball of dung, and horrible things can happen for no reason, there are positive outcomes too, sometimes. I'm not going to say things balance out, because of course they don't—life is not fair—but it's not just awful, either.

I'm not crying out for slapstick, here. You know that's never done it for me. And I'm certainly not saying that I want you to be shallower.

If anything, I'm asking you to be deeper—to embrace more of the range of human experience. Not just the bad times. I mean, sure, we need to acknowledge the bad times, and I've deeply admired your recent willingness to explore new perspectives, to take on issues of race and gender and sexuality that once you would have shied from.

I have never doubted your courage.

But look at Terry Pratchett. (I know, we should all be Terry Pratchett. But then what would *he* read?) He manages to be incisive without being pretentious. He manages to be sharp and illuminating *by* being funny. Look at Neil Gaiman. Here's a guy who can tackle some hard subjects and still have a good time. He makes people like him, and because they like him, they listen when he says hard, important things.

I almost hate to bring it up, but . . . J.K. Rowling? I know, you don't take her seriously. She's a woman, and she writes for kids, and in fairness some of the later books . . . could have used a closer encounter with the blue pencil. So it's easy for you to dismiss her. But what you can't dismiss is that she reaches people—and whether you agree with the way she discusses issues like class bigotry or not, the fact is, she does discuss them. Her awareness of them saturates her work, and it gets into people's heads—because millions of people *read* her work.

I guess what I'm saying here is, look at Lenny Bruce. Look at George Carlin. The angrier they got, the less fun they got—and the less effective they got, because nobody wants to listen to an old man cat-yell at the kids on his lawn.

Oh, honey, I'm not saying you're old. And I'm not leaving you. You're a big part of my life, and I will always be here for you. I'm just trying to make sure that you're always here for *me*, and sitting there in a toxic stew of your own bitterness . . . it's not good for you. *Look* at you. When was the last time you left the house? When was the last time you read something because it was *fun*, not because you thought it was good for you?

Stern-lipped moral uprightness is not a literary value, darling. Sure, theme is. I'm not disputing that. But did you know that John Gardner talked about this thing he called "disPollyanna Syndrome?" He considered it a literary vice—the cynical fallacy that the real world is unrelievedly bleak—and he considered it as great a disservice to art as its opposite. And . . . he cited Harlan Ellison as a chief practitioner in this mode.

Oh, I heard you gasp. But the New Wave is one of the primary influences on the way we live our life and do our work today. And also, I hear you say, Harlan was popular! And funny!

Well, yes, he was funny. That's why he got away with it. But you? I feel like all we have anymore is pus and severed limbs and the eschaton. And that's not something we can build a future on, is it?

Kind of by definition.

I'm just saying that it's right—and humane and morally correct—to harbor a deep and abiding concern for the world around you. And that it's a perfectly normal—even laudable!—trait to express that concern and draw attention to problems by being savagely trenchant, witty, and sarcastic. Caustic, even. I want you to speak out. I want you to say what you mean.

But sometimes lately, spending time with you is like having my face pressed down into a trough of human misery until the bubbles stop.

You can have a sense of humor too. It's *okay*. We'll *still like you*. We'll still take you seriously. We just think it'd be best for all of us if you could let yourself unbend just a little.

I know. It's easier to get people to take you seriously when you're all grit and pus and urban decay—or all gut wounds and bureaucratic incompetence, for that matter. It seems like a quick route to street cred. But the thing is, real people generally aren't miserable all the time. Even in horrible situations, they find ways to take a little pleasure, to crack jokes. Dying people and homicide cops and soldiers are generally really funny.

I want us to have a little pleasure again too.

And maybe we'd have more friends if you weren't such a downer to be around all the time.

INTRODUCTION

It all started with a letter . . .

Yes, that letter. The letter from Elizabeth Bear. The one published in *Clarkesworld* Issue 68 (May 2012), which we've reprinted in this anthology. Her open letter to Speculative Fiction.

After reading her letter, we could have applauded like many others and blithely wandered off with our hands in our pockets. Instead, we decided to *do* something. This is the result—a new anthology that is fun to read and embodies many of the elements found in classic, Grand Tradition science fiction. In short, we decided to put our money where our heart is.

So what is Grand Tradition science fiction? I am not going to give you the Wikipedia answer, I am giving my answer. Your mileage may vary.

Grand Tradition stories were full of ideas, optimism, inspiration and respect for science. Grand Tradition SF showed us that science was cool. Like many others, I chose a career in science because it was the most exciting thing in my universe. The wonder of discovery; the satisfaction that comes from building new things; and the knowledge that you can make a difference through intellect (or cleverness), hard work and perseverance are heady experiences. There are no magic wands, fairy godpeople, or Miracle Max creations. Grand Tradition stories inspired many of our current technologies and they continue to help scientists understand how these technologies might interact with the real world.

Grand Tradition stories were fun to read. In her open letter to SF,

Elizabeth Bear asks why "[SF seems] to think that nothing fun can have value." I obviously agree with her sentiments. I am sorry to say that a derisive public wrote off Grand Tradition SF as mere escapism—as if escapism was something unsavory. This escapist "dreck" taught me about Dyson Spheres, red-shift, general relativity, and put entire cultures and belief systems under the intellectual microscope. Not too bad for escapist literature.

Grand Tradition stories embodied a sense of adventure and expectation. I realize that adventure is a relative term. One man's adventure may be a normal day to another. *Communicating* this sense of adventure is the important thing. Readers of Grand Tradition stories have a gleeful expectation that interesting things are about to happen; that "normal" events will not remain that way for long.

And finally, the best Grand Tradition stories had a strong human element. Great SF is not just about gizmos and spaceships, it's about us and how we are shaped by, and relate to our environment. Human elements are the Velcro that makes stories stick in our brain. They make them enjoyable, approachable, and memorable.

The stories in this volume embody one or more of these elements.

Far Orbit is truly a labor of love, but no matter how much I express my ardor, it's all about the stories. We endeavored to provide a broad mix of SF stories by established, award-wining authors and newly emerging authors. Their stories embody a variety of SF motifs including those from 1940s pulp-fiction, realistic hard SF, noir fiction, spaceship fiction, alien encounters, and action-adventure. The range of subjects is astonishing and includes slimy alien babysitters, an angry sentient bear, walking plants, alien bunnies, and a barbecue. If that is not enough to pique your interest, the anthology also features a cello-playing assassin, high-stakes poker emancipation, space ship crashes/rescues, alien artifacts, and fights with space pirates. We hope every SF fan can find a favorite within these pages.

So here it is, our latest creation. We obviously want the *Far Orbit* anthology to be successful for financial reasons but just as importantly, we know a successful approach will be emulated by more conservative publishers. The net result could be a future where there is a wider variety of fun, Grand Tradition story choices and story markets—good things in my estimation.

This anthology isn't just about us and our desires; it's also about you, the new SF reader, the SF fan, the aspiring (or established) writer. Let me know what you think of this anthology and where we should go from here. I will be "listening" at: farorbit@worldweaverpress.com.

Bascomb James
Anthologist, Far Orbit: Speculative Space Adventures

OPEN FOR BUSINESS

Sam Kepfield

"Open for Business" could have been ripped from today's headlines. As I write this, humankind has reached a turning point in space exploration—a point where funding for big government space projects is decreasing and private funding for practical, goal-driven business ventures, like the one in this story, is increasing. Recent headlines have touted the successful launch and recovery of SpaceX's commercial launch systems, the onset of space tourism, and Golden Spike's plans for profitable commercial flights to the moon. In contrast with some of these more grandiose space business plans, two companies, Deep Space Industries and Planetary Resources, have announced measured initiatives to begin asteroid prospecting operations using small CubeSats and off-the-shelf technologies. "Open for Business" floats effortlessly on this sea of current events. The story reads like mid-century science fiction of the Grand Tradition, but there is a twist: Rather than following the steely-eyed lead scientist, the author provides a more human approach by telling the story through the point of view of a slightly neurotic attorney.

Sam Kepfield was born in 1963, and raised in western Kansas. He graduated from Kansas State University in 1986, and received his law degree from the University of Nebraska in 1989. He practices law full-time in Hutchinson, Kansas, in order to support his writing habit. His work has appeared in *Science Fiction Trails*, *Aiofe's Kiss*, *The Future Fire*, and a number of anthologies. His first novel, *Magic Man, Gold Dust Woman, and the Dream Machine,* was published in March 2013.

"This is what ten trillion dollars looks like," Terry Raines said. I was into my second beer at Hannigan's, an upscale restaurant in downtown

KC, with several dozen other yuppies. The Power and Light District was a renaissance neighborhood in the 21st century, after falling to the hookers and drug dealers in the 1970s. The lighting was low, the music was soft jazz, the beer was Boulevard (brewed right here in KC), and the food was, of course, barbeque. It was a great venue for a weekend get-together by three old college friends, one flown in from out of state and two others who'd driven up on a Friday afternoon.

"It's a dot," I said, peering at the laptop screen on the table.

"Not just any dot," Terry replied confidently, flashing that toothy Kennedyesque smile.

"What are you up to?" Greg asked Terry over a wheat beer. Greg was tall, with blond hair that he wore long in the back, swept back from a high forehead, a strong, angular face and a body built the old-fashioned way, lugging hay bales on his dad's farm out by the Colorado line. He wore faded jeans and denim shirt, gray Tony Lamas, which was about as dressy as he got at whatever super-secret division he toiled for at Boeing.

"This is Asteroid 2009 BT," he said, pointing to a small light smudge in a starfield. "It's a near-earth asteroid. Makes a loop around every fifteen years or so." Terry worked as a subcontractor to NASA for their near-earth asteroid tracking program.

"How big?" Greg asked.

"A mile in diameter. Classified as stony-iron, meaning it's mainly nickel-iron ore, but with a good amount of precious metals mixed in. Look here," he said, hitting a couple more keys, producing a spectrograph. "Over 75% nickel-iron, but plenty of palladium, titanium, platinum, cobalt and—gold."

"How much?"

"Nickel? About equal to three year's world production. Iron, about the same. Gold—enough to make whoever mines it the fifth largest holder in the solar system. Conservative estimate is ten to fifteen trillion dollars' worth."

"Aaaannnd?" I asked, beginning to see where this was going.

"And it's there for the taking. 2009 BT makes an approach to within 45,000 miles of the Earth in eighteen months. All it needs is a little nudge to put it into orbit."

"So NASA's going to send a mission to intercept it?"

"No," Terry beamed. "We are."

I nearly choked on my baby-back ribs. Terry plowed on after I cleared my windpipe with a beer. "You're insane," I finally gargled out.

"Remember your history classes about the old West? The government did nothing in the West but give peace medals to Indians and catalog plants and animals. They were trying to *hold back* settlement."

"They wanted order," I added. "A sensible policy."

"If you're an Indian. Or a control freak politician who knows a dispersed population is harder to govern. Shay's Rebellion, the Whiskey Rebellion, both of them started with farmers out on the frontier wondering how they'd fought a Revolution and wound up with taxation without representation."

"So?"

"So, William Becknell loaded a wagon train right here in 1821," he thumped the floor with his foot, "at Westport Landing, sent it to Santa Fe, unloaded his goods, hauled more back here, and made a killing. A couple years later, *everyone* was hauling on the Santa Fe Trail. All without a bit of help from the government. After that you get the fur trade, the Oregon Rush, the Gold Rush, the first settlement of the Lousiana Purchase—"

"And Bleeding Kansas," I piped up.

Terry ignored that. "Other than surveying and titling the land, the government didn't have much to do with settlement."

"It cleared out the Indians. And built the railroads," I countered.

"No natives up there," Terry shot back. "NASA doesn't have a monopoly on the Iron Horse anymore."

"And this has to do with a big chunk of rock how?" I asked skeptically.

"Space is the new Old West. We're Becknell. We're the first. It's a wagon train to the stars."

"What about Virgin Atlantic?" Greg asked. They were a couple of years into regular orbital flights to orbital hotels.

"Tourists—phooey! Go on a vacation for a few hours or a couple of days, screw in zero-gee and go back to brag about it. There's no value added. We're going out there to stay, to make money, not just stare at the scenery ooohing and aaahing."

"Just how do you propose to physically accomplish this historic feat?" I asked, thinking it was still a joke.

"That," he announced, "is what we're going to do this weekend. You in?"

It was insanity, even after Terry's explanation, but a very seductive insanity. I was ready to listen to any crazy damned scheme that would get me out of a low-paying public defender position. I was tired of the ingratitude and the long hours.

Terry was in his third postdoc after graduation, a research position at the University of Chicago, working at the Yerkes Observatory. Jobs for astronomers and physicists weren't exactly plentiful, and Terry was getting burned out on moving every couple of years. He wanted security, didn't see it materializing, and was willing to take a risk. He'd been talking this way for a decade, chafed at being held back.

Greg was no problem. He lived for challenges like this, creating a space program on a napkin or placemat. Greg figured out whether he could do it, not whether he should.

We wound up back at Terry's hotel room with a twelve-pack and a lot of wild ideas, Greg's drafting kit and Terry's manic energy.

How does one move an asteroid?

"Nukes?" I began offhandedly. I was a history major, but I'd read plenty of science fiction as a teenager.

"Unless you know some terrorists, buying stray Soviet warheads from Trashcanistan is out. Try again."

"Rocket motor?" Greg said. "Get a large enough booster engine, attach it, fire, and you're in business."

"Know where we can get some?"

"You can get one on the surplus market. But the fuel requirements are huge, so you'd have to include that in the payload. It'd take an Atlas or Proton rocket to put it in orbit."

"Too expensive. Plus paperwork, telling the launch contractor what we're doing, which gives them opportunity to stop us. Or beat us to it. No good."

"An ion drive would be best," Greg continued. "They've got a higher specific impulse, makes them more efficient. A VASIMR or plasma-based drive can use almost anything for propellant. But those are still in the trial stage. And there's one other thing you've overlooked. We need *two* direction changes. One to move it to earth orbit, but first you gotta stop the asteroid's rotation."

"I know that," Terry said impatiently. "Our target has a pretty slow tumble rate."

"Yeah," Greg countered, "but something that big's gonna take a lot of force to stop. And we just ruled out rocket engines."

"Use the asteroid as its own reaction mass," I said. "Like with an ion drive."

"Huh?"

"I read somewhere about moving killer asteroids, you could start venting gases to change orbit."

"That was for carbonaceous chondrites," Terry said. "They're full of water, other organics, easy to outgas. This is solid rock."

"I see where you're going," Greg said to me. "Get a big mirror, focus it at one point on the rock, eventually you start vaporizing the surface, and you've got your own rocket motor. It's definitely doable," Greg said, making marks on a borrowed legal pad. "But how do we get it there in the first place?"

"Yeah," I said, hoping this would close the topic. "I mean, we don't have our own rocket and a launch pad. NASA is booked up solid for years in advance. Same with Arianespace and the Russians and the

Japanese. By which time 2009 BT is long gone."

"And the rates," Greg added, "aren't cheap. NASA's charging a hundred grand a pound on a Titan."

"Let me worry about the money," Terry said. "How much would something like this weigh?"

"Depends," Greg replied. "Big mirror, figure a kilometer across, make it out of Mylar or some other light material, and we'd need some way to spread out the material, or inflate it, and a way to anchor it . . . call it a ton at most."

Terry frowned, deep in thought. "Sorry to bust your balloon, Terry, we tried. No wagons for sale." And I would get to go back to my lousy job. I turned to Greg, and saw him staring ahead, eyes unfocused. "Greg?" I said, but quickly quieted. Back in college, we called it The Trance, when Greg got an idea and devoted his entire brain to solving the problem, everything else shut down. The world could end and he'd never know it. We sat still and quiet for several minutes. Finally he spoke.

"A balloon."

"Huh?" Terry and I said.

"A balloon. That's how you get it into orbit. Lift it up to near-space, say 100,000 feet, cut it loose, a rocket lifts the payload into space. Since you're launching from the edge of the atmosphere you don't need as much fuel, the engines are smaller and more efficient. And cheaper."

Terry's eyes were aglow, as he sat in front of Greg. "How much would we need?"

"Depends. One ton payload?" He began mumbling. "Cube the radius multiply by four-thirds, multiply by twenty-eight two, divide by four-four-eight . . . Get a 100-foot diameter helium balloon, you can lift sixteen tons. More than enough."

Terry began flashing through websites on his laptop. A couple of minutes later, he looked up. "Helium's no problem. The Bureau of Land Management's selling off a bunch from the helium reserve, for

$70 per million cubic feet."

"I got that much in my wallet," I said, instantly hating myself for enabling Terry.

"Okay, that's your share of the investment capital."

"I know where we can get a mirror," Greg said. "The Air Force was running an experiment with space-based mirrors for ground-based lasers, some ABM project that got scrapped."

"So there's unused surplus sitting around," Terry finished eagerly. "Who was contracting it out?"

"I'll make some phone calls Monday."

"And a rocket motor to send it into deep space—" Terry said.

"I can get those, too," Greg said. "More surplus. Lying around from the moon programs that got cancelled."

"More expensive yet," I replied.

"I figure we need five million." Terry sat back, smiled. "It's time to hit up the old man for money."

* * *

Terry Raines majored in physics and astronomy because it fascinated him, but also because he saw a frontier waiting to be opened—and commercially exploited. He needed a working knowledge of finances so any boom wouldn't go bust, at least not immediately. His father was an investment banker. As a seventeen-year old intern, Terry told his dad to dump every last financial and banking stock he had, put every penny into precious metals and wait two-to-four years. His father had laughed, asked how Terry could go against the Street.

As Terry told it, he took an afternoon to show his dad the foolishness of securitized mortgages and credit default swaps and the housing bubble's imminent burst. The bank sold its securities the next week, Raines' *père* unloaded some from personal holdings, put it all into gold, silver, platinum, and waited all of nine months before the stock market and the U.S. economy did a belly flop into a depression.

Then he turned around, began gobbling up the same bank stocks that he had sold at a hundred dollars for a nickel a share and re-sold them for a hefty profit when the economy came roaring back in the late 'teens. He bought gold at $300 an ounce and sold it for $4000 an ounce near the peak in 2017. Whereas before Raines had been upper-class comfortable, he was now, thanks to his son, filthy *nouveau riche*.

Since his old man was more than fixed for life, and Terry figured he was owed for having a hand in it, asking for the money didn't take quite the balls one might think. Terry reminded his old man that if he'd gone on his it's-different-this-time happy-skippy mindset they'd be living in a single-wide in Wyandotte County instead of a Tudor-style spread on a couple hundred acres the wealthiest county in the region. Terry walked out with five million, cash.

I filed incorporation papers with the two hundred dollar fee at the Secretary of State's office in person two days later. I put down a year's rent on a small office in a Wichita office park, used it as a business address, and opened a checking account.

Cosmodyne, Inc. was in business.

* * *

We had a launch window six months away, so things moved quickly. A balloon supplier in Arizona custom-made a hundred-foot diameter balloon for two hundred grand with the rigging and delivered it to a large warehouse that we rented on the edge of KC. Communications equipment and the computers for our mission control were all commercially available, as was the TRAKSAT software.

As for the probe itself, that was a bit harder. Since the early 'teens, a small DIY aerospace industry had sprung up. A couple hundred thousand bought a small rocket engine to propel the probe into deep space and an aeroshell to house the core and the mirror. Greg was, in fact, able to find a surplus laser-reflective mirror at Boeing's Seattle plant, and for a half- million it was ours. We shelled out some more cash for a small shop in Wichita, half-dozen skilled workers, no questions asked or answered, and with Greg supervising the spaceship was done in two months.

Since I spoke Legalese as a second language, my job was to check the Code of Federal Regulations and FAA pubs for flight plan requirements. The safety guidelines in 14 CFR §101 meant we couldn't launch it in the middle of a city, that we had to install two independent payload cut-down systems, a radar reflective device in the 700 to 2700 MHz range, no trailing antennas, had to have running lights visible at 5 miles, flash frequency between 40 and 100 cycles per minute. Oh, and we couldn't launch it where the clouds or other "obscuring phenomena" were more than five-tenths coverage, and where the horizontal visibility was less than five miles. In plain language—launch it in the middle of a field ten miles from the nearest town on a clear fall day after sunrise with lots of big flashing lights and a radar reflector, you're okay.

Add an FAA flight plan, filed with the local Air Traffic Control Center in Denver six to twenty-four hours before launch, with basic info like launch time, trajectory, estimated time of ascent to 60,000 feet, weight of the payload (but not, fortunately, its nature or purpose), duration of flight and estimated time of return to Earth.

That was just for the balloon. The launch vehicle, which we'd named *Conestoga* 1, required a whole separate license to launch, under 14 CFR §415. Most of them applied to a traditional Atlas or Delta or Saturn V-style launch, from a fixed launch site. The balloon launch saved a small forest of paperwork. What was left was bad enough— detailed rundown of the payload, the propulsion system, safety measures, detailed rundown of the flight plan, among other things. Plus a risk assessment. We fudged a lot on that one, limiting it to what happened if the craft itself crashed and burned (might take out a barn or a quarter section of wheat). I emailed it all to the FAA with all fingers crossed and a prayer.

* * *

"At least if we fail, no one's gonna know," I said as the sun came up over the horizon, glinting off the half-inflated balloon that sat in the middle of a stubble-filled wheat field in Logan County, Kansas. Greg had grown up around here and had talked a cousin into turning his half-section into Cape Canaveral for a day.

"It's not going to fail. Think positive, ferchrissake," Terry growled, squinting into a small videocamera.

The Western Kansas Sport Balloon Club was being paid enough to help us and to keep their mouths shut. A tank truck with helium was parked near the farm plug leading to the gravel road. The gondola, with the payload and the rocket boosters, drew a few curious stares and comments, but no more.

The sun cleared the horizon and climbed into the cerulean fall sky, glinting off the silver sphere. The balloon floated lazily at its tethers with the oddly-angled irregular payload beneath. The crew moved away, save for three men at each of the lines holding the balloon. Greg joined us, wiping his hands with a rag and orange pumice soap.

"We're set, Terry. Anytime you're ready."

"Here," he said, handing me the videocamera. He walked towards the balloon, head high and shoulders erect, with a confident stride (in addition to financial acumen and scientific know-how, he had a sense of theater and of History; MacArthur wading ashore at Leyte Gulf had nothing on Terry). He stopped, legs planted firmly on the ground, raised one arm, and brought it down in a knife-chop. The lines fell away, and the silver sphere began rising quickly into the air, to a small cheer from the ground crew.

Greg went over to our mobile Mission Control, a used Ford panel van stuffed with tracking and communications gear. The van had cost ten grand, the electronics three times as much. The only giveaway was the small retractable satellite dish that poked up through the roof.

We watched, craning our necks until the balloon became a speck in the morning sky. Greg was already in the van, seated at the left console, tracking it. "So far so good," he told us.

The ballooners would follow us and help with retrieval, which we had figured would be about fifty miles east of here, given the prevailing winds.

I drove, keeping under the speed limits on the two-lane roads, leaving Greg and Terry to monitor the launch, wearing headphones and squinting at LED displays.

"Pull over," Greg told me as we neared Hays on I-70, close to the projected touch-down. I steered the van off onto the shoulder, parked it. "We're at 100,000 feet." Too far beyond this and the balloon would burst before we launched the payload.

"Separation sequence keyed," Terry said, suddenly all business, hitting buttons on the keyboard in front of him. "In ten . . . three, two, one." Bright lights flashed, it was completely quiet for about thirty seconds.

"First firing complete," Greg said. "All readings nominal. We're on course." They both let out their breaths, and I realized I'd been holding mine, too. "Bleeding off helium." Another pause. "Altitude 101,000 feet. Dropping . . . 100,500."

"There's a McDonald's up here," Terry said. "Let's grab some breakfast, see where it comes down." We pulled into the golden arches along the interstate, parked in the lot (the antenna ruled out the drive-through), and devoured McMuffins while we tried to pinpoint the landing site.

Per FAA regs, we had to transmit data on the flight every hour, so Terry sent the first update via email. The entire flight was going to take four hours. The FAA took our updates without asking any questions. Three hours later, the balloon came down in a field six miles south of Victoria.

* * *

We hadn't struck the Mother Lode yet, so we couldn't quit our day jobs. Greg went back to Boeing in Wichita, Terry was back at Yerkes, and I was back to the Sedgwick County Public Defender's Office. We kept in constant contact by e-mail, and were wired into the control center, which was Greg's basement.

On weekends, I would do the legal work for Cosmodyne, or pop into Greg's Mission Control. Then it was back to work, visiting jails and dealing with ingrate clients and arrogant prosecutors and self-deified judges, all the while thinking that if this worked, I was done with the lot of them.

It was like being eight years old again, just after Halloween, with Christmas in sight but too far away to begin making up a list. There were times when the thought of a bonanza made life more bearable, providing a light at the end of a tunnel, and there were times when I wondered who I was fooling, that it couldn't possibly pan out. The old travelers on the Santa Fe Trail must have felt the same way about the time they crossed the Cimarron River into the dry country, too far to turn back and doom and forever in front of them. Can't turn back, plowing forward only by inertia, and have a few drinks and laughs over it at trail's end. Day by day, we endured.

Six months out, *Conestoga* 1 rendezvoused with 2009 BT. Terry, Greg and I burned three days of vacation time to gather at mission control. I arrived a little late, owing to a hearing that ran long, and found Terry and Greg in the basement. Becky, Greg's wife, had served up pizza. They had met in college, and married after graduation. She was a big, rawboned country girl with a blond mane and an earthy, unpretentious manner. She also knew about the project. It would have been impossible to keep it from her. Becky knew how to keep a secret, though.

"Brought it out of hibernation twenty-four hours ago. All systems nominal," Terry told me as I devoured a pepperoni and sausage slice.

"Five thousand kay out." *Conestoga* was approaching from behind, on a heliocentric orbit. "Deceleration burn in ten minutes." I watched as the seconds counted down, and then saw delta-vee and velocity numbers dance and change on the LED screen.

At fifty kilometers out, the retrorockets began a series of burns, bringing the ship to a halt one hundred meters from the surface of the asteroid. A dart fired, dug into the surface, anchoring it to the asteroid with a monomolecular-fiber cable.

That completed, Greg keyed in a series of commands to unfurl the mirror. This was the nerve-wracking part; the mirror had to unfold without a glitch after a months-long journey in absolute zero, or we'd just wasted a few million dollars. We waited in nervous silence for ten minutes while it emerged like a Japanese fan and spread out. Greg broke the tension. "Mirror deployed." A few more commands aimed the focal point of the mirror to a spot on the surface, which Greg had calculated would halt the asteroid's rotation and provide a slight course change in the bargain.

Stopping the rotation took a week. Moving its path by a few degrees for insertion into Earth orbit took a couple of months. 2009 BT was on course, estimated time of arrival five months and ten days out.

* * *

What does a dog do when he catches the car he's chasing? That's what faced us over the next few months.

First order of business would be to lay claim to it. Mining law on earth was well-developed, and every country had a system for filing claims. But, as I discovered after hours of research on the internet and in the law library, there was no mining law for outer space as such. The Outer Space Treaty of 1967 forbids countries from laying claim to celestial bodies. It doesn't prevent corporations from laying claim to a moon or comet or asteroid. It doesn't outlaw extracting resources from these places, either. The drafters had realized that would destroy any incentive for space colonization. To be safe, I filed a mining claim in Sedgwick County, where we had our offices.

Next dilemma—a mining claim is only patented after the claimant performs work on it. Failure to work the claim for six months amounted to abandonment. The Mining Act of 1872 required $100 of work annually or improvements. So we had a short window in which to start working the claim.

At least ten nations were capable of launching unmanned vehicles to 2009 BT; at least three were able to put men on it. Three corporations claimed the ability, but had a spotty track record. We could initially send an unmanned vehicle and begin mining and smelting operations. Greg went to his drawing board and had a serviceable model done up in a month that could be built for under a million dollars.

All of which led to the final, and maybe most vexing, problem, that of how to finance it all. We were talking about a million for a teleoperated smelter, and maybe as much for payload fees to NASA or ESA or Roskosmos or JAXA. Add on a few more million for return vehicles and we were talking serious money.

The orbital mechanics to get the asteroid to Earth were one thing. Debt servicing was quite another.

It turned out that leveraging was the answer. Divide the asteroid up into neat little tracts, and lease portions of the mineral rights to whoever wanted them, for a hefty fee up front plus royalties. Whether the lessee carted his own equipment or not was optional, but we would be more than happy to provide the equipment, for a percentage of the profit. We figured to clear enough in the first rush to be able to book payloads on a booster within a year.

All of which begged another question—how to prevent a crash in the precious metals market? Part of it was logic—it would take years to fully mine 2009 BT, so we weren't going to be dumping three years' worth of nickel production on the world all at once. The market would dictate the rest, to a degree. Everyone knew the stuff was there, but not in circulation, and it would pay to hold back rather than dump it.

In my off hours I pored over oil and gas law, downloading royalty and lease forms, modifying them to what I hoped was an acceptable degree, sending them to my law school buddies who did oil and gas for review. I also slogged through contracts, launch service agreements and sale of rights contracts. I learned more about commercial law in five months than I ever had in law school. I had a nice file of ready-to-ink paper on hand within several months.

And then the feds found out, and we were nearly thrown in a dungeon.

I was in the lobby of the Sedgwick County Jail, waiting to visit a couple of clients, when my cell phone buzzed. It was Terry, sounding worried.

"Where are you?" he asked me.

"The jail. For a visit."

"Get out. Now. While you can."

"What's this about?"

"Not on the phone. Meet me at the rest area at Mile 320 on I-70 in eight hours." It was just after nine in the morning.

"Okay. I need to get some stuff at home."

"No," Terry ordered. "Don't go home. Don't even go back to the office." He hung up, leaving me there in the jail, panic creeping over me. The drive to the rendezvous and the wait only served to feed it.

I got some cash at an ATM by the courthouse, threw my folder in the car, called the office and told them I had a family emergency come up and could someone handle the preliminary hearing I had set for that afternoon? There was some grumbling, but I bore up. I took the Turnpike from Wichita to Topeka, and got lunch downtown. Arriving at the designated point a few hours early, I put the seat back and took a nap.

A tapping on my window woke me up after sunset. I started, half-expecting a State Trooper or FBI tactical squad. Instead, Greg's grinning face looked down at me. "Terry should be here in a half hour."

I got out of the car, stretched. The blue van was parked nearby. "What's the panic?" I asked.

"Our secret's out," Greg said. He was a Kris Kristofferson album cover, faded Levis, denim shirt and scuffed boots. "Terry had me pull all the hard drives from mission control and clear out. I sent Becky to her folks' for a couple days. Someone's concerned about a large rock heading towards Earth, and drawing parallels with dinosaurs."

"It's not going to impact, though, right?"

"Right," Greg said. "If we make final course corrections in the next couple of days. Otherwise the current trajectory is within a margin for error for an impact."

We spent the next half hour speculating on our fate, going from a short stay in a county jail to life at Guantanamo Bay. Terry showed up in a rental Honda before we got to the death penalty.

"Terry, what in God's name is going on?" I asked him.

"I gotta take a leak," he said, brushing past me. He looked disheveled, hair mussed and his clothes looked slept-in. "Been chugging Diet Coke and coffee since I hopped a flight to KC." So we stood awkwardly in the tiled men's room while Terry stood at a urinal and explained.

The Jet Propulsion Laboratory's Near Earth Asteroid Tracking project caught on first, catching 2009 BT when it was about seven months out. When they saw that it was headed straight for Earth, they panicked. The long-range telescopes detected an unusual spectrum, from the outgassing caused by the mirror. This convinced NASA to re-task the Hubble to take a look. Some of the wilder theories bouncing around JPL and Houston involved alien attacks. Then they called NORAD, and recovered the tracking data from the launch of *Conestoga* 1; by this time, with several private spaceports in the continental U.S., commercial space launches weren't all that unusual. From there it was a simple matter to backtrack from the telemetry data to the FAA flight approval forms I had filed a year ago, which contained our home addresses. No doubt search warrants had already been prepared, if not executed, for our homes.

The buzz about a dinosaur-killer had reached his ears quickly, but not until guys in Air Force uniforms started showing up did Terry spring into action. He ducked out of Yerkes and booked a flight to Kansas City.

"Now what?" I asked. "Greg says we have to make some last minute course corrections to keep this from hitting the Earth."

"We can do it from the van," Terry said. "It's got everything we need, tracking software, Kμ-band transmitter. I got the data we need on flash drives. We're set." Greg and I looked at one another, but there was nothing else we could do. "In for a penny," I muttered, and we got in our cars and hit the road.

We set up shop about ten miles south of the interstate, parking by an abandoned farm house enclosed by a shelterbelt of red cedar and cottonwoods with a quarter-mile long driveway. The dirt-and-gravel road led to a truck stop, which provided us with water, Diet Coke, chips and burgers. We slept in the van, or in the back of Greg's pickup, making it a big camping trip.

Meanwhile, in the outside world, all hell was beginning to break loose. A graduate student at the Australian Astronomical Observatory in Sydney spotted 2009 BT while doing routine blink-comparator work, reported it to the Royal Greenwich Observatory, Berlin and Paris, and somewhere along the way a press release was issued, and the circus was on.

I was buying burgers and fries from the truck stop Burger King when the words "killer asteroid" flashed on the big-screen television. I had just paid for the food, and glanced at the screen as I headed for the exit. DINOSAUR KILLER was the subtitle by the CNN logo. The blond anchor's words were barely audible over the din of the restaurant, but were close-captioned underneath. Pictures of 2009 BT flashed over her shoulder, followed by a serious-looking bearded man identified as an astronomer with Mount Palomar. "ONE MILE IN DIAMETER . . . COLLISION COURSE . . . DEFENSE DEPARTMENT . . . WHITE HOUSE . . ." scrolled by on the screen. My gut dropped to my feet. We were in deeper than I thought, and I left the store in a rush.

At least they hadn't shown our pictures. The feds probably didn't want to tip us off that they knew who we were. I fumbled my keys out of my pocket, and drove back to the farmhouse, nearly sideswiping an eighteen-wheeler on the way I was so distracted. The AM newsradio station was full of babble about the Russian and Chinese ambassadors paying a visit to the White House, and both countries placing their missile forces on high alert.

Halfway there, my cell phone rang. The caller ID showed a 202 area code, for Washington D.C. I thought about hanging up, since nothing out of D.C. was going to be good—but would the FBI call before raiding us? But there was one person it could be . . . I pulled over, and answered.

"If you're doing this just to impress me, okay, I'm impressed, I'll take you back," a female voice said. The tone was weary, but not severe.

"Honestly, it wasn't my idea, Jen," I pleaded.

There was one voice I was overjoyed to hear at that moment, and it belonged to Jennifer Gillespie. Six years ago I had come close to marrying her. Beautiful—raven hair, olive skin, deep liquid brown eyes. Brainy, and cool but not aloof, laughed at my stupid jokes, and a tigress between silk sheets. Three years with her had been the best of my life. But we had different career plans. She thought she could save the world by going to Washington, where she currently served as an aide to Senator Byron Morgan (D-Colorado). I thought I could do it by not selling out and fighting for the poor and downtrodden. Right now, her way looked pretty good.

"I know. I've tried telling everyone you don't have the smarts to cook this up," she gently teased. "I'm on a semi-secure line, so I've got about thirty seconds before Homeland Security traces you. Listen up. You've got everyone scared stiff here. All they know about this is what they saw in the movie *Armageddon*."

"How bad is it?" I asked in a weak voice.

"The President's ordered the Air Force to re-target about three dozen missiles on your asteroid. Same with the Chinese and Russians. The rest are pointing at us and their trigger fingers are mighty itchy."

"Wonderful," I said despondently. I had unhappy visions of 2009 BT vaporized in a nuclear flash, all that work—and profit—down the drain. That was replaced by mushroom clouds right out of bad sci-fi movies from my youth.

"Homeland Security and the FBI have been called in to track you." With that, I put the phone down, opened the door, and threw up on the gravel road. "Are you hiding?"

"Are you okay?" she asked as I finished with the dry heaves and put the phone to my ear again.

"As a matter of fact, I'm not. Look, tell Byron that we're not terrorists. We're entrepreneurs. He's a Republican. He'll love that."

"I'll try," she said. "I don't want to get caught up in this. But I don't want to see you go to prison for life."

"I'm touched that you still care," I said.

"Thirty seconds are up. Now go hide."

Terry and Greg took the news in stride, as they downed cheeseburgers on the rickety porch, listening to locusts in the late summer air. I'd lost my appetite. "I'm not surprised it leaked," Terry said. "I was hoping it wouldn't, but it was always a risk. Kinda hard to hide a mountain-sized rock heading towards you."

"Why didn't you let me in on this beforehand?" I sputtered. And why hadn't I thought of it?

"I didn't think it was likely," Terry finessed. "And I had doubts about your ability to withstand torture. Anyway, not to worry. Once we get the final corrections, we'll inform NASA that it's not going to plop into the Pacific."

"And how do you plan to do that?" I asked, my voice rising in alarm and anger.

"Dunno," Terry said, around a mouthful of fries. "Probably do it through work. Press conference, something."

"How thoroughly did you think this through?" I asked, now

thoroughly mad at Terry and at myself. "Did you have a plan for what to do if we got discovered and caused a national panic?"

"First off, it's not a national panic," he said, finishing a burger. "The government and the media are doing what they can to downplay it. They don't *want* a panic—it causes all sorts of nasty things, like riots and civil disorder, they gotta mobilize the National Guard, it's a hassle, costs money they don't have. Second of all," he stuffed fries into his mouth, "do you plan for every contingency in a trial? You get surprised, or things take a wrong turn, what do you do? You wing it, and because you're trained, you get away with it. Right? So quit worrying. Trust me."

Terry and Greg went back to the van. I milled around the shelterbelt surrounding the house, enjoying the quiet of the countryside.

I heard the faint *whup-whup-whup* of a helicopter from the east. I squinted and saw dust clouds kicked up by a convoy of vehicles barreling down the road from the north. Spun around and saw another convoy approach the crossroads half a mile south.

All at once I had the overpowering urge to run through the stubbled cornfield, to scream and break down crying, to simply faint dead away, and/or piss my pants. I wondered how my clients managed to keep from becoming a blubbering mess when cops in ninja suits kicked in their doors to serve search warrants. I guess after you've had a few no-knock warrants served at midnight, you get used to it.

My legs felt like lead as I turned and sprinted back to the van, shouting at Terry and Greg. I threw open the back door to the van, blabbering and pointing something about cops—I can't remember my exact words. I found both of them in their seats, calmly typing commands into guidance control, switching out flash drives. They were still at it when the first black Suburbans and Crown Vics skidded to halts in a cloud of dust and clean-cut All-American types in dark suits and ties and Ray-Bans jumped out and stormed the van. My bladder got an extra challenge when they drew 9mm glocks and Uzis.

"Terry Raines?" one of the men, a blonde crewcut linebacker in Brooks Brothers asked. He held a Beretta with his right hand, displayed a black leather ID case with a badge.

"Speaking," Terry said, casually crossing his arms, swiveling in his chair and facing the law enforcement arrayed behind the van.

"Special Agent Gordon, FBI. You're wanted for questioning on suspicion of terrorist activity."

Terry let out a bark of laughter at that. Gordon frowned, and his brows furrowed over the Ray Bans. "Where's your warrant?"

"We're working on it," a second, thinner and bespectacled, said. "NASA's tracking a mile-wide asteroid on a collision course with the Earth. We regard it as a weapon of mass destruction."

"Wrong," Terry said. "It's a private enterprise venture. We're planning to orbit it and file a mining claim on it. Destroying it is contrary to our mission statement."

"You might want to tell that to the Chinese and the Russians," the second man, who showed an ID from the Defense Department, said. "They're picking up your rock on their deep space radars, and they're going apeshit. The President has been on the hotlines to Moscow and Beijing, assuring them that we're not trying a sneak attack."

A bleak prison cell, iron bars and graffitied walls and taking a crap in a stainless steel toilet in front of three drug dealers and rapists, swam before my eyes.

"We're not."

"You'll have to explain it to the U.S. Attorney," Gordon said. "You're under arrest." Several of the suits began reaching for handcuffs.

"That's a bad idea," Terry said calmly.

"Really?" Gordon said sarcastically.

"Really. Right now, the asteroid is on a course that has a fifteen percent chance of landing it somewhere on Earth's surface—"

"Eastern Siberia," the DoD suit chimed in. "We ran the trajectory."

"Unless, of course, we can tilt the mirror attached to it in such a way that the outventing moves it further from its path. That *has* to be done from here."

"We can get NASA to take over," another suit said. "Jason Young. I'm with NASA."

"No," Greg said, taking off his headset. "The controls can only run from here. And we've just finished locking them out. You need a special password to get back in. If you try hacking from another connection, there's a self-destruct command in the software."

Young's eyes got wide. "You mean there'd be no way to control it?"

"Right. It burns out the receiver, so there's no way to receive commands from ground control." Insane. And, I realized, for that little subroutine to be installed, Terry had to have had some inkling it might come to this. "And the asteroid drops into Siberia or the Pacific. If you're lucky."

"You're bluffing," Gordon said brusquely.

"I'm not," Terry said softly, steel in his voice. "But go ahead and cuff us, and try to get into the system. The corrections have to be made within the next seventy-two hours at the outside. After that, nothing we do will avert a direct hit."

Gordon looked torn for a few minutes, talked with Young, and faced us again with a resigned distaste on his face. "All right. Make your course corrections. We won't interfere with you before that. Afterwards . . ." his voice trailed off, and the threat was real. Terry and Greg got back to work, while I sat in the back seat of a Crown Vic.

When it happened, the orbital insert of 2009 BT was anticlimactic. The video monitor in the van showed two dots converging, velocity and distance counting down, the dot representing the asteroid approaching at an oblique angle, and gradually assuming a wide ovoid orbit around the earth.

That, of course, was when they took us into custody.

* * *

Over the next couple of weeks, the earth's new moon was a hot topic on the airwaves, over the net and in the blogosphere. We were either bold entrepreneurs who had seized the day, or dangerous lunatics who had nearly wiped out humanity. No in between.

The feds were in a quandary. They had toyed with terrorism charges, but realized it was a weak case. Even Terry's threat wasn't so clear cut that the U.S. Attorney wanted to prosecute. They looked for FAA violations, found none; we'd done our homework. After a month, the whole matter was quietly dropped.

Terry was busy fielding phone calls and doing interviews. Greg did a couple of appearances, but he hated the exposure and unobtrusively went back to Boeing, where he lasted another month. I returned to the office a week later, to an awkward silence from co-workers and office staff. No one was quite sure how to handle having a staff lawyer who was a bigger celebrity than some of our more notorious clients.

After a week, though, I turned in my two weeks' notice and burned two weeks of vacation time, with the blessing of my boss. The calls over lease opportunities were pouring in. Mining companies like 3M and Alcoa were banging at the door, offering enormous sums of money and begging to start operations. 3M offered ten million up front for leasing rights, Alcoa twice that. I posted ads for good mineral rights lawyers and contract attorneys, made some hires. Cosmodyne, Inc. was becoming more than a shell corporation.

There was no procedure for filing a mining claim on a celestial body. The UN didn't have one; the U.S. Government didn't have one. I'd done the next best thing, by filing a claim in Johnson County, where our offices were located. The Chinese-led UN uproar over treaty violations was short-lived, since everyone realized that the treaty didn't apply to us.

The U.S. Government still wasn't completely sold. They sent a crew from BLM and State to meet with us. Getting them on board wasn't all that difficult.

"The early estimates on this," I told them, "are about two million tons of nickel ore, a million-five iron, with titanium in significant quantities, along with plenty of gold, silver, and palladium."

"We're worried it could get dumped on the market and depress prices," said a Treasury suit.

"Won't happen. It'll take a couple of years to get going, and the process will be slow at first. I suspect a good portion of the production is going to be used in space construction."

"The environmental impacts—"

"Are negligible," I responded. "I have one reason why you should help us."

"What would that be?" said the head suit, from State.

"We, and the corporations we lease to, have to pay taxes on everything that comes out of there. Do the math. We've got a few trillion dollars sitting up there. You get a cut. Last I heard, Uncle Sam needs the money. We're even willing to lease space to NASA. I could even dream up a discount rate, if you're interested." They were. The mining claim was approved in short order, and Congress amended the mining laws for future outer space claims.

* * *

"A thing of beauty, isn't it?" Terry asked. It was several months later, the excitement had died down. The money from leases was now rolling in. Terry moved to Wichita, our headquarters, from Chicago. I had purchased an old farmhouse in the Flint Hills and was in the process of rehabbing it.

Terry and Greg and I were in a wheatfield gone back to grass behind the house, a cooler of beer sitting beside us and my other new purchase, a 15-inch reflecting telescope. There was nothing but starlight above, giving a perfect view of our property through the eyepiece.

"It is," Greg said, peering at the small brilliant dot hovering in the center of the field. "Any ideas on what to call it?"

"Avalon," Terry said. "Where Excalibur was forged, where King Arthur recovered from his wounds received while fighting Mordred. An island that produces everything from itself, fields of grain with no need for sowing, apple and fruit orchards that merely rise from the soil."

"Been doing some research lately, have we?" I said. I hadn't known Terry to be a high-literary type when we were younger.

"Maybe," he said, staring at the sky. "But it fits."

"Hardly able to grow everything it needs, though," I said. "No water, no oxygen to speak of. Teleoperated mining probes are fine, but sooner or later men are going to have to live there."

"We've got that one covered," Terry said nonchalantly, tapping a few keys on the telescope motor. The motor whirred and the tube moved to the right and down. Terry motioned for me to look through the eyepiece. "You can't see it, but in the middle of the field of view is a carbonaceous chondrite asteroid. In twenty-seven months, it makes a five-million mile pass from earth. We're going to grab it. There go our atmosphere and water problems."

"I'll alert the bail bondsmen," I said dryly.

"No need," Terry said. "The first time is always the hardest. We've opened up a new frontier—us, ordinary people, not some lantern-jawed heroes riding an expensive government rocket. We've shown it can be done. There's no going back. Once people realize that it's within reach, they'll take it, because it offers freedom."

"The IRS may have a different opinion."

Terry snorted. "Transitory. Let them think they can control this," he said, waving his arm at the sky. "It's like the internet—space is inherently chaotic. The distances, the physics, all defy easy control. It'll be another gold rush. We've given people something they've always needed—freedom." He lowered his arm, looked at both Greg and I. "The people want stars, we've given them stars. Space is now Open for Business."

COMPOSITION IN DEATH MINOR

K.G. Jewell

Noir science fiction emerged at the end of the Golden Age (1938-1950) when a number of established writers began to explore new themes and new science fiction styles. The cynical and stylized perspective of classic noir fiction became increasingly popular in the 1950s and 1960s. Jack Finney's *The Body Snatchers* (1955), Harry Harrison's *Make Room! Make Room!* (1966), and Phillip K. Dick's *Do Androids Dream of Electric Sheep?* (1968) are some of the best known examples of noir science fiction of the era. Noir SF had a significant impact on science fiction films and the cyberpunk movement that emerged in the early 1980s. "Composition in Death Minor" continues the noir tradition and infuses it with modern tech-based world building. Author K. G. Jewell introduces us to Sophie Devine, a hard-as-nails assassin and concert cellist. She has a job to do and doesn't like assholes.

K.G. Jewell lives and writes in Austin, Texas. His stories of short speculative fiction have appeared in *Daily Science Fiction, Orson Scott Card's InterGalactic Medicine Show,* and *Unidentified Funny Objects*. He's working on a novel relating the further adventures of Sophie Devine, cello player and intergalactic assassin. His website, which is rarely updated, is lit.kgjewell.com.

Playing classical cello was a lot like assassination. The threads of a good composition and the components of a reliable plan were surprisingly similar; just as years of cello rehearsals and performances had taught Sophie Devine to catch an off note before it could be heard by the audience, years of successful hits allowed her to recognize that her plan had gone wrong.

The entry agent's eyes barely flickered at the passport, but they flickered. Sophie tensed; she'd been made.

"Purpose of your visit?" Perhaps the note could be turned, the piece salvaged.

She discarded her cover story as a commodities vendor.

"Espionage." Not quite true, but espionage was slightly more socially acceptable than assassination.

The entry agent raised his eyebrows and chuckled. "At least you Earthers are finally open about it. That's new. Welcome to Callisto, look around. We have nothing to hide."

He set a pill bottle on the counter between them. "Two-hundred Ds."

She tossed the cash on the counter. The container of Callisto-Ripture anti-bacterials would last Sophie five days, which was longer than she planned on being on this backwater moon. She picked up the container and popped one of the red tabs. The room grew crisp and warm as the drug dissolved in her mouth with the faint taste of butterscotch.

"Just remember this isn't a tourist town." He handed back her passport, his attention shifting to the man in line behind her, a ship's steward. "Next."

She stepped past the agent, carefully compensating for the low-G. The exit lock was a single bounce away. The customs building was small, a pre-fab module ill-designed to handle more than the odd passenger.

Sophie acknowledged she was an odd passenger. She'd hitched a ride to Jupiter's eighth moon on a freighter loaded with luxury Earthside food for the CallistoCom executive cantina. She had a contract on a female CallistoCom agent named Quail. Quail had stolen valuable goods from Sophie's client, who wanted payment from the woman in cash or blood; preferably both.

Sophie slid the rebreather mask hanging around her neck over her nose and mouth. The metallic tang of converted air filled her lungs. She stepped into the exit lock and activated it. Stale breathable atmosphere whooshed out the ceiling, raising her short hair. A carbon-dioxide-hydrogen mix of pressure-form rose from the floor, the temperature dropping as the freezing-cold atmosphere filled the room. The exit door opened.

Her first glimpse of the Callisto landscape was a crush of humanity. A dozen, maybe two dozen, pedicab and rickshaw operators jockeyed for her business. Behind them loomed the dark-maroon cliff wall that enclosed Landing Crater Twenty-Seven Alpha.

"Fast, Fast, Fast!" shouted a pedicab operator, flexing his muscles.

"Direct to Job Center, cheap!" a woman said, pounding on the hood of her rickshaw.

"Whatever you need. I've done it all," an elderly man whispered in her ear, his mask in his hand.

A short kid with a rebreather covered in duct tape didn't say a word, but leaned against an auto-rickshaw decked out in glowing racing stripes. Sophie nodded at him, opened his passenger side door and ducked inside the small space. She wanted speed.

The kid slid into the driver's seat.

"Where to?" His voice was muffled, filtered through his mask. He was maybe fifteen.

"A hotel."

"Business or cheap?"

"Cheap."

The rickshaw accelerated, bouncing off in a burst of energy. Sophie glanced back at the plume of dust in their wake. The other drivers turned to protect their eyes, maroon grit bouncing off their backs.

The road, a dirt trail marked with orange flags and tire tracks, led around the crater and over the rim. The cramped auto-rickshaw prevented her from getting a good look at the sky, but as they rose up the crater wall, Sophie saw a cloud of purple dust covered the crater floor behind them, wrapping the cube of the processing center and two bulky freighters in a light haze.

Then they passed the crater lip, and Jupiter commanded the

horizon, glowing with reflected sunlight. The swirled orange planet was the landscape's only notable feature—everything else was rock. Maroon rock.

Sophie had jumped at the chance to take a contract on Callisto. She'd never been here, and CallistoCom had a reputation for being one of the most morally corrupt corporations in the system. In the three decades since they'd colonized Jupiter's second largest moon, CallistoCom had broken five unions, withdrawn from the System Convention on Human Rights, and legalized child labor, claiming kids were the best workers.

Sophie took special pleasure in executing contracts on assholes.

The monotonous landscape and hum of the motor threatened to put Sophie to sleep. She'd been up for twenty hours; the time zone of the White Sands-based ship meshing poorly with Gamma Station's time zone. Local time was mid-afternoon. It was going to be a long night.

"How is the pressure-forming coming?" Sophie asked. She knew the official answer—not well—but she needed conversation to help keep her awake. CallistoCom pumped heat, hydrogen, and carbon dioxide, processed from surface ice, into the atmosphere from a seeding station controlled from Gamma Station. The process prevented the necessity of full enclosure suits and allowed the growth of the silicate algae that was Callisto's main export. The pressure-forming was continuous, offset by atmospheric leakage from the weak-gravity well that was Callisto.

"The Cripture still infects." The kid didn't take his eyes off the road. "The company shouldn't allow any new arrivals until they fix it."

"Why? Too much traffic?" Given the empty road, this was Sophie's attempt at humor. She needed sleep.

"No. Too many bodies—they're driving up the price of the Benediction."

CallistoCom held a monopoly on the anti-bacterial that protected residents against the anaerobic bacteria that infected the pressure-forming atmosphere. The locals called the drug the "Benediction." It was mildly addictive, the tab's grip on its users growing over time.

Sophie doubted demand had anything to do with the price.

The rickshaw rounded a set of rocks, heading towards a field of silver metal panels. Gamma Station was underground, below the huge array of solar panels powering the facility. Gigantic mechanical spiders darted across the field, continuously removing the ever-present maroon grit.

A freight truck emerged from a hole in the ground beside the solar array, headed at them. The rickshaw swerved to the right to give the truck a wide berth. Even with the maneuver, a rock spit out of the truck's wheel and ricocheted off Sophie's window.

Then they were underground.

The passageway was dim, barely lit by a string of bulbs down the center. They turned down an even dimmer side passage. The glow of the rickshaw's racing lights reflected off the bare rock walls, its single headlight casting forward into the darkness.

The rickshaw stopped in a desolate passage of blank rock and the engine went silent.

"You have payment?"

Sophie tensed. She dropped her hand to her boot and fingered the collapsed baton clipped to her shin. A mugging by a rickshaw driver wasn't worth live ammunition.

"Sure. Twenty Ds." She kept her voice even. According to an official sign at the processing center, twenty Ds was the price to Gamma Station from Landing Crater Twenty-Seven Alpha.

"Twenty Ds and half your Benediction."

"Nope." She didn't plan on sticking around long enough to need all her tabs, but she wasn't going to take that chance for some punk taxi driver.

The kid's hand went to the door-handle, but Sophie was quicker. The baton was in her hand, flicked to full extension, and around the kid's throat before the handle turned.

"I have a better idea. Turn the rickshaw back on without any trouble, and we'll pretend this conversation never happened." The kid probably had friends waiting in the passage to take the easy mark in the rickshaw. She didn't intend for that to happen.

Two decades of cello practice had given her very strong biceps. She tightened the baton against the kid's carotid artery.

The kid turned the motor back on and they accelerated forward. When they re-entered a tunnel lit by faded work lights, Sophie relaxed the pressure—she didn't want him passing out and crashing into a wall. When she could see masked pedestrians on the sidewalks, she removed the baton from his neck altogether, collapsing it back into its holster.

They stopped in front an establishment with a worn sign reading "Quality Boarding House: rooms by the hour or the day."

"Play nice." Sophie threw a twenty D bill at the kid. "I'll need a ride in about an hour." If she got a new driver, she'd have to go through the whole mug-the-tourist thing again. This kid wouldn't be that stupid twice.

A pair of beggars confronted Sophie as she stepped out of the rickshaw—a man and a woman, probably in their thirties, wearing the gaunt skin and scars of life on the street. The couple shared a rebreather, handing it off between huffs. The tell-tale roseola of stage-one cripture crept down both their cheeks. The paralyzing seizures of stage-two wouldn't be far behind.

"Benediction! Just one tab. Please!" the man knelt and laid his hands on her feet in supplication. Sophie kicked off his grip and strode into the hotel. She had a job to do.

After getting a room and freshening up—a shower was worth at least half a night's sleep—she returned to the street. The beggars were gone. The kid leaned against his rickshaw, a scowl on behind his mask. "I wasn't going to mug you. I was just going to tighten the headlight."

"Sure kid, whatever." If he needed to save face, she'd let him. She didn't need him looking for revenge. "Do you know where the El

Dorado is?"

The kid shook his head. "That's not a place for ladies."

"My mother has always wanted to me to be a lady. Take me there anyways."

The kid kept shaking his head.

"Fifty Ds and three tabs." Sophie said. Everyone had their price.

"Ok, but I warned you."

"You didn't warn me, you insulted me." Sophie got in the kid's vehicle. He hopped in the driver's seat and the rickshaw took off.

"The El Dorado isn't licensed, so the company busts it up every couple of months. If the company busts it while you're there, you're in trouble," the kid said.

"Who hangs out there?"

"Smugglers. I've never been inside, but it's got a rep as the place with the toughest smugglers on Callisto. I bet if you walk in there with a bottle of meds, you aren't walking out with it."

"I'll take that bet."

The rest of the drive was in relative silence, the whir of the motor the only conversation. They passed through lit tunnels, and then unlit ones before re-emerging back onto the Callisto surface. Jupiter still governed the horizon, stars filling its sky-court. After another half-hour they turned into a crevice containing a modular building surrounded by some twenty vehicles. The vehicles ranged from auto-rickshaws to sleek sport transports to dump trucks.

Sophie paid the kid, throwing in an extra tab as tip. "Stick around."

Sophie had been in gangster hangouts on four Earth continents, three moons, and two of the five space stations. But as the airlock opened and she stepped into the module, she realized she hadn't been in one quite like this.

No music. No smoke. No billiards. Not even a bar. Instead, a clerk with well-coifed blonde hair sat across from the door, a smile on her face and a fashion magazine on her desk.

The illegal gangster hangout of Callisto was a day spa.

"May I help you?" The clerk wore no face mask.

"Um, yeah. I'm looking for a Deborah Vilmese?" Sophie peeled off her mask and tasted the air. Fresh and sweet. This place smelled like money. Dirty money, perhaps, but money.

"Do you have an appointment?"

"No. But she was highly recommended by a mutual friend." That being her client, who had said Deb the Reb could help Sophie track down Quail.

"And you are?"

"Tell her Joanne Digeo is visiting." The name was a passcode from her client.

"I see." The clerk's lips pursed and she picked up a phone. "Have a seat."

Sophie declined the plush easy-chair that half-filled the tiny lobby. She stayed on her feet, taking in the faint scent of lavender and the small Zen sand garden on the coffee table.

Her job was so weird.

"Come on back."

The clerk led her through a door, down a brightly lit hallway, and directed Sophie into a side room. She entered, the door sealing behind her.

A massage table filled the room. A large woman stood beside it, perhaps twice Sophie's weight but only two thirds her height. She wore a pink mumu, her hair short. She was fifty or so—it was hard to tell.

"It doesn't help me with the authorities when an announced Earther spy makes her first order of business a visit to my establishment," the woman said.

"It must be a small town. I hear good things of your operation, Ms. Vilmese. I wished to meet you for myself."

"Call me Deb. Lie down. You're buying a massage."

"OK." If that was the cover, she'd roll with it.

Sophie shrugged out of her jacket, shoulder holster, and shirt and lay across the massage table. She folded them in a neat pile on the corner of the massage table, making sure her gun was within reach. She left on her pants and boots—she *was* working.

Deb squirted oil on her hands and rubbed them together. "The company might know of my operation, even occasionally tolerate it for the right kickback. But it doesn't help to wave it in their face. Your driver is probably filing a report as we speak."

"The kid?" Despite herself, Sophie realized she had started to grow fond of the punk.

"That kid is company bought and paid for, as is everyone in this town." Deb's hands were thick and strong as they worked up her back.

"You?"

"When I need to be. Why are you here?"

"I need assistance."

"What do you need?" Deb's hands worked her shoulder blades, and then the base of her neck. Sophie could feel the tension in the muscles fighting a losing battle against Deb's firm touch.

"I'm looking for Quail."

Deb's hands stopped kneading, her grip tightening on the back of Sophie's skull. Sophie realized Deb could snap her neck at will. She forced herself to relax. She had to trust her information. She was not the only player in this orchestra.

"For what?"

"We have business to transact. I have things she needs, including the instruction manual for a recent acquisition she made Earthside." Deb didn't have to know that the other thing Quail needed was a lesson in morals that would end her life, preferably in a high-profile, messy way.

"Quail is a very secretive individual." Deb's hands remained still, firmly gripping Sophie's neck. Perhaps she'd played an instrument once herself.

"That is why I need help."

Deb resumed the massage.

"I'll let Quail know that you are looking for her, but tell your friends this is their last favor. This one repays my debt in full. Where are you staying?"

"The Quality."

Deb snorted. "I bet it is."

The lights flickered.

"It looks like your friends are coming to check in on you. Three minute warning."

Shouts and footsteps in the hallway indicated the other guests were making a break for it.

Sophie didn't even bother to lift her head from the table. "I don't suppose my ride is still here?"

"I very much doubt it."

"Well, can you get that knot above my left shoulder blade before the cops arrive?"

* * *

Not getting thrown in jail required four bribes and three different forms signed in triplicate by three different police officers. She promised herself to pay CallistoCom back by closing out her contract in spectacular style. She hated assholes.

The kid was waiting outside her hotel.

"Welcome back!"

"No thanks to you. How did the cops know where I was?"

"This is Callisto. The Com knows everything."

"How much did they pay you to know where I was?"

"Enough." The kid smirked. "But I've got better gig. Quail wants to meet you. Get in." He pointed at the auto-rickshaw.

Sophie looked longingly at the hotel and imagined her bed inside, empty.

She got into the rickshaw. This was her job.

The kid drove around the block, and then turned into a doorway framed by glowing biohazard signs. The stacked yellow barrels indicated this was a storage facility.

"This is your stop." The kid motioned to the auto-rickshaw's door.

"Pardon me if I don't tip." Sophie stepped out onto a concrete floor. Even through her mask, she could sense the air here was thick and bitter.

The kid gunned his engine and darted off, wheels spinning on the concrete. The door rolled shut behind him, leaving half-dozen pale bulbs failing in their attempt to light the space.

"Sophie Devine." A woman's voice rang out. A tall, thin figure stepped out from the behind a stack of barrels. The stern, taut, face matched the file on her target: Quail.

"Today I go by Joanne." Sophie evaluated the angles. She could make the shot, but not without puncturing a barrel of whatever was behind that biohazard label. This wasn't the moment. The music was still building.

"What brings you here?"

"I have the release protocols for the anti-Cripture biotech your organization recently acquired." The bait. "The protocols will save you a lot of trial and error."

"My organization? Sophie, you are mistaken. I work alone."

"CallistoCom is the only organization with the infrastructure to use what you stole. If you work alone . . ."

BOOM!

The door crumpled open behind Sophie. She dove to the side.

The crescendoing climax had arrived.

Sophie drew her gun mid-roll. She took a bead on Quail and watched over the gun barrel as the containers behind Quail exploded. Sophie hadn't squeezed the trigger—someone else had beaten her to the shot. Or tried to—they'd missed; Quail still stood.

Sophie scrambled back to her feet as a tank rolled into the warehouse, CallistoCom purple. It turned, its rail gun arcing as it charged for another round. Shit.

"This way." Quail ran past Sophie, blood streaking down her back.

Sophie looked at the tank, and decided she'd wait to finish off Quail. They had a mutual enemy.

A large, armored, mutual enemy.

Sophie followed Quail out a side door of the warehouse, then up a ladder. As they climbed, blood from Quail's wound dripped onto Sophie's face. What a mess.

The ladder ended at a service hatch in the solar field that lined the surface of Gamma Station. Sophie pulled herself onto the metallic surface. It was dark outside.

"Now what?" It wouldn't take long for the Com's forces to find them. It was their facility, they must know about the access hatch.

"I radioed for backup. We'll be picked up in a moment." Quail sat next to the hatch, clutching her side.

"I thought you worked alone."

"Working alone doesn't mean I don't have friends."

Sophie wondered if Quail's friends would extract Sophie if Quail was dead when they arrived. She didn't risk it. There would be plenty of time to kill Quail after they escaped.

Clickity clickity click. A maintenance-spider approached, dusting the array behind it.

"Here's our ride." The spider stopped in front of them and knelt. Sophie helped Quail mount the small platform atop the robot, and then scrambled aboard herself.

Then they were off.

The stars spun as the spider danced across the array. Sophie felt a little dizzy; she couldn't imagine what Quail was experiencing. Blood loss and carnival rides were not a good combination.

"I don't work for CallistoCom." Quail's voice wasn't as strong as it had been in the warehouse.

"So it appears. Or at least, if you did, they are ready to terminate your contract. Where is the biotech?"

Quail reached into her shirt, withdrawing a small pink vial. "This anaerobic bacteria will displace the niche of the bacteria that causes the

Cripture. CallistoCom infected this land with the Cripture, this can free it."

"Are you saying the Cripture infection is intentional? The cost of treatment is enormous!"

"They didn't create it, but they've done nothing to stop it since they realized the addictive power of the counteragent. The Com maintains control though their monopoly of the Benediction. If the Cripture bacteria is eliminated, they won't own every moment of every life. Without the addiction's grip, their cheap workforce might leave. There might be more value, but the company will control less of it."

The spider spun to a stop beside another access hatch.

"This is the pressure-form control center. From here, power and chemicals are pushed to the atmospheric seeding station. Callisto has been infected with the Cripture for almost three decades. With this bacteria and your protocol, we can break free of the Com."

Sophie's music teacher had once noted the distinction between an improvised solo and the composition of a new piece as a matter of theme. If the theme was maintained, a solo could always be tied back to the original composition.

Regardless of her client's sheet music, Sophie's theme was screwing with CallistoCom. She decided it was time to bust out a solo on her contract.

"Let's get that biotech pushed out." Sophie hopped off the spider and popped the access seal to the pressure-form control center. "You first." She didn't want any more blood dripped on her than necessary.

Quail descended the ladder. Sophie glanced up to the Callisto sky, stars twinkling through the infected pressure-sphere. Kids like the rickshaw driver shouldn't grow up in a world of beggars dying from societal indifference, their biggest hope a lifetime of drug addiction. She could stop that, right here, right now.

The control center was empty and dark. Laboratory instruments and screens lined the walls. Quail twisted the bacteria sample into a tank, and tapped commands at a central console.

"The protocol?"

Sophie handed Quail a chip with the dispersal specs. She'd demanded the specs be real, live bait, in case Quail had decided to pay. Quail placed the chip into the console, and typed a few more lines into the command terminal.

"It's in the breeding chamber. Two minutes of incubating and it will be ready to push." Quail pointed at a big red button on the console interface: release compound.

"Once this goes, it is irreversible?"

"Nothing is impossible, but they'd have to invent a new bacteria to displace this one, and CallistoCom isn't that smart. They stumbled on the Cripture during the initial pressure-form, and just decided to encourage its growth rather than stop it."

Sophie cracked her neck. Time for business. "When will you be paying for the tech and the protocol?"

Quail looked pained. "This release doesn't cost Earth anything. They have plenty of this bacteria. This is just a sample."

"It's my client's intellectual property. They want payment."

"I'm not going to be able to provide that." Quail broke eye contact and turned back to the console.

They were both silent.

The screen flashed green, Quail punched the button.

A cellist knows the ending coda must echo the original exposition, even when the performance includes an improvisational solo off the printed music.

Sophie drew her gun and shot Quail.

Playing classical cello was a lot like assassination, and Sophie Devine believed it was the secret of her success. It made sure she ended on the right note, every time.

SPACEMAN BARBECUE

Peter Wood

"Spaceman Barbecue" fully embraces the pulp fiction adventure stories of the 1940s, 50s and 60s. I am not talking about stories with lurid covers of scantily clad women being carried off by horrible monsters. I refer instead to stories found in *Boys Life* and other "Adventure" magazines. These stories usually had a softer science element and an underachieving protagonist who found new focus and confidence as the adventure progressed. I loved those stories and practically grew up on them. In "Spaceman Barbecue," the adventure begins with the event I prayed for as a child: a crippled spaceship landing in the nearby woods.

Peter Wood, an attorney in Raleigh, North Carolina, lives with his surly cat and forgiving wife. Growing up in Ottawa, Canada, and Tampa, Florida, he watched *Star Trek* and *Outer Limits* episodes and listened to vintage radio shows like *X Minus One*. Pete's literary heroes include Bradbury, Vonnegut, and Hemingway. His stories have appeared in *Stupefying Stories, Daily Science Fiction,* and *Bull Spec.* He hopes "Spaceman Barbecue" heralds a new genre, Southern Fried Science Fiction.

Hank followed the smoke the rocket spewed as it dove into the pines behind his trailer. He tripped over a rotten stump and fell into the clearing. His ex-wife was bringing their son over for his biweekly visitation. With a spaceship in the woods, even she would understand if he wasn't outside waiting.

A silver rocket almost as tall as some of the nearby trees listed like a drunk at closing time. A slot in the ship's side hissed open. A man in a sparkling gold space suit stepped outside and gestured to Hank.

"Citizen! How far to the Mentone space port?"

Hank had lived in the backwoods town his entire thirty years. Mentone didn't even have an AM radio station.

"There's no space port around here," Hank yelled back.

There was a rustling from the woods. The spaceman pulled out what resembled a ray gun from an old science fiction television show. A deer bolted through the pokeweed and brambles.

Hank didn't want to discover the weapon's powers. "Easy, bossman."

The spaceman exhaled loudly. "You have to watch for mutants."

"Not much of a mutant problem around here," Hank drawled.

"I'm Commander Matt Brannigan of Space Command. I need to find the space port."

"You're in Mentone, North Carolina. We have three filling stations and six Baptist churches. But no space port."

* * *

Hank's battered pickup stopped on the main highway and he and Matt stared at the expanse of corn fields and cow pastures that stretched in both directions. Things sure didn't look futuristic. Hank was late for his son, but if a space port lurked somewhere in Mentone, it would be worth it.

"Where's this space port?" he asked Matt.

"One moment, citizen."

Hank smiled. "My name's Hank."

"Sure, Hank." Matt waved his hand over a silver object the size and shape of a pen. A tiny three dimensional ravishing redhead in a form-fitting spacesuit materialized.

Hank blinked. "What's that?"

"Omnivac computer. It communicates through the girl. Transmitting Interface something or other. The troops call her Trixie."

"Your request?" Trixie cooed.

"Where's the Space port?"

Trixie blew him a kiss. "No signal detected. But the port should be one point four miles west."

"Matt turned to Hank. "Can you find that?"

Hank shrugged. "I don't usually drive as the crow flies."

Matt pointed to the gear shift. "Just shift into fly."

"You want me to fly like the Jetsons or something?"

"Faster than driving. Space Command flies everywhere."

Hank cleared his throat. "My truck just drives."

Five minutes later Hank's pickup sputtered into a trash-strewn parking lot where a hamburger stand had been back in his high school days.

"This isn't the space port," Matt said. "There are no rockets, no landing pads."

Hank stared at Matt. If there hadn't been a rocket ship in his backyard, he would've assumed that the stranger was a lunatic.

* * *

Arms crossed, Hank's ex-wife, Darlene, sat with their six year old son, Billy on rusty lawn chairs on the concrete slab that passed for Hank's front porch. "You're late."

Hank winced. She was annoyed again. He forced a smile. "How y'all been?"

Billy's oversized Barbecue Barn T-shirt proclaimed "If You're Tired of Barbecue, You're Tired of Life." Hank hugged him. "Good to see you, sport."

Billy giggled.

Darlene picked up the dog-eared Ernest Hemingway novel Hank had dropped on the porch. "You ever going to finish that Master's?"

Hank snatched the book from her. It was just another thing that stonewalled him. He used to make A's at NC State, but since his Dad passed five years ago Hank couldn't get anything done. He was still working a stopgap job at the Barbecue Barn and living in Daddy's old doublewide. "I just need to finish my Hemingway thesis."

Darlene rolled her eyes.

Matt stepped out of the truck. The sun glistened off his metallic suit. "Good evening, citizens."

Darlene's eyebrows rose. "Evening." She turned to Hank. "Who's your friend?"

"Matt works with me," Hank lied.

Matt gave Darlene a half salute. "I'm Commander Matt Brannigan from Space Command."

Darlene's nose crinkled. "Is that so?"

Hank just smiled. He wasn't sure what else to do. "He's joking."

"Are you a spaceman?" Billy gasped.

"Yes, citizen." Matt patted his ray gun. "Protecting the cosmos."

Billy's eyes opened wide. "Is that gun real?"

Matt nodded. "Yes, citizen, but photon guns aren't for children."

Darlene turned to Hank. "Billy and I want to show you something in the car."

Hank didn't want to hear again how he was screwing up. Darlene didn't care that he was doing the best he could, living on his Daddy's land, selling timber once in a while. She kept pushing him. "Sure, let's go see."

Darlene smiled at Billy. "Show Daddy your new toy." When Billy raced to open the car door, she walked through knee-high grass until they were out of earshot of Matt. "Okay, what's the deal with the spaceman?"

Hank suspected it would take more than a rocket ship in his back yard to convince her. "Matt loves kids. He gets a little carried away sometimes."

Out of breath, Billy ran up. "Daddy, see what Mommy got me." He brandished a bright red toy ray gun.

"He says everybody has ray guns in those TV shows you watch," Darlene said.

A loud clanging came from the side of the trailer. A raccoon sprang off the garbage can with a half-eaten fast food hamburger in its mouth. It had undone the bungee cords holding down the lid.

"Scat!" Hank yelled.

Matt ran to the trash cans, his gun cocked. "Are there mutants?"

Darlene glared at Hank. "Mutants?"

"No mutants," Hank muttered.

Darlene, in a very sweet and controlled voice, said to Billy, "Wait in the car. We'll see Daddy later."

"I want to play with the spaceman!"

Darlene's voice was firm. "In the car now."

"It's not fair." Billy stuck out his lower lip and stomped away.

"I know this looks crazy," Hank said.

"Don't even start. I don't want to hear about your pothead friends. I thought you were maturing, Hank."

Hank exhaled slowly. She just didn't care how hard it was to lose Daddy from cancer. "Maybe there are mutants where he's from. I saw him fly down in a rocket." He pointed to the pine trees. "His ship's in the woods."

Then he noticed Darlene filming him with her mobile phone.

"What are you doing?" he asked.

Her eyes showed more exasperation than anger. "Just stop it, please. I can't leave Billy with some drug addict. Don't make me show my lawyer this film of you talking about spacemen."

Hank threw up his hands. "Last time you got pissed, because I let him watch Star Trek."

"You spend more time learning about fantasy worlds than the real one. You can name every Star Trek episode, but you can't get a real job."

Hank swore under his breath as he noticed Matt carefully examining the trash can.

"What are you doing, Matt?" Darlene called out.

Matt picked up the trash can lid. "Checking for radiation burns.

My Geiger counter's in the ship. Mutants always leave signs."

"It was a raccoon, not Mothra," Hank muttered.

Matt pushed the trash can to the side. "Mutants start out small. But they get out of hand quick. Last year Birmingham had dragonflies that flew off with city buses. And those monster ants in Phoenix about destroyed the city."

Darlene was breathing hard. "Damn it, Hank. Now you're hanging around some loser who dresses up and goes to science fiction conventions? Except he can't wait for the convention so he wears a costume every day."

"Or he's telling the truth," Hank said.

Darlene marched away without another word.

* * *

Matt glanced about Hank's cluttered living room. Pushing some textbooks aside, he sank into the sofa. "You must be rich. I haven't seen this many books out of a museum."

"Y'all read much?" Hank knew he should be angry. Darlene said he rolled with the punches too much about everything. But he felt sorry for Matt. Wherever he was from, he had nowhere else to go.

Matt put down the most recent Hemingway Monthly and passed his hand over the omnivac. "Tell me a book," he said to Hank.

Hank shrugged. "*The Sun Also Rises?*"

Trixie appeared in a flash before them. She wore a Roaring Twenties flapper dress and pearls. She easily could have slipped into Hemingway's novel about rich Americans wandering around post World War One Europe. She started talking about fly fishing in Spain.

Hank laughed. "Stop. I've had it with Hemingway and fishing. He wrote an entire book about it."

"Hemingway never wrote a novel about fishing," Trixie said.

"Sure. In 1951. The Old Man and the Sea."

"Hemingway died in a German atomic attack in 1946," Trixie said.

Hank shook his head. "Germany surrendered in 1945."

Trixie paused momentarily like she might be stumped. "This is an alternative reality."

Matt stared at Trixie. "What the hell are you talking about?"

She put her hands on her hips. "It's obvious. Nobody here has heard of mutants. There is no radiation. Hemingway apparently lived longer in this world than in ours."

Matt turned to Hank. "Did you have an atomic war?"

"No."

"We did," Matt said. "That's why we colonized space."

* * *

A couple of days later Hank yawned as he trudged through the woods. He sipped a jumbo Jiffy Mart coffee. He had a shift at the Barbecue Barn in three hours.

He heard Matt's deep voice singing. "Every man does what he can. All for the good of the Space Command!"

He entered the clearing Matt had spent the previous day sprucing up. The ground was freshly mowed and branches were stacked in neat piles.

Matt was polishing the rocket, as he had done last night at sunset. "The space drive's fried. Trixie thinks a space rift somehow interacted with the anti-matter flux and caused the reality shift."

Hank swigged his coffee. He hoped the caffeine kicked in soon. "Is it fixable?"

Matt wiped the sweat off his face. "No, sir." He slapped the ship's side. "Her flying days are over. But Space Command will find a way. They always do."

Hank swatted a mosquito. "You think another ship's going to slip through?"

Matt grinned. "Trixie's listening for ship signatures."

"You know you can only clean up your ship so much. In the

meantime you think you want a job?"

"Matt squinted. "A job?"

"At the Barbecue Barn. You'll make barbecue."

"What's barbecue?"

* * *

Hank sat on a cracked plastic chair beside the Barbecue Barn's smoking pit. He glanced occasionally at the whole hog that sizzled on the grill. Every so often he poked it with a metal spatula or sprinkled it with the restaurant's special rub of salt, black pepper and cayenne. In a couple of hours he and Matt would lift it off the smoldering cedar fire and chop it up for sandwiches and barbecue plates.

Wearing Hank's sneakers and jeans and a Barbecue Barn t-shirt, Matt picked up trash in the gravel parking lot. He had told Hank he couldn't just sit. He needed to feel productive.

Hank heard a loud beep. Matt pulled out the omnivac.

Trixie appeared. "Signal detected from a Mars Transport." She paused. "The signal is gone." The last few hours she had detected a dozen signals, but none had lasted more than seconds.

"You'll get another signal soon," Hank said, although he had no idea what he was talking about.

Matt sighed. "Trixie says the rift's weakening." He half-heartedly whistled a few bars of the Space Command theme. "But, Space Command will find a way."

Then Darlene's car pulled around to the back of the restaurant. It kicked up gravel and parked.

Billy jumped out and ran to Hank. "Daddy!"

Hank picked up his son. "Hey, buddy!"

Darlene walked slowly towards the fire pit. She allowed herself a small smile. "So, Matt really works here."

"Told you he did," Hank said.

Billy's eyes opened wide. "I see the spaceman!"

"He's not a real spaceman, honey," Darlene turned to Hank. "Tell him, Hank."

Hank shook his head. "Can't do that, Darlene. Matt just might be the real thing."

Darlene glared.

"He told me about his spaceship last night," Hank said to Billy.

"Did he bring his ray gun?" Billy asked.

Hank winked at Billy. "He left it at home."

Darlene watched Matt toss a grease-stained Styrofoam to-go box into a bulging garbage bag. "Your spaceman friend works pretty hard. He doesn't just sit around and read and call it work."

Billy walked towards Matt and pulled out his toy ray gun. "Gotcha!"

Matt grabbed his chest. "Good shot!"

"I'll get a degree," Hank said to Darlene.

"You know, Hank, you do a lot of talking. You've been promising for five years you'd finish school."

Hank frowned. "I've had a lot happen."

"I miss your Dad too. But you got to move on." She laughed. "It's funny that you think a rocket landed in your yard. You've been waiting a long time for something to fall out of the sky and tell you how to live your life."

* * *

Matt took a long sip from his fourth bottle of Pabst Blue Ribbon as he and Hank listened to the NC State game on the porch. "Watch this," he slurred. He tossed the bottle in the air and fired his ray gun. The bottle glowed bright red and vaporized before it hit the ground. "Fastest gun in Space Command."

Hank let out a low whistle. "Holy Crap." He reached into a battered cooler and pulled out two dripping wet beers. He handed one to Matt.

Matt uncapped the bottle. He held out the gun. "Want to take a shot?"

Hank took the weapon. "How's it work?"

"It's got different settings. Lowest setting will just warm things up. We use it sometimes in the ship's cafeteria. Damned kitchen staff serves cold food half the time. Highest setting disintegrates."

Hank studied the weapon. "You use this in battles?"

Matt laughed. "Nah. Target practice. Sometimes the gun loosens up the molten ore down in the ship's hold." He winked at hank. "But that's not official."

"Molten ore?"

"Yep. Dangerous work, scooping up molten metal from Mercury. We lose a man every run or so. Hoping for a cushier job someday. When I get back." He sipped his beer. "If I get back."

Hank cocked the weapon and pointed it at an abandoned mower that had rusted away in the yard since his Dad died. "What do I do?"

Matt belched. "Squeeze the trigger."

The old mower glowed and vanished.

* * *

The next Saturday Hank sat by the smoking pit. He nursed a Jiffy Mart coffee. *The Sun Also Rises* sat on his lap. Flapper Trixie narrated.

She paused to explain a passage. "Hemingway is talking about the upcoming war."

Hank had only been half listening, but he sat up straight "Four drunks playing bridge is about war?"

"Hemingway's death had to mean something. Most critics agree that his novels expound atomicism."

"What the hell are you talking about?"

"Atomicism is the worldwide philosophy that arose after the atomic war. A third of Earth was in radioactive ruins. Give up or build for the future were the choices. The basic tenets of atomicism are: One, accept the past. Two, everybody has worth and is productive. Three, all things must lead to a better future."

And Hank wondered how productive he had been. Then he realized the book's real message. It was about crippling fear. The main characters were so traumatized by WWI that their lives were stunted and pointless. It was all too familiar. "Thanks, but I think I know what I'll write about." He started flipping through the book.

Frowning, Matt came around the corner of the concrete restaurant, holding a bucket of soapy water and a brush. He was sweaty and dirty. "What are you doing?"

"Working on my thesis." Hank handed the omnivac to Matt. "I won't need this anymore."

"You haven't been using it, have you?" Matt snapped.

"For about half an hour today." Hank felt bad for Matt. It had been a stressful week. Trixie had nothing but bad news. After a flurry of calls the first couple of days she had detected only three ships the last week. And they had blipped in and out in the wink of an eye each time. Trixie almost seemed to enjoy reporting that the dimensional portal was dissipating. "Matt, do you believe in atomicism?"

Matt sneered. "Yeah, everybody does."

"Trixie said-"

Matt didn't let him finish. "Yeah, I know what Trixie said. Atomicism is the philosophy that saved humanity. All I know is I work my tail off hauling molten ore so I could send my wife and kids off-world."

"I didn't know you had a family."

"Why the hell would you care about my family when you don't care about your own? I'll never see them again. They'll lose the house and Space Command's death benefit will be just enough for passage back to Earth."

"I'm sorry."

Matt sat down on a lawn chair and let out a harsh laugh. "Atomicism. Everything must lead to a better future. Everything has a purpose. What's my purpose in being here?"

"I don't know."

Matt scowled at Hank. "But at least I had one once. I don't think you ever had a purpose."

"My Dad died and I-"

"Do you have any idea how many people died in the atomic war?"

Hank looked at the smoking pork and wondered how much time he had wasted, making barely minimum wage. And then he had a thought. Hadn't Matt told him they had used the photon guns to warm up food and blast dirt off walls? Maybe the gun could help him. He turned to Matt. "Can I see your ray gun?"

Matt shrugged and handed it over.

Hank twirled the controls and stopped somewhere between the setting for warming food and blasting mildew off the walls of the Barbecue Barn. He fired the gun.

The rich smell of roast pork filled the air. The aroma was more pungent than any Hank had smelled before.

Hank pulled out his pocket knife and sliced off a thick piece of barbecue. The outside was crispy and spicy and sealed in the meat's succulent juices. Barbecue was often dry and had to be soaked with sauce. It was hard to get just right. But this batch was better than perfect. Somehow the rub had infused the entire roast. "This may be the best barbecue I've ever had. How long will that ray gun hold out?"

Matt looked puzzled. "Forever. They're solar powered."

Hank smiled. "Bossman, I have an idea."

* * *

A week later Hank whistled the Space Command theme as he drove his truck onto his property. It had been a good week. After not setting foot on campus for two years, Hank finally handed his thesis to his advisor. The professor seemed surprised to see him.

Then today he started the next phase of his life.

He slammed the truck door. He wore his only suit, the clothes he had donned for Daddy's funeral. He'd never cook barbecue for another ungrateful boss.

The bank loan officer today was impressed with the plate of photon-infused pork Hank had brought by. He just wanted to inspect his land and see where Hank planned to build the restaurant.

He loosened his tie. He had a lot of work to do if he was going to clear those trees from the road up to the spaceship. Matt's rocket was going to be the centerpiece of the new restaurant.

The spaceman sipped a beer on the front porch.

"Hey, bossman," Hank called out. "Looks like I might get that mortgage."

"Good news, citizen," Matt said without enthusiasm.

There had not been a signal in almost a week. Hank hoped Matt hadn't given up trying. "Look, I got to run down to McCrae's hardware. I'm getting some lumber to fix up the house a bit. And I need a new blade for a bow saw. Come on along. It'll be good to get out for a little bit."

Matt sighed. "Sure, citizen. Why not?"

* * *

Hank parked at the hardware store. Matt had silently looked out the window for the thirty minute drive. The Omnivac lay on the floor of the truck, almost like it was trash.

It beeped loudly. Trixie appeared. "Incoming transmission."

A staticky voice said "Commander Matt Brannigan, we are approaching your vessel. Be prepared for immediate rescue. Our time in this world is limited. We'll be lucky to last twenty minutes."

"Damn!" Matt snapped. "We don't have enough time."

Hank whipped the steering wheel around. "We'll make it."

* * *

The first ten minutes of driving thirty miles over the speed limit on two lane country roads were relatively simple. Then the cop pulled behind Hank. Two minutes later as Hank gunned the engine and passed a semi a second police car, lights flashing and siren screaming, joined the pursuit. Then a third cop car appeared.

Hank's mobile phone rang. "Hello?"

"Billy and I are at your place," Darlene said. "I thought I'd surprise you with an afternoon visit. Where are you?"

Hank laughed. "I'll see y'all in a minute." He hit the brakes and swung onto the dirt road that led to his trailer.

Matt had been talking with the rescue ship's Captain. Trixie had been right. The space anomaly was weakening fast. This was probably the spaceman's last chance.

"What's wrong?" Darlene asked in that too serious tone she reserved for Hank.

"I might be going to jail."

Darlene's voice almost drowned out the sirens. "What did you do?"

"I got a mess of police cars behind me. A spaceship is coming to get Matt. I broke a bunch of traffic laws to get him to the trailer on time." The speedometer said ninety.

"I hear the sirens," Darlene yelled. "I warned you about these stories." She hung up.

Hank saw an old-fashioned flying saucer hovering over the forest.

"I see the ship. I'm leaving the truck," Matt said over the omnivac.

"We're lowering the gangway." The Captain's voice crackled and faded.

Hank slammed on the brakes.

Matt jumped from the truck. "Thanks, bossman." He handed Hank his photon gun. "Take this. It might come in handy."

The gangway touched ground and Matt scrambled on board the ship.

A half minute later the gangway slapped shut. A crimson ray fired into the woods. Flames shot into the sky.

Hank guessed that Space Command had destroyed Matt's ship. They probably didn't want to risk leaving advanced technology on this world.

The flying saucer flickered and blinked away.

Three police officers gawked at the sky. One was filming with a mobile phone.

Then Hank saw Darlene and Billy.

"Where'd the spaceman go?" Billy asked.

"You were telling the truth," Darlene said.

Hank picked up Billy. "He went home, son."

* * *

Hank handed a plate heaped with piping-hot barbecue, Cole slaw and creamed potatoes to Darlene. Since he had opened Spaceman Barbecue four months ago she always got a free meal when she dropped Billy off.

She smiled. "Thanks."

Hank smiled back. They weren't together, but they were getting along. And that was good enough for now. He gave Billy chicken tenders. "One junior spaceman plate."

They sat in the replica of Matt's spaceship Hank had constructed. Darlene pointed to a photo on the wall of Matt's rescue saucer. "You ever wonder about Matt?"

Hank sipped his sweet tea. "All the time."

"What do you think he's doing?"

Hank doused his pork with hot sauce. "I hope he's opened his own barbecue joint."

OBSIDIANITE

Kat Otis

Trader-adventure stories have always been well-received by readers of Grand Tradition stories because of their action-adventure elements. Some of the best-known SF Trader tales are those of the Polesotechnic League series by Poul Anderson, featuring sweeping tales of the well-heeled Nicholas van Rijn and his associate David Falkayn who use their wits and a whatever-it-takes approach to make a profit. Another take on the trader-adventure story is epitomized by Andre Norton's novels describing the travails of the crew of the *Solar Queen*, a small independent interstellar trade ship whose owners always appear to be teetering on the edge of insolvency. Author Kat Otis' story "Obsidianite" fits well within the merchant adventure profile. In "Obsidianite," Janessa's profit, pride, and personal history mix explosively on the side of a volcano.

Kat Otis lives a peripatetic life with cats who enjoy riding in the car as long as there's no country music involved. Her fiction has appeared in Orson Scott Card's *Intergalactic Medicine Show*, *Daily Science Fiction* and Marion Zimmer Bradley's *Sword & Sorceress XXVI*. She can be found online at katotis.com or on Twitter as @kat_otis.

The moment the *Bonadventure* emerged from FTL, Janessa began calling up system reports.

It wasn't that she didn't trust her newest pilot—Darion was better than her last three pilots combined. But Darion was also still young and didn't have much experience with interstellar travel. Anyone with half an understanding of calculus could throw together coordinates for a basic FTL jump; the difficult part was making the dozens of ship-specific adjustments required to make the jump without damaging said ship. One of the *Bonadventure's* aft sensor arrays was especially prone to shearing off in transit—she'd owned the ship for seven years and lost as many arrays in the same time period.

"I didn't botch the calculations, Jan." Darion drummed his fingers on the arm of his chair. "All systems should be green to go. Will you stop fussing and check out the planet? I think that transmission really was a distress call."

"*Should* be," Janessa muttered, even though the reports all seemed to be agreeing with him. Still, as a freelance trader—and occasional treasure hunter—her entire livelihood depended on her ship's welfare, which meant she checked every single system report and made certain her ship was in perfect working order before allowing her attention to be diverted to the visual he'd plastered across all four of the bridge's viewscreens.

At first glance, the viewscreen only appeared to show what they already knew. The mysterious transmission they'd received five hours earlier had originated on this solar system's only terrestrial planet. The Interplanetary Database supplied them with its name—New Galilee— and classification—Luddite, which meant it eschewed all spacefaring technology and was closed to interplanetary commerce. The latter was particularly obvious from space as its orbits remained uncluttered by stations, ships or even space debris. The planet was pristine, all greens and blues, the way historic Earth was always portrayed in holovids.

Of course, in the holovids there usually wasn't an enormous cloud of ash spewing out of an erupting volcano near the horizon line.

"You think that's their problem?" Janessa pulled up the full Interplanetary Database's entry on New Galilee and began scrolling through, looking for information on the planet's communications capabilities. "The transmission didn't mention a volcano." Then again, the transmission hadn't said much of anything; it had mostly consisted of apocalyptic ranting that didn't bear so much as a passing resemblance to a distress call, for all that it had been broadcast on the dedicated emergency frequencies.

"What else could it be?" Darion asked. "I'll put us in low orbit and see if we can get a response back on the same frequency."

Janessa paused as a line of text caught her attention. The planet's only settlement had been built near the summit of a landform that the New Galileans called Mount Sinai, but it wasn't really a mountain—it was a volcano. She cross-checked the settlement's coordinates with the sensor data and her stomach lurched. "Don't get your hopes up. I doubt there's anyone left down there."

"What are you talking about?"

She flipped the text up onto the starboard viewscreen and enlarged the pertinent sentences so Darion could read them easily. All color drained out of his face. "That can't be right—why would they do that? It's insane!"

"The volcano was supposed to be extinct." Janessa scanned the next few lines. "Initial exploratory surveys suggested it hadn't erupted in over twelve thousand years."

"But they must have put seismometers in place—"

"Luddites," Janessa reminded him. "By the time there were visible signs of volcanic activity, it was probably too late to evacuate." Though there'd apparently been enough time to send off a transmission about the redemption of repentant souls and the smiting of the wicked.

"All those dead," Darion whispered.

Janessa didn't particularly want to think about the New Galilee population estimate she'd seen in passing, nor the percentage of that population that had been under the age of sixteen. No good could come from crying over an empty oxygen tank, after all. Instead she tried to refocus on what she did best: making money.

The New Galilee volcano was as good a treasure trove as any ancient ruin. That was how she had to think of it—as an ancient ruin, its inhabitants long dead and far beyond the need for anyone's help. And the treasures from that volcano would be worth enough to earn back all the costs of their detour and more.

"We'll call it Galilean Obsidian," she decided, scrolling to the mineralogy reports. High silica content, good. Gold, copper, iron and aluminum were all listed, as well. It looked promising enough that she dared to hope they'd find some brilliant colors in the volcano's obsidian flows. Black obsidian could be made into nice, saleable jewelry; rainbow obsidian would make stunning and very expensive jewelry, especially when coupled with a tragic story like New Galilee's. Every socialite in the Sharman Sector would be desperate to get her hands on a piece of Galilean Obsidian, at least until the next fashion trend eclipsed it.

"We . . . what?" Darion stared as if she'd lost her mind.

Janessa shook her head. "Don't worry about it." She'd hired him for his piloting skills, not his business sense, though she'd had hopes he would eventually develop the latter. He hadn't. He'd still managed to last longer than most of her post-Ethan pilots—almost five months— but she was probably going to have to find herself a new pilot soon. Hopefully, they'd earn enough off this venture that he wouldn't object to being ditched at Jemison Station. "Just focus on your flying—we're going planetside."

* * *

The *Bonadventure* had originally been designed as an in-system yacht and only later modified to function in deep space. The finicky sensor arrays were one of the more irritating consequences of not buying an exclusively purposed tradeship, but Janessa had been more than willing to put up with such quirks because her ship had one feature that tradeships lacked: it could handle atmospheric flying and even planetary landings. It would take a ridiculous quantity of fuel to escape the planet's gravity well, afterwards, but every good trader knew you had to spend money to make money.

Darion took his sweet time bringing them down, allowing them to slowly adjust to the increased gravity while he scanned every available frequency for any sort of communication. Janessa did her own scans, looking for signs of human habitation that might have served as a refugee camp, but without much hope. There wasn't even a trace of New Galilee's original settlement—it had probably been buried when the volcano erupted.

Janessa consoled herself with the knowledge that none of them could have suffered long—there were far worse ways to die. Then she turned her attention back to the mineralogy reports. "Find us a safe landing spot, a klick or three away from the crater. You can keep monitoring the comm for survivors while I check out the lava flows."

"Check *what* out?" Darion demanded, but obediently began searching for a place to land while Janessa went to gear up.

She didn't have a proper heat suit, but she wasn't expecting to hit temperatures of more than 700 Kelvin. Instead, she made sure almost every inch of her skin was covered, from her thick-treaded boots to her gloves and hard hat. She carabinered a laser scalpel and gas mask to her climbing harness, hoping to use the former but not the latter. Last, but not least, she shrugged into the straps of her backpack, making sure to distribute its minimal weight evenly over both shoulders.

To his credit, Darion didn't laugh when she reemerged on the bridge, though he did give her a sidelong look that showed his thoughts clear as crystal. He thought she was mental. Well, she probably was, a little bit. The *Bonadventure*'s safety was one thing; her own was another matter entirely. Fourteen years of risking life and limb to turn a profit had definitely skewed her definitions of *acceptable personal risk* to the extremities of the human bell curve.

"Three standard deviations of crazy," Janessa said, though she knew it would confuse Darion. Unlike some of her other pilots, he'd never implied she was merely the brawn of their operation, so she'd mostly broken her habit of randomly lapsing into brainiac jargon. Maybe she should hold onto him a little while longer. If Darion made it to six months, that would break her post-Ethan record of five months and three weeks, which was almost reason enough in itself to keep him.

"Say what?"

"Never mind." Janessa checked her consoles again, trying to get the lay of the land. There were some promising-looking lava flows a quarter klick east of their landing site. She reeled off the coordinates. "I'm going to head that way. Keep a comm channel open to me, you know the drill." Not that Darion had ever monitored her planetside, but he'd supervised enough of her space walks that he ought to be able to translate the skill.

"And if I make contact with any survivors?" Darion asked, with relentless optimism. Or maybe it was just denial. Either way it made her feel old, reminding her that she was almost twice his age. That annoyed her; when the human life expectancy was almost a hundred and ten, she shouldn't feel old at thirty-eight. No, it really was time to get rid of him and find a new pilot.

"If," she bit off the word, "they've survived this long, they can last an hour or two longer. It shouldn't take me too much time to look around and get back here." Hopefully with a backpack full of souvenirs, though it wouldn't do to bring too much obsidian back. An object's value was in direct correlation with its scarcity, after all.

Darion bit his lip and looked unhappy, but he didn't protest as she went back to the airlock and cycled herself out onto the surface of the volcano.

The heat hit Janessa first, sweat popping out from every pore and trickling down her skin. The overwhelming stench of sulfur registered next, nearly making her gag. Her boots sank at least a decimeter deep into the ash lining the ground and even more ash was falling from the sky, dusting her clothing and clinging to her eyelashes. Every time she breathed in, she could taste the ash coating her tongue and drying out her mouth. She hoped she didn't end up coughing up that crap for the next several days.

She toggled the comm channel open and cleared her throat, "You read me?"

"Loud and clear," Darion said.

She glanced around, trying to orient herself in the right direction, but anything more than ten meters away was obscured by a thick curtain of falling ash. The *Bonadventure*'s landing gear had left two deep furrows in the ash, which probably stretched out a good quarter klick or more, but of course they led in the wrong direction. "Visibility officially sucks out here."

"No problem, I'll give you a shout if you go off course."

That was the kind of thing only a pilot could say, holed up safe and sound aboard the *Bonadventure* while she took all the risks. It would never occur to him that she wasn't concerned about getting lost so much as stumbling into an active lava flow or getting crushed by a volcanic bomb she hadn't seen in time to dodge. But standing in place wasn't going to get the job done—and her back to safety—any faster, so she began to carefully pick her away across the surface of the volcano. If there was such a place as hell, it had to be very much like this.

Once upon a time, she'd believed in heaven and hell and till death do us part. That faith had died in a burst of gamma radiation, along with her unborn child, her fertility and—though she didn't realize it at the time—her marriage. Ethan had sworn he didn't care about children; he claimed they were a bloody expensive hobby he could do without. She'd believed him for two years before she realized he was having an affair. Knowing her own recklessness was at least partially to blame for their estrangement hadn't made the ensuing fall-out any easier to deal with. She should have known better than to spacewalk pregnant, and the New Galileans should have put seismometers in place, and either way it was the children who somehow ended up paying the most for their parents' stupidity.

Not the cheeriest line of thought while she was climbing around on an active volcano. "Darion, you still with me?"

There was a crackle of static, barely audible over the dull roar of the eruption, then Darion's voice came through. "You're still on course, maybe fifty meters still to go."

"Getting a bit of noise in the signal."

"I'll keep an eye on it," Darion promised. "Might be why I haven't heard so much as a peep on any other frequency."

Or he wasn't hearing anything because there wasn't anything to hear. Janessa bit her lip and didn't say it; if he hadn't already considered the possibility, nothing she said was going to convince him.

Up ahead, she thought she caught a glimpse of something red-hot and glowing. She slowed her pace, moving even more cautiously and squinting to see through the ash falls. Despite what she'd told Darion, she didn't actually want to find a lava flow. Or rather, she didn't want to find an *active* lava flow; she wanted a nice little river of felsic lava that had already solidified into obsidian. With this much ash, it wasn't strictly necessary to find real obsidian—she could use an acetylene torch to melt the ash into obsidianite that would net her enough to recoup her landing costs—but obsidian would be a hundred times more valuable.

As she got closer, it became clear that she'd found a partially solidified flow, glowing streaks of red-hot lava standing out against the darker, solidified lava like veins in a man's arms. If she could afford to wait until later, she might be able to mine it safely, but even she wasn't fool enough to start poking around at it now. "This one's a bust. I'm going to follow it and see if it forks anywhere."

"Sensors show something maybe a hundred meters south-southwest of your current location," Darion offered, helpfully.

Janessa refrained from pointing out to him the impossibility of her judging south-southwest. "Just keep an eye on my location and give me a shout if I'm about to go *into* the lava, okay?"

"Roger that."

She backed a respectable distance away from the lava flow, then turned and began following it. Within thirty meters, it split in two. The other fork was no more solid than the first, so she didn't bother branching off after it. There had to be something better, if only she could *find* it.

After a good half an hour of walking, though, she had to admit she was no closer to finding the right kind of lava flow than she had been when she left the ship. That and she was getting perilously close to the edge of comm range—the static had grown exponentially. She was just about to give up on finding natural obsidian, and go back for an acetylene torch to make obsidianite, when there was a crackle of static over the comm that resolved into Darion's voice.

"We've got company."

Darion would have sounded much happier if he'd found survivors. "Someone else responded to the distress call?"

"I don't know, they didn't open communication when I pinged them. Um, ship's transmitter is broadcasting its registration—Alpha Six Niner Quebec Echo Delta. The *Sundancer*, registered to-"

"Ethan." Janessa's stomach lurched. "Ethan d'Lacour."

"That's right, how did you know?"

"Don't ping again—I'll be right there."

* * *

Janessa cursed her misfortune all the way back to the *Bonadventure*.

Of all the people to be in the sector, it had to be her ex-husband. Most people would have ignored such an odd not-distress call, but she'd worked with him for long enough that their mind ran along similar tracks. He was doubtless here for the same reason she was—to make a quick profit. Unfortunately, every penny Ethan made off of New Galilee would be a penny less for her to pay her bills. There were only so many rich socialites willing to pay whatever it took to have the latest in fashionable accessories the moment they first became available; most people would wait until a horde of eager treasure hunters had brought down the price by flooding the interplanetary markets with Galilean Obsidian.

She cycled through the airlock and headed for the bridge, wincing a little at the ash she was shedding all over the place. Darion's eyes went wide when he saw her and she held up her hand, palm-out. "Not one word—there'll be plenty of time to clean up once we're in FTL. Sitrep?"

Darion flipped an image of the planet up onto the viewscreen. "The *Sundancer*'s in a geostationary orbit. They launched a lander and it headed straight for the volcano." He zoomed in and traced out the lander's trajectory on the screen; whoever was piloting had done a flyover of the settlement's coordinates before setting down dangerously close to the crater. "I haven't pinged them again. They seem to be ignoring us."

Of course Ethan was ignoring her—every second was precious, now, if he wanted to beat her off the planet and back to civilization. The lander was little more than a rocket attached to an escape pod; it could take off much faster than the *Bonadventure*, but he'd lose at least a quarter hour with docking procedures, no matter how much he hurried them. So long as they left before the lander did, they ought to be in the clear. If the lander beat them off the volcano . . . all bets would be off.

"All right. Start on the pre-launch checklist. I'll be back before you're done."

"You going to tell me how you know this guy?"

"Tick tock," she said over her shoulder as she turned away. "We're on a tight schedule and time's a-wasting."

"Janessa—"

She pretended not to hear him and headed back towards the airlock. It would only take Darion maybe ten minutes to do the pre-launch checklist, so she wasted no time in finding an acetylene torch and cycling back out of the airlock.

This time she was grateful for the ash that was still thick in the air and even thicker on the ground. She went a few meters from the *Bonadventure*, to give herself a safe working zone, then turned on the gas and lit the torch.

It wasn't long before the ash began to melt into chunks of reddish glass. She gave the chunks time to cool while she filled her pack with more ash, in case she ruined this batch and needed to make more obsidianite once they were back in civilization. Then she gathered her meager bounty, wincing at the heat that radiated through her gloves, and hurried back inside.

Janessa stowed everything carefully and stripped off the worst of her ashy gear before heading back to the bridge. "Please tell me we're ready to go?"

"Just waiting for you," Darion said, powering up the engines.

Janessa dropped into her seat and strapped herself in. A quick check of the sensors showed that the *Sundancer*'s lander was still on the volcano. She smiled at the readings. Even if the lander took off, right that instant, she'd still have a lead in the race back to civilization. *Eat my exhaust cloud, Ethan.*

While Darion taxied the *Bonadventure* into position for take-off, she turned her attention to composing the message she would send to all the local treasure hunters once they reached Jemison Station. With Ethan right on her tail, there was no point in trying to keep the planet a secret. She scaled the fee she was asking, depending on the amount of information they wanted. The planet's coordinates alone would be relatively cheap; details on the disaster would cost them significantly more. The smart ones would be able to extrapolate the volcanic eruption from the Interplanetary Database entry on New Galilee, but there were always people willing to pay someone else to do their thinking for them.

A hiss on the emergency channels broke her concentration, then Ethan's voice came in loud and clear. "Mayday, mayday, mayday. This is *Sundancer, Sundancer, Sundancer*. Mayday, *Sundancer*. I require immediate assistance, over."

"Now *that* is a proper distress call," Darion said, reaching across the console.

"Was it?" Janessa swatted his hand away. "I didn't hear anything."

"Jan!" Darion protested.

"It's a ruse," she told him. "Oldest trick in the book. Well, one of the oldest, anyway." Ethan had probably noticed Darion start the engines and was trying to cut into their head start, delaying them with a fake distress call.

"How can you be sure? Who *is* this guy?"

Janessa considered ignoring the question a second time, then took in the determined look on Darion's face and sighed. "My ex-husband. We were married for nine years and I taught him everything he knows. Ungrateful bastard."

"You were *married?*" Darion stared at her, mouth dropping open slightly. "For nine *years?*"

"Yes, I was married," she snapped. Why was that so hard to believe? Just because her recent track record with pilots wasn't great didn't mean it had always been that way. "And yes, I'm sure it's a fake distress call. If it was real, he'd have told us what was wrong."

Another hiss of static. "Damnit, Janessa, I know you're out there, listening! It's an emergency, so come in, over!"

"Maybe we should still answer?" Darion bit his lip, but didn't take his eyes off his console to look at her again. "Just in case?"

"Not on your life. Or your hope of being paid."

"But—"

"Janessa, I'm begging you, I need help!"

She felt the first twinge of nervousness—Ethan never begged. Reluctantly, she hit the comm. "What is it, Ethan?"

"Thank God!" That made Janessa even more nervous—Ethan prayed as much as he begged—until he added, "The lander was hit by a bomb and now Avari's trapped down there."

It didn't take a genius to figure out why Ethan's new wife and partner had ventured into an area being pelted by volcanic bombs—she'd found a vein of real obsidian. If they were going to take suicidal risks, let them deal with the consequences. There was no point in Janessa risking her ship, or her life, to bail them out. "And how is any of that my problem?"

"But the bombs—"

"Tell her to hide behind a spur or something."

"Janessa, she could *die*—"

Cry me a river. Was Janessa really supposed to care about the tart who'd stolen her husband? "She's got at least a fifty-fifty chance of surviving even if she was stupid enough to go out without a helmet—"

"Avari's pregnant!"

A coal of hatred she thought she'd long ago smothered flared back to life again. Whether or not he was telling the truth, it was low of him to bring *that* up. "Then what the hell is she doing on an active volcano? You damned coward, can't you ever do your own dirty work? If they die, their deaths won't be on *my* conscious, they'll be on yours. Assuming you even have one, which by now I seriously doubt!"

Janessa toggled off the comm. "Let's get the hell out of here."

Darion stared at her, wide-eyed with shock. "We're not going to help?"

"He'll come down for her."

"But that's a tradeship—it doesn't have any planetary landing gear!"

Janessa felt a glimmer of satisfaction. "I know. They'll be stranded for a day or two, until the treasure hunters start overrunning this place and they can bargain for passage off. Serves the bastard right."

"But—!"

"We're taking off, now, or I'm getting a new pilot as soon as we dock," Janessa snapped.

Darion bit his lip and looked like he wanted to argue more, but finally started down their improvised runway.

The engines began to whine as he boosted their fuel intake, a loud, obnoxious sound that out in deep space would have signaled some sort of problem. She could feel the engines straining to break free of the planet, the moment when they reached the tipping point and the *Bonadventure* began to move upwards. Acceleration dragged at her limbs, making her feel even heavier than the planet's gravity did. She didn't let that distract her from monitoring the ship's systems, though.

As Ethan himself had drilled into her: there were old pilots, there were bold pilots, but there were no old, bold pilots.

Ethan was going to be an old pilot, the coward.

Speaking of Ethan. . . . Janessa frowned at her consoles. As she'd expected, the *Sundancer* was breaking orbit, but it wasn't headed towards the planet. "What does he think he's doing?"

Darion barely glanced up from his own consoles, preoccupied with keeping the *Bonadventure* on course. "He's too close to the planet to enter FTL."

Janessa shook her head, certain she must have misheard. "He *what*?"

"Either he knows you better than you think he does, or he cares more about his ship than her," Darion said. "Can I adjust course now, or do I keep wasting fuel?"

Darion was wrong. He'd only known her five months and was still young—naive, even. Ethan, on the other hand, had been her pilot and husband for nine years. He knew how reckless she could be with her own life, and with others' lives as well, especially when money was on the line. He wouldn't leave Avari—pregnant or not—at Janessa's non-existent mercy.

A bright white light flashed across the forward viewscreen; the *Bonadventure's* sensors went crazy, reporting a burst of radiation that spanned the electromagnetic spectrum, but that white light was the only visible portion. Then it faded, leaving only the blackness of space where the *Sundancer* had once been.

Janessa stared in disbelief. "He left. He really did it. The *bastard*."

"I'm adjusting course," Darion said, not bothering to wait for permission. "Don't suppose you have any idea of what comm frequency she'd be listening for?"

She should tell him to stop. They didn't have time to waste on a rescue operation, not when they were already going to lose precious time breaking free of the planet's atmosphere. Ethan wouldn't just beat them back to Jemison Station—he'd preempt her selling the location of the planet to the other treasure hunters. The value of her obsidianite would begin to plummet before she even made it to the station, much less made contact with her buyers. With the way her luck was going, they might not even make enough to refuel.

"Jan?"

"I got it." Her hands danced across the consoles, finding the right frequency and coding in Ethan's old encryption algorithm. He liked to think that made his communications more secure, as if it wasn't child's play to break an encryption that never changed. "Avari, it's Janessa, can you hear me? Over."

"Janessa?" Avari's voice—and the anxiety within it—came through loud and clear. "Something's wrong with my comm, I lost contact with Ethan."

That's because he abandoned you. But Janessa suddenly found she couldn't say it. "Little birdie told me you were pregnant." It had to be a lie—Ethan would never have left her if she was really pregnant. "That so?"

"Three months," Avari answered, without hesitation. "You've been talking to Ethan? Can you relay a message for me?"

Janessa felt like someone had punched her in the stomach. Her whole life, everything she'd believed, had been a lie. Ethan didn't care about children any more than he'd cared about her or Avari. He'd let her believe it was all her fault, just so he could get his hassle-free divorce and move on to a newer model of wife. Once they'd found out she was pregnant . . . had he been setting her up for failure? Deliberately pushing her to take greater risks than usual? *One more job, Janessa, it should be an easy one. You know babies are bloody expensive, Janessa, we need the money . . .*

She dug her fingernails into her palms and ground out the words. "Kind of hard to relay a message to someone who's gone into FTL."

Dead silence greeted her words, and for a moment Janessa thought she'd lost the connection. Then Avari said, "Oh."

"That's what you get for trusting a guy who cheated on his first wife." There was so much else Janessa had wanted to say to the woman who ruined her marriage, so much she had been *waiting* to say when she got the chance, but suddenly she felt like she was kicking a puppy. Besides, she wasn't sure Avari was the enemy, not anymore; Ethan had screwed them both over. "What's your sitrep?"

"FUBAR?" Avari offered, with a shaky little laugh. "The lander's a total loss, the bombs are still falling everywhere. . . ." She swallowed, audibly. "And I'm pretty sure my leg is broken."

Janessa swore, a long string of profanity that used every curse she knew and a few she made up on the spot. If Avari couldn't walk off the volcano by herself, they really were in trouble. It wasn't as if Darion could just set the *Bonadventure* down right beside her; even in the best case scenario, they'd somehow have to transport Avari over at least a hundred meters of unstable ground while being pelted with bombs thrown out from the still-erupting volcano. FUBAR, indeed.

Abruptly, Janessa became aware that silence had stretched out on the comm and that Darion was frowning at his consoles. It didn't take a genius to figure out why—the situation was bad enough that no one could possibly blame her for deciding it was impossible to attempt a rescue. Here was her perfect opportunity to see the home-wrecking tart dead.

"Avari, you still there?" Janessa asked.

"Yes?"

"Just sit tight. We're coming for you."

* * *

Darion flew over the crater twice, searching for an adequate landing site. The *Bonadventure* was at least ten times the size of Avari's lander and it quickly became apparent that there wasn't enough solid, lava-free ground to set down anywhere near her. Finally, he pointed out a little promontory, over half a klick away. "I think that's the best we're going to get."

Janessa bit her lip. That was a hell of a distance to haul a wounded woman. "Best as in nearest or best as in safest?"

"Nearest. It's not at all safe," Darion said, bluntly. "I'm going to use the incline to dump speed so I won't need as much space to land, but it's still going to be dicey. You want something safe, we might as well head back to where we landed originally."

Janessa actually considered it, but if she wasn't sure she could carry Avari half a klick, how was she supposed to carry the woman five times that distance? "Nearest it is, then."

"Look on the bright side," Darion said, adjusting course. "Worst case scenario, I wreck the ship and we all hang out inside, safe and sound, until help comes."

"I suppose that's slightly better than *we all die*." Janessa unstrapped herself and rose. It would be a rough landing, the kind she ought to be safely strapped in for, but she couldn't bear to watch this. "I'm going to go put together a first-aid kit. Try not to wreck my ship while I'm gone."

"Right."

While the ship shuddered and lurched around her, Janessa queried the computer to confirm that pregnancy didn't alter the necessary first-aid procedures for a broken leg. She dumped all the ashes from her pack into whatever containers she could scrounge up, then began refilling the pack with bandages and drugs. It wasn't exactly sanitary, but given all the ash outside she didn't think a little more would hurt. She did well enough with the rough landing until she tried to climb back into her ash-covered gear; then she fell over twice, sending clouds of ash flying into the air. Assuming they survived this insanity, she was going to have to scrub every nook and cranny of the entire ship.

The *Bonadventure* finally touched ground, hopped twice, then settled down with an agonizing groan of stressed metal and strained engines. Janessa shuddered at the sound and laid one hand on the nearest panel. "I know, Bon, I didn't much like that either." She waited a few seconds longer, as they slowed to a shuddering halt, then carabinered a pair of hiking sticks to her pack and went back onto the bridge.

Little red lights were blinking all over the consoles. Janessa winced and forced herself to focus on Darion instead of those lights. "What's the damage?"

"It could be worse?" Darion said, his hands flying over the consoles as he checked the system reports.

Janessa fought down a growl of annoyance at his non-reply. "Can we take off again?"

"Definitely."

"Are we space-worthy?"

"Um, sorta. We'll be a bit . . ." Darion hesitated, clearly searching for the right word. "Leaky. But we should still be able to go FTL."

Leaky. Janessa didn't even want to imagine the repair bill they were going to have. "Fine. Rig up some extra shielding around my quarters, to be on the safe side. We'll put Avari there." She and Darion would be safe enough on anti-radiation meds, but they couldn't chance giving them to Avari, not while she was pregnant.

"I'm on it."

This planet was definitely some sort of hell, Janessa decided, as she cycled back out onto its surface. She made a quick trip around the *Bonadventure*, checking out the extent of the damage. The landing gear was fine and the aft sensor arrays were intact—for once—but that was about the only good news. Darion must have hit a couple of bombs, coming in, because there were clear impart craters on the hull. They were going to be leaky as a sieve until she could afford to pay for repairs. At least it *could* be repaired.

"Bloody expensive," Janessa muttered, then toggled the comm channel open. "Darion—whatever shielding you were planning on, double it. Avari—we've landed and I'm on my way."

Half a klick gave Janessa plenty of time to appreciate the monumental stupidity of going this close to the crater of an erupting volcano. Bombs were falling all around her, not that she could see them; most were hidden by the thick ash falls, their existence betrayed only by the explosive sound they made when they hit the ground. One did get close enough to see—and close enough to hit her, too, if she hadn't dived for cover. The sound of its impact, only a few meters away, was deafening.

It was a relief when she finally caught sight of the ruined lander, though the giant bomb that had crushed it was a sobering reminder that even the *Bonadventure* wouldn't survive a direct hit from a large enough bomb. This one had probably been over a meter in diameter, though it was hard to tell for sure given the way it had deformed on impact with the lander. Avari was crouched in the shelter provided by the wreck.

Janessa hastened to join Avari, appreciating the irony of the giant bomb protecting them from the lesser bombs that still flew all around them.

"God, you have no idea how glad I am to see you," Avari said, wrapping her arms around her stomach. She was a mess; her right leg was stretched out in front of her—probably the broken leg—and brown streaks on her cheeks marked where tears had washed away the gray ashes that coated the rest of her.

Janessa dug her canteen and ace bandages out of her pack. She tossed the canteen to Avari. "Drink this. I'm sure you need liquids by now and I doped it up with pain meds."

Avari had the canteen uncapped and to her lips before Janessa finished speaking, but then she hesitated. "It won't hurt the baby?"

"I double-checked with the computer," Janessa assured her. "It won't hurt the baby."

Avari nodded and chugged the canteen's contents.

"I'm going to splint your leg," Janessa said, unclipping the hiking sticks from her pack. "And then we're going to get the hell out of here." She laid out a stick on either side of Avari's broken leg, extending them until they were the right length, then began using the bandages to tie them in place.

"I . . ." Avari lowered the canteen and sniffled, rubbing at her face.

"I don't th-think I . . . I just, I can't—"

"Girl or boy?" Janessa only realized she'd tightened one of the bandages a little too far when Avari hissed in pain. She loosened it and tried again. "Your baby—is it a girl or a boy?"

"I don't know yet. Ethan—" Avari faltered for a moment. "We were going to let it be a surprise."

And didn't that sound achingly familiar. "He probably didn't want to pick out names, either, did he?" Janessa shook her head and went on in a sing-song voice. "A name is one of the most important things a parent gives to a child, we shouldn't rush this decision. How can we know what to *call* the baby until we *meet* the baby?"

Avari frowned. "That sounds like Ethan, all right."

"Mine was going to be a girl—I had the technician tell me when Ethan wasn't in the room." Janessa had to force herself to be gentle as she tied off the last of the bandages. "Bonnie. Ethan didn't know it, but I was determined her name was going to be Bonnie."

"That's a nice name." Avari laughed, shakily. "Ethan would have hated it."

"So," Janessa said, sitting back on her heels. "Are you going to get up off your ass, walk out of here with me, and choose a name for that baby that Ethan will hate? Or are you going to sit here sniveling until you die and free Ethan to screw over wife number three?"

Avari stared, eyes wide. "God. You really are as much of a b-bitch as Ethan said." But then her face hardened and there was a new determination in her voice as she added, "But bitches survive."

"Atta girl." Janessa held out a hand and tugged Avari to her feet. Well, foot. Even with the painkillers and the splint, Avari wasn't putting any weight on her injured leg. "Put your arm over my shoulders and lean on me."

Janessa was still a little worried that Avari might collapse again, the first time they took a lurching step forward. Avari whimpered and clenched her hand painfully tight on Janessa's shoulder. But she kept moving.

After four or five steps, Janessa felt confident enough to signal the *Bonadventure*. "Darion, we're on our way back."

The static on the comm drowned out half of Darion's reply. "Rog… done with . . . ding in . . . the bridge . . .watch your six."

"Watch my six, like I've got eyes in the back of my head," Janessa grumbled. Not that it was bad advice—the bombs were now coming from behind her, after all—but at the moment it was all she could manage to keep them moving in the right direction.

"He's worried—ow—about you. 'Scute," Avari managed to say, through gritted teeth. "Boyfriend? *Ow!*"

Janessa rolled her eyes. "He's half my age."

"So?"

Avari was probably just trying to distract herself from the pain, but her questions still annoyed Janessa. "So *no*. But don't get any ideas about stealing another one of my pilots, I'm sick of training new ones."

"Well." Avari looked slightly taken aback. "Don't think I'll—damnit *ow*—need another one soon, anyway."

It seemed like hours before a smudge in the distance began to resolve itself into a larger blur that was probably the *Bonadventure*. Janessa sighed in relief—she wasn't sure how much longer they could have lasted. She was about to signal Darion, to confirm, when the ground gave a violent shake that nearly knocked them both off their feet.

"Jan," Darion said, his voice strangely flat. "If you can run, now would be the time."

The ground kept shaking and Janessa had to stop for a second to brace herself against the motion. She *could* run, but only if she abandoned Avari. "Not going to happen."

"Crap."

"If you have to leave me—" Avari tried to let go, but Janessa clamped her hand on top of Avari's.

"Shut up and move."

Two more steps and Janessa was sure they were only a few meters away from the *Bonadventure*. They might as well have been a few klicks away, for all the good it would do them.

Then the airlock cycled open and Darion dashed out. It was insane—he wasn't dressed for the heat and his lightweight deck shoes were little better than going barefoot. But he hardly seemed to notice as he skidded to a stop beside them. He grabbed Avari's free arm and pulled it over his own shoulders, lifting her off her feet entirely.

"Okay, run *now*," he said.

Janessa dredged up the strength to run the last few meters to the airlock. The instant they were inside, Darion dropped Avari and kept on running through the already-open inner airlock door.

"You jammed open the airlock?" Janessa shouted after him, but he was already gone.

Swearing, she helped Avari to the ground then looked back at the outer door. The ever-present ash falls had actually cleared a little. Now she could see all the way back to the lander and beyond—to the avalanche of darkness roaring towards them.

A pyroclastic flow.

"Oh, God!" Janessa dashed to the control panel whose cover Darion had removed. The floorplates beneath her feet began to vibrate as she frantically uncrossed and recrossed wires to fix the short he'd created. The outer doors slid closed with a little whine of protest for their mistreatment, drowned out a moment later by the angrier whine of the engines.

Janessa grabbed Avari under the arms and hauled her through the inner airlock, then hit the controls to shut those doors, too. "Brace yourself!" She followed her own command, sliding down the wall of the corridor and pressing her feet against the opposite wall. Avari awkwardly mimicked her.

Her stomach gave a little lurch as the whine of the *Bonadventure*'s engine increased in pitch and they began to win their battle with New Galilee's gravity. "Come on, Bon, you can do it—"

Then the pyroclastic flow slammed into them.

The *Bonadventure* spun like a child's top—once, twice, part of a third time. The motion stopped almost as abruptly as it had begun, though Janessa could still hear the deafening roar of the flow surrounding them. She wasted no time in staggering to her feet and grabbing Avari again, dragging her two meters down the corridor to the door to her quarters. She slapped the door controls and pitched Avari inside. "Strap into my bunk if you can."

She didn't wait for a reply, just turned and ran for the bridge.

Darion was fighting with the controls, desperately trying to gain altitude while keeping the *Bonadventure* level with the horizon. The viewscreens displayed radar instead of visuals, probably because there was nothing that could be seen in the dark cloud of superheated gases that had engulfed the ship. If it had hit them while they were out in the open, they'd have died instantly. Though they still might die—the engines were screaming in protest.

"I'll monitor for bombs." Janessa flung herself into her seat and pulled her straps tight.

Darion nodded, without ever taking his eyes off his own console.

As agonizing as it was to quietly sit there and let Darion do all the flying, Janessa kept her hands to herself and her eyes on the sensors. She had to trust him; he was her pilot, this was what she had hired him to do, and he did it well. She only had to warn Darion about incoming bombs twice, and both times he managed to narrowly avert impacts that would have compromised the structural integrity of the ship. The second time, the bomb in question sheared off their aft sensor array. Janessa nearly laughed. She should have known better than to think that bloody array was going to make it through this mess, intact.

Suddenly, Darion gave out a shout of triumph. A moment later they broke free of the bomb-filled darkness, moving into the clear air—and then clear vacuum—above it.

* * *

Once they achieved low orbit, Janessa took over the controls and sent Darion off to take care of his burns—the heat had begun to melt the synthetic fabrics of his jumpsuit and the way he limped off indicated he probably had worse burns beneath his shredded deck shoes. He'd laughed off his idiotic act of courage on New Galilee, saying at least he'd gotten to rescue two survivors, but he wouldn't be laughing once the adrenaline wore off and pain of those injuries really hit him.

Janessa took advantage of her temporary privacy to run a full set of system reports, wincing at what she found. The damage to the *Bonadventure* was extensive and it would be more than her obsidianite was worth to pay for any of the repairs, much less all of them. Some things could wait—the landing gear was more of a luxury than a necessity—but the essential repairs alone were going to eat up all of her savings. She didn't know how she was going to pay for the docking fees and refueling, too.

At least she could take comfort in the fact that Ethan wasn't going to come out of this any better; once Avari was done divorcing him, he wouldn't have a penny left to his name.

Darion returned to the bridge, still limping but in a new jumpsuit. "Our passenger is fine—or, at least, no worse than she was before. She seems to be fascinated by our database of baby names?"

He sounded so puzzled that Janessa had to laugh. "Glad to have *some* good news."

"You're both completely mental, you know that?" Darion shook his head. "Oh, before I forget, she wanted us to have this, as a thank you for saving her." He reached into his pocket of his coveralls and pulled out a piece of shining red glass. It looked just like obsidianite, but there was one important difference—it was real. "She said it was the only piece she got. Does that make sense to you?"

Janessa took the obsidian, carefully, and cradled it in her palms. "Yes. Yes, that makes perfect sense." It was unique. Priceless. She could sell this for enough to repair the *Bonadventure* and then some. They'd come out ahead on this voyage, after all.

"Well, that makes one of us."

Darion was never going to develop a business sense, but Janessa wasn't sure she cared anymore. He was a good pilot. And he had saved her life. "What do you say about heading out towards the Tereshkova Sector, once we're done with repairs?"

He eyed her, thoughtfully. "That's almost a four month round trip."

"Yes, yes it is."

Darion grinned. "Sounds like a real adventure."

STARSHIP DOWN

Tracy Canfield

Alien life-forms and encounters with extra-terrestrial beings have been an important part of science fiction writing since the inception of the genre. During the pulp fiction era, most aliens were world ravagers and mortal adversaries. Thoughtful alien stories didn't come into their own until the end of John W. Campbell's tenure as editor of *Astounding Science Fiction*. In his famous dictum to his writers, Campbell exhorted them to "Write me a creature that thinks as well as a man, or better than a man, but not like a man." Campbell's dictum has some merit, but to be truly believable, an alien culture must exist within a logical and consistent world as "Starship Down" does. The planet's native population certainly doesn't think like humans . . . on most matters.

"Starship Down" first appeared in the October 2008 issue of *Analog Science Fiction and Fact* where it won an Analytical Laboratory (AnLab) Award. AnLab is the annual readers' poll to determine the favorite stories, articles, and cover art published each year in Analog Magazine. "Starship Down" was chosen as the best *Analog* story of 2008.

Tracy Canfield is a computational linguist from Indiana whose fiction has appeared in numerous magazines, including *Analog, Strange Horizons*, and *Fantasy Magazine*. In her biography, Tracy notes that she is the voice on the Klingon audio tour at Australia's Jenolan Caves and CNN called her a "Klingon scholar." You can read more about Ms. Canfield by visiting her website tracycanfield.com.

The mobile medstation doorlight buzzed, and Okalani Yee opened the door without setting the viewscreen to the outside camera feed. It was a bunny, of course. The nearest non-bunny was at Aoi Station, currently six hundred kilometers away.

"A bunny tripped by the orchard wall and broke its ankle," said the visitor. Bunnytongue had no greetings.

"How far away?"

The bunny spoke a single word, which the translator bud in Yee's ear rendered as "Two to six kilometers."

"Wait a minute." Yee grabbed the medkit and pulled on a lightweight mask with a portable aerator that clipped on her belt. The Myosotis atmosphere was breathable enough—a bit high in CO_2, a trifle light in O_2—but on long brisk walks she preferred to breathe Earthmix. The mask was comfortable. With the temperature and humidity regulation, she'd forget she was wearing it.

The bunny loped off over a blue hill. It wasn't even Genius Bunny, who was the only Myosotian Yee could tolerate any more.

* * *

Looking at the bunnies clumped on the blue hills around the medstation, Yee wouldn't have known there was an emergency. They were sitting placidly, mating vigorously, grooming their "ears," chasing their round little children away from the stone walls, and playing the copycat game. This was one of the few bunny recreations that did not involve mating. The rules were simple: two bunnies faced off and imitated each other's gestures. Yee had been refusing to play for six months now.

She trotted on the springy blue mat of grass—in an Earth year on Myosotis, she'd lost the mental quotation marks—and dodged between orrum trees heavy with orange bulbs: the orchard. The bunnies did not tend or plant the orrums. The orchard had sprouted from discarded rinds the bunnies had left after scavenging outside their pastures and bringing back foods they liked.

Myosotians—bunnies—were technically sentient, the only such

race on Myosotis. They were "herbivores"—evolution on Myosotis had never erected the rigid barriers between plant and animal that Earth had, but the term conveyed an accurate approximation of the bunny ecology. Everything bunnies ate was sessile. They were not hunters.

There was the wall, a precarious stone heap built by the bunnies to keep other herbivores out of their pastures. Yee knew she had reached the scene of the accident when she saw a circle of bunnies squatting so they faced outward. The injured one would be at the center—a hardwired defense mechanism against a long-extinct predator.

The defenders were so close together that Yee had to step on a shimmering blue-scaled knee to get to the gap between their shoulders. The bunny patted her ponytail but made no move to help or hinder her.

In their usual resting posture, sitting on their hind legs, bunnies presented an egg-shaped silhouette three meters high, not including the waving "ears," a bifurcated ornamental crest that could add another fifty centimeters. A slit in the chest between the forelimbs concealed the sex organs. The vrith, one of the two bunny sexes, also had a white or pink stripe down their backs and small white nipples under their armpits.

Yee clambered down into the enclosed circle and took a look at her patient.

* * *

Humans had invented FTL technology—and never used it.

The first test of the Slominski Drive had inspired an immediate outburst of optimism that completely drowned out the voices droning about rocky planets where no one could live, the possible lack of Van Allen belts and consequent frying by cosmic radiation, the prohibitive cost of colonization. Then the Kairians made contact.

Yee had been old enough to read the headlines and understand the significance of the enormous fonts and sidebars overflowing with unanswered questions. And she had been young enough to find a mandatory class on Coalition history waiting for her when she reached high school.

The Kairians had been watching Earth via never-noticed ansible-enabled satellites (or, more likely, some other member of the Coalition of Planets had been watching, and reported to the Kairians when the Slominski drive became feasible; interstellar security guards working in exchange for some piece of Kairian technology—cold fusion, weather control, the ansible itself.)

The Kairians had had FTL for over five thousand Earth years and considered themselves to be running this part of the galaxy. It could have been a lot worse. They had a hands-off approach. They appreciated it if sentient races joined their Coalition of Planets (and what the Kairians appreciated, everybody did.) They discouraged interplanetary war and interspecies exploitation (and what the Kairians discouraged, nobody even considered doing). They handed out technology generously. But there was a catch. Advanced species had to help less advanced species adapt.

The bunnies were not, by even the broadest definition, advanced.

* * *

Yee recognized the downed bunny. She called it Baron von Bunny, though she would have had to query the translation database to know how that came out in bunnytongue. One of the Baron's hind ankles was clearly twisted. The Baron writhed in evident pain, though Yee still saw little in its faceted black eyes except stupidity.

In the safety of the circle the Baron's thumbclaws had retracted, as if for locomotion. Yee stuck an analgesic pad over its breathing orifice to let it inhale the drug, then straightened the ankle and tied a splint on with slow-dissolving bandages. Bunnies' hind legs were larger copies of their upper limbs. The thumbclaw on all four limbs, which had presumably evolved for dealing with food, provided an opposable digit.

Bunnies usually moved by bounding on their hind legs. On rough terrain they dropped to all fours. They did not build roads.

The flesh around the injury was seriously abraded. Yee wiped up the clear bunny blood and covered the wound with a strip of synthflesh, which immediately let out a puff of ozone and began to fuse to the Baron's scaly skin. She sprayed the outer layer with a fixative to prevent the Baron from finding itself fused to the wrong side of its dressing.

She waited for the Baron to get up and take a few tentative hops on its splinted ankle. With unnecessary slowness, the circled bunnies came to the realization that there was no injured comrade to protect and they could disperse. Yee trudged back to the medstation, allowing herself to contemplate her usual futile plan for bunny education.

By Kairian standards, bunnies were intelligent. They used language and made tools—well, they built ramshackle stone walls, and long ago they had made weapons. Their language, as Yee had just observed, let them refer to things that were distant in space and time; they could say *A bunny tripped by the orchard wall.* But it was weak in other areas. Many, many other areas.

Yee still had an old Intro to Xenobiology file about bunnytongue. At first she had assumed it was a joke, like the file on "Sex Life of the Caobotes" (which was empty; the Caobotes were parthenogenetic.) The bunnytongue file was intended to be used as an insight into Myosotian thought, not as a phrasebook. No humans could actually speak bunnytongue—the sounds were too unsuited for the human vocal apparatus. Yee's portable, wireless translator synthesized bunnytongue words for her.

Bunnytongue had three numbers: one, two, and many. (Desperately bored medstation biologists had programmed numerous synonyms for this last into the translator, from "a lot of" to "veritable metric shitloads." Yee preferred not to enable them, but there were . . . many.)

Bunnies were good about expressing time, especially past and present. (The future was often hazy.) They weren't bad at aspect— whether an action was in progress or completed. They were hopeless at counterfactuals. Statements like *If I were hungry, I would eat* were beyond them. This made it improbable that Yee's plans for founding the first Myosotian school of medicine would succeed.

The flocking on the medstation walls looked grubby, but installations on Myosotis couldn't have shiny metallic walls or even reflective windows. Bunnies would spot their reflections and play the copycat game with them until they fell over from exhaustion.

Speaking of the copycat game, there was Genius Bunny, playing it with another bunny—Flora Bunny, Yee thought. Genius Bunny was toting an empty orrum rind. Flora reacted to something—Yee was too far away for the translator to pick up its words, but it had doubtless lost in a way that seemed stupid even by bunny standards. Flora retracted its claws and began cuffing Genius Bunny's face. Genius Bunny dropped the rind and shielded its eyes.

Yee felt a pang. She liked Genius Bunny and, she admitted to herself, probably encouraged it to follow the medstation on its circuit through the bunny pastures. Like so many scientists-to-be she herself had been, or at any rate had felt, excluded by others as a child because of her brains. Here, far from Earth or humanity, the same pattern played out for her daily as farce.

Flora finally gave up abusing Genius Bunny and ran off to mate. Yee noticed that Flora had very long ears. Long-eared stong were very desirable to vrith.

The two bunny sexes could be mapped onto "male" and "female," if you stretched, but no one on Myosotis ever did. Stong produced eggs internally, and vrith fertilized them. After mating the stong would immediately lay the fertilized egg and give it to the vrith, who would carry the offspring to term in a pouch and then care for it until it was old enough to graze on its own. Offworld biologists considered the Stong female, but no human who had seen a group of vrith nursing their infants could quite bring themselves to call them "male."

Bunnytongue itself didn't mark gender. Much as Japanese can indicate plural, but usually doesn't, bunnytongue didn't have separate pronouns for vrith and stong. The automatic translator handled both pronouns as "it," since there usually wasn't enough context to disambiguate the two, and humans followed suit.

Yee reeled the collapsible bunny dummy she used for practice out of the medstation and laid it on the waving blue grass. *This time it will work*, said the optimistic part of her brain. She was doing this solely to shut that part up for another few days.

"Come here," she said to a nearby bunny, Yoshihisa. She would rather have tried this with Genius Bunny, but Genius Bunny was so little respected by other bunnies that they might not have let it try this on them for real.

Yoshihisa bounced over and faced Yee. It took no interest in the dummy. Yee held up a splint.

"If a bunny had a broken leg, you would fix it like this." The Kairians discouraged exploitation and manipulation of client species, but this technology sharing was the whole point.

"A bunny has a broken leg?" Yoshihisa tapped its hind feet. Yee knew that meant the onset of panic.

"No, no bunny has a broken leg." Yoshihisa looked relieved. It had abandoned the unwelcome idea so quickly that it wasn't even mad at her for lying. Bunnies never lied, after all.

"If this bunny had a broken leg, you fix it like this." She held up the splint again.

"That's not a bunny."

"If this was a bunny, you could help it."

"This isn't a bunny."

Yee gave up again and took the dummy back inside. In her opinion you didn't need a starchart to find Myosotis: it was smack in the gap between sentience and intelligence.

* * *

Yee checked the biologists' forum for messages. Due to a loophole that excepted the forum from the normal technology regulations, it tended to be chatty. Unfortunately most of the new squirts were in Bengali.

The first English post was an update from Sirinen Station on Pythagoras Bunny, who was something of a Sirinen mascot for its ability to perform the Lo rock-counting test for numbers up to fourteen. Pythagoras had been killed by a collapsing wall.

Yee sent her condolences. Genius Bunny could do the Lo Test up to ten more often than could be accounted for by chance, but it seemed insensitive to mention it.

The other English post was a new overlay for the translation database, promising one hundred and five new synonyms for "to mate." There were dozens of user-created overlays for this single term, but Yee never enabled them. Given the pre-eminence of the subject in bunnies' conversation, the cruder forms made a crowd of them sound like sailors on leave.

According to Yee's old Applied Xenolinguistics prof, machine translation was one of those computational linguistics proposals that, on Earth, had never really been persuaded to work—human languages have too many ambiguities of the "Time flies like an arrow, fruit flies like a banana" variety. Bunnytongue, though, was simple enough to model, and if you were careful to restrict your speech to things bunnies understood, it could handle it. The bunnytongue translator was based on Kairen technology—they'd been looking after the bunnies for centuries, after all, and had compiled the definitive corpus of bunny utterances—but it hadn't been necessary to build dams or design highway systems on some backwards Coalition world to earn it. It was so trivial a human grad student could have built it.

A centralized database allowed the translator to be consistent about words, especially proper names. If a human slipped and used a word with no bunnytongue equivalent, the translator would generate a legal sequence of sounds that did not collide with an existing word and store it. The neologism would at least come out the same way every time.

The translator's attempt to overlay prosody to simulate perceived emotion was much dicier. As with the synonym inserter, Yee preferred to disable the feature and figure out bunny emotions from context. To her the default bunny voices sounded pleasant and emotionally neutral. Admittedly, this probably made them sound even stupider. Individual bunnies could be tagged with distinctive voices—Yee had set Genius Bunny's to a simulation of movie star Rui-Lian Ducrot, who specialized in adorable nerds.

But Rui-Lian's stories always ended in triumph, and Genius Bunny's didn't. Yee could identify.

* * *

The failed first-aid class had left Yee grouchy, as usual. She decided to make a phone call. First, she closed her door and sealed it. Her tiny bedroom contained a full-length mirror, which over the course of the past year had revealed a dourer and dourer Yee.

She called Lizzy Srisai at Azzura Station, on the Half-Cracked Continent. Srisai was the most senior biologist on Myosotis, and her five-year hitch was nearly up.

Bunnies occupied all eight continents. Archaeologists did not agree how this had been achieved, except that it was an accident. The medstations were distributed among bunny settlements, and their routes were designed to bring every bunny in range of medical treatment several times a year. Allowing contact between humans was not a requirement.

Half of the stations were currently staffed by Bengali speakers and half by English speakers. Earthservice had originally tried sending qualified xenobiologists regardless of their language background. Only two of the original team could talk to each other, and that was in schoolbook Latin. There had been suicides. One of the Latin speakers had traveled a thousand kilometers to assault the other one. Earthservice changed the policy.

Yee was considering learning Bengali just so she'd have more people to talk to. Besides the bunnies.

Srisai offered the usual sympathy with Yee's woes. "Have I told you the story about the bunny I taught to apply analgesics?" she said. Yee smiled. Of course she had heard the story several times, but right now she just wanted to have a conversation at an adult human level. It didn't have to be novel.

Apollo, the bunny, had learned to do a few basic tasks under Srisai's supervision and her scrupulous avoidance of the word *if.* "Differential diagnosis was always the stumbling block," said Srisai. To look at a case of thebba-leaf poisoning and realize it wasn't geriatric gastric inflammation, you had to be able to imagine something not present. That ability had always eluded Apollo, who was now dead of geriatric gastric inflammation.

Yee kept the conversation short. After she and Srisai had said their goodbyes, she stuck her head out the door and shouted "Does anyone want to talk on the phone?" Of course they always did.

Kairians disapproved of using advanced technologies on a client world without giving the native population a chance to share. With a last check of her bedroom door—evacuating a bunny from the medstation was a non-trivial task—Yee flipped the phone into bunnymode so it would shut off when they'd used it as long as she had.

She opened the door. Her Earthmix air would smell a little odd to the bunnies, but shouldn't do them any harm in the—she glanced at the timer—eighteen minutes they'd be inside.

A bunny she called Izzy lumbered up to the viewscreen. Onscreen, another bunny nodded vigorously.

"It's raining," said the remote bunny.

"No it's not," said Izzy.

"Yes it is."

"No it's not."

"Would you like to mate?"

"Okay."

The onscreen bunny pressed its chest up against the screen. Srisai was giggling uncontrollably. At Yee's end, Izzy did its best. Yee turned away. Explaining to the bunnies why this wouldn't work was a lost cause. Earthservice had settled for making the screens sturdy and easy to clean.

Yee wandered outside and sat on the grass. In the distance, tall blue fronds waved and sang in sweet harmonies. The orrum trees raised their orange bulbs high like an armful of sunsets. The grass wiggled.

What appeared to be a lavender flower on a blue stalk nuzzled Yee's ankle. The flower was actually a mouth. With more ambition than sense, it was trying to devour her, but lacking teeth or tongue it could only tickle. It was, in its alien way, cute. Then a bunny hopped over and ate it.

Myosotis such a beautiful planet, she thought, except for being full of bunnies.

* * *

When Yee had decided on a xenobiology career, she had imagined Coalition work as an interstellar Peace Corps. She would dive beneath methane oceans in her Earthservice-issue envirosuit-uniform to teach glowing globular Therakass how to program their first computer and ditch their circular slide rules. She would fly on a collapsible harness among the Dwala and explain strong cryptography. She would disseminate bioengineered toxophages with the slithering photosynthetic Orsho. Maybe she'd publish the occasional academic work in xenobiology, or give interviews to the popular press on alien cultures and diplomacy.

But she'd been assigned to the Myosotian protectorate instead, to look after a race that was never going to develop FTL on its own and qualify for full Coalition membership. Medical care was the only technology the bunnies could benefit from. They did not need energy sources, pollution clean-up, or FTL. They toiled not, neither did they spin.

And they weren't intelligent enough to treat themselves. That's where Yee came in. She, along with the biologists scattered among the Myosotis medstations, looked after their fellow client race. In return humanity got an improved FTL technology that made the Slominski drive look like a four-stroke engine.

And all the scientific work on the bunnies had already been done by the Kairians back when humans were still trying to figure out how to keep thieves out of their pyramids.

According to Kairian archaeologists, bunnies' ancestors were a large herbivorous species. Their sheer size and groups discouraged most predators. Only one had ever been large enough to pose a threat. Bunnytongue no longer had a word for it. Humans called it the elmer.

Bunnies seemed to have begun to build stone walls as protection from the elmers. Language ability left no hard parts to fossilize, of course, but a pre-existing communicative system—perhaps used for warnings or when food was discovered—had probably developed into proto-bunnytongue, and bunnies who could talk could better organize defenses. Archaeologists had found clubs and even spears, invented by some bunny Oppenheimer. Armed with these tools, the bunnies had defended themselves against the elmers until the elmers were extinct.

The elmers had been gone for millennia before the Kairians had come to call, but the conflict had left its mark. What the first Kairians on Myosotis had taken as religious practice, the burial of the dead at the ends of the stone walls and the extension of the walls over the graves, seemed to be instinctive: a way to deprive the elmers of their kills. Bunnies would flee unthinkingly—even more unthinkingly than usual—from a shape that suggested an elmer. The human biologists sometimes took advantage of this for emergency crowd control.

Az-Zarqaa' Station had tried an elmer suit. Bunnies, it turned out, could still make clubs. Now the biologists used a projector.

Yee wasn't going to say it would have been a good thing if elmers were still eating bunnies, not publicly, but in the long run it might have been better than the alternative. With the end of competition, bunny evolution ceased.

Bunnies didn't even compete with each other for territory. Egg fertilization and implantation rates decreased as population density increased. The population would grow to what the environment would support, then stop. A wonderful solution for individual bunnies, who only invested resources in offspring that were likely to survive, but it also eliminated the one other possible source of evolutionary pressure.

* * *

After the phone call had ended it took Yee nearly an hour to shoo the bunnies out of the medstation and ten minutes to squeegee off the viewscreen to her satisfaction. She celebrated with a lukewarm shower in her bedroom.

When she came out to take the evening air, Genius Bunny had re-appeared and was approaching a vrith not known to Yee.

"Will you mate with me?" said Genius Bunny with a syncopated bounce Yee could not help interpreting as hope.

"No.

"Mate with me."

"I don't want to mate with you."

"Genius Bunny, come inside," said Yee. Maybe she could give it a lesson on the dummy. It was probably just as much of a waste of time as the last lesson, but at least it wasted time for a different reason, since Genius Bunny might learn something.

Genius Bunny ambled inside. It still had that orrum rind in its hand and was dribbling spore pouches on the clean floor. Yee decided she didn't care.

Yee slid the dummy out of its wall niche, but Genius Bunny wasn't paying attention. It was leaning over to stare intently at—oh, hell, she'd left the bedroom door open. She could have smacked herself.

Genius Bunny squeezed through the bedroom door so that the

reflection was at the favored bunny focal distance. It held the rind up in front of the mirror and took out a black rock.

That must be what had made Flora so angry. Genius Bunny had figured out a way to win the copycat game every time—even if its opponent had an orrum rind of its own, it couldn't predict what Genius Bunny was going to pull out of it. It was the bunny equivalent of discovering a new forced mate in chess. No doubt Genius Bunny had expected this to make the game more fun and was surprised to find its inspiration rewarded with cuffs.

And now, Yee supposed, it had found an opponent that wouldn't be angry—but couldn't be beaten. Since she couldn't squeeze into her room and get a shot of ethyl alcohol with artificial lemon flavor, she consoled herself with a long drink of distilled water from the dispenser.

But when she finished, Genius Bunny was backing out of her room and looking at her—not the mirror.

"Nobody can see what's in the orrum rind," said Genius Bunny in Rui-Lian Ducrot's voice. "Nobody can know what's in the orrum rind. Nobody can take out the same color. It took out the same color. That's not a bunny. That's me."

Yee had just witnessed the bunny equivalent of *Cogito ergo sum*. The thought made everything that much more depressing. She let Genius Bunny outside, then went in her room for that drink.

* * *

She decided to watch the sunset and came out just inside to see Genius Bunny getting rejected by Izzy for the second time in one day. Genius Bunny bounced off to eat some ferns. Yee decided to interrogate Izzy a little.

"Why didn't you mate with Genius Bunny?" she asked.

"I don't like Genius Bunny."

"I like Genius Bunny."

Izzy scratched the back of its neck with its thumbclaw. "Did you mate with Genius Bunny?"

"No.

"I like you."

"You don't want to mate with me."

"You're not stong." That was the least disturbing possible response, now that she considered it.

Genius Bunny probably wasn't a mutant. It was at the high end of bunny variation, not a quantum leap forward. Bunny evolution may have been in equilibrium, but Genius Bunny wasn't about to punctuate it. If only it wasn't suffering the same fate as so many of its Earth counterparts—if only it could get laid, and pass on that nice collection of genes to its offspring—

Yee, for the first time in her career, recalled an offhand reference from a froglike (though human) biology prof whose lectures had heretofore been useless to her. It gave her a wonderful, awful idea.

She was so excited she was tempted to snap on the ansible and try to reach a former classmate who might have the exact reference, but resisted. The FTL comm channel was for Kairian-approved business only, and it's not as though there was anyone offworld who wanted to talk to a bunny afterwards, or vice-versa. She searched the electronic library instead. Eventually she found the article she wanted.

Now for the forbidden experiment. She could hardly wait.

* * *

Yee unrolled the largest-sized sheet of synthflesh on the worktable and cut out a meter-long leaf shape with a pointed tip and squared-off bottom. It seemed a little floppy, so she reinforced it along the back with a thin length of splint that extended about ten centimeters past the square end. She gazed upon her creation, and saw that it was good, so she made a second one. Finally she masked off the bases and sprayed them on both sides with fixative so that only the bottom three centimeters were reactive.

She lay awake in her bed all night, unsleeping, drumming her fingers, staring at the ceiling, waiting for dawn.

* * *

Genius Bunny was its usual affable self. Yee was suitably impressed. She certainly wouldn't have been at her best if an alien with a flashlight had awakened her at sunup and ushered her into a hospital room.

"Lean forward for me," she said. It did, puzzled, she thought, by the untranslatable "for me." She gently applied the synthflesh to its ears, with a few supplementary strips along the splint to hold it them in place. The tips of the prosthetic ears brushed the ceiling.

To her, the results looked fine: a bunny with unusually long ears. For all she knew, though, other bunnies would find the effect grotesque. She had one last test, and it wasn't a very good one. She opened the bedroom door.

Genius Bunny looked in the mirror for a long time. It retracted and extended its thumbclaws, it rocked from side to side. Yee was not sure how to read that emotion. At last, it spoke.

"If I were vrith, I would mate with me."

* * *

Yee nervously held her finger on the projector button. What worked with Earth birds might not work with bunnies.

Generations ago, a pre-Kairian zoologist, Malte Andersson, had studied the widowbird—a Kenyan bird with such extreme sexual dimorphism that males' tails were twice the length of their bodies. Andersson had snipped off some of those tails and pasted them onto those of other male widowbirds, with results never before seen by female widowbirds—who preferred the enhanced males to normal ones by a factor of two to one. Size did matter—and you could improve on what Mother Nature had to offer.

Yee didn't know how the bunnies would take to a similar imposture. She hated to risk Genius Bunny for it—but at least she had a backup plan: the projector, the tranquilizer, the self-cauterizing scalpel.

* * *

"I can't believe I'm hearing this," said Srisai. "You're saying you performed a cosmetic medical procedure, without informed consent, on a bunny?"

"I doubt you can get an objection out of it." Yee glanced at the viewscreen. Genius Bunny was lying happily on its back, paddling its hind legs in the air, exhausted. "We should edit its entry in the translation database and change its name to Playboy."

"I don't even know how many rules this violates."

"Want me to ship Genius Bunny to you? It should make a tour of all the stations. It could be the first sex tourist on Myosotis."

"You need to take a long deep breath."

"I'm going to take a long deep drink instead." Yee slugged down a third shot of lemon alcohol. Another happy thought occurred to her. "The counterfactual! Did I tell you what it said? 'If I were vrith, I'd mate with me.'"

"There's no word for 'if' in bunnytongue—wait, I get it. From the translator, right? *We* say 'if,' and the translator always handles it the same way."

"I'm so proud. I'm going to train it to be a doctor. And all the smart little baby bunnies, too. In a couple of years we'll be starting the Genius Bunny School of Myosotian Medicine." She snapped the phone off. With the vaguest sense that she was overlooking something, she fell asleep on the bed.

* * *

Something buzzed Yee awake. Not the door—the communicator in the other room was going off. She couldn't have been asleep that long; she wasn't quite sober. She stumbled out to take the call.

That red light—the ansible was on. An offworld call. She looked back over her shoulder, smoothed her hair, and switched on the viewscreen.

Her caller was something few humans ever saw. Most of its body was a flattened white cylinder, flexed into an arc. The carapace was open at the end and a knot of many-jointed black fingers extended to work what must have been Kairian comm controls. The glossy round red braincase was at the center of the screen. The writhing black tube extending from the braincase served as sensory and communication organ. Its tip writhed and a fine mist sprayed out.

"Mavi Station. This is Akolani Lee."

"Ms. Yee," said the speaker. Kairian speech was usually described as "warbling"; the audio output must be coming from a computer. Kairian machine translation was, unsurprisingly, excellent. "This is Margaret Abraham Whetu Zukisa Cheong-Chi Rowtag of the Coalition of Planets.

"Ms. Srisai contacted us on the ansible to report your recent actions." *Bitch*, thought Yee groggily. "She stated that you have performed an experimental procedure on a Myosotian without said Myosotian's consent. She further stated that you did this with the belief that said Myosotian might be exposed to danger as a result of the procedure—again, without said Myosotian's consent. She said this was done in an attempt to manipulate said Myosotian's mating potential."

"Said Myosotian is named Genius Bunny. I can get its Myosotian name from the translation database." Yee was not moved to deference. Might as well be hung for a sheep as a lamb.

"I have not finished reading the charges. Your medstation logs show that you used a long-distance communication device without allowing the Myosotians to use it as well. Ms. Srisai stated that you performed all of these discouraged acts, except the last, in order to achieve a long-term change in the Myosotian gene pool. This is a strongly discouraged act."

"It's true," said Yee. It occurred to her that she didn't have a will. She wondered if she owned anything that her brother and sister would consider worth fighting over. On the bright side, she supposed that she had found a way to get out of four more years of bunny service.

"In keeping with Coalition recommendations, I remind you that Coalition members have never experimented on humans, have never deliberately exposed humans to increased risks, and have never permitted technology introduction and application teams on Earth to use technologies without sharing them with humans. Furthermore, Coalition members have not engaged in selective breeding of humans, except for that incident in Dallas, and the team involved was immediately and thoroughly discouraged."

Yee thought about that for a moment.

"You have not acknowledged the reminder." The simulated voice was implacable.

"I acknowledge it."

"I served on Myosotis myself, two hundred twenty-four Earth years ago, long before humans knew of the Coalition of Planets. I know the Myosotians well. I know how this will change them." The black tube waggled. "It's about time, isn't it? And don't forget to let the Myosotians use the phone for twelve point four minutes."

BACKSCATTER

Gregory Benford

Gregory Benford needs no introduction to SF readers. He received his first Nebula Award in 1974 for "If the Stars Are Gods," a novelette he wrote with Gordon Eklund. His 1980 novel *Timescape* won the Nebula Award, the John W. Campbell Memorial Award, the British Science Fiction Association Award, and the Australian Ditmar Award. Among his many notable SF achievements are the *Jupiter Project, Artifact, Against Infinity, Eater,* and the six Galactic Center novels.

Benford is a professor of physics at the University of California Irvine and has published extensively in the areas of plasma physics, particle physics, and condensed matter. His wide-ranging contributions also include several papers in biological conservation. The consummate storyteller, Benford has the ability to make scientific principles approachable for nonscientists. In the space adventure "Backscatter," Benford spins a tale of survival and discovery that is very much in the SF Grand Tradition. It left me yearning for the chance to upload Claire's AI assistant, Erma, to my desktop. "Backscatter" was originally published by Tor.com.

She was cold, hurt, and doomed, but otherwise reasonably cheery.

Erma said, *Your suit indices are nominal but declining.*

"Seems a bit nippy out," Claire said. She could feel the metabolism booster rippling through her, keeping pain at bay. Maybe it would help with the cold, too.

Her helmet spotlight swept over the rough rock and the deep black glittered with tiny minerals. She killed the spot and looked up the steep incline. A frosty splendor of stars glimmered, outlining the peak she was climbing. Her breath huffed as she said, "Twenty-five meters to go."

I do hope you can see any resources from there. It is the highest point nearby. Erma was always flat, factual, if a tad academic.

Stars drifted by as this asteroid turned. She turned to surmount a jagged cleft and saw below the smashup where Erma lived—her good rocket ship *Sniffer*, now destroyed.

It sprawled across a gray ice field. Its crumpled hull, smashed antennae, crushed drive nozzle, and pitiful seeping fluids—visible as a rosy fog wafting away—testified to Claire's ineptness. She had been carrying out a survey at close range and the malf threw them into a side lurch. The fuel lines roared and back-flared, a pogo instability. She tried to correct, screwed it royally, and had no time to avoid a long, scraping, and tumbling *whammo*.

"I don't see any hope of fixing the fusion drive, Erma," Claire said. "Your attempt to block the leak is failing."

I know. I have so little command of the flow valves and circuits—

"No reason you should. The down-deck AI is dead. Otherwise it would stop the leaks."

I register higher count levels there, too.

"No way I'll risk getting close to that radioactivity," Claire said. "I'm still carrying eggs, y'know."

You seriously still intend to reproduce? At your age—

"Back to systems check!" Claire shouted. She used the quick flash of anger from Erma's needling to bound up five meters of stony soil, clawing with her gloved hands.

She should have been able to correct for the two-point failure that had happened—she checked her inboard timer—1.48 hours ago. Erma had helped but they had been too damned close to this iceteroid to avert a collision. If she had been content with the mineral and rare earth readings she already had . . .

Claire told herself to *focus*. Her leg was gimpy, her shoulder bruised, little tendrils of pain leaked up from the left knee . . . no time to fuss over spilled nuke fuel.

"No response from *Silver Metal Lugger?*"

We have no transmitters functioning, or lasers, or antennae—

She looked up into the slowly turning dark sky. *Silver Metal Lugger* was far enough away to miss entirely against the stars. Since their comm was down *Lugger* would be listening but probably had no clear idea where they were. Claire had zoomed from rock to rock and seldom checked in. *Lugger* would come looking, following protocols, but probably not before her air ran out.

"Y'know, this is a pretty desperate move," she said as she tugged herself up a vertical rock face. Luckily the low grav here made that possible, but she wondered how she would get down. "What could be on this 'roid we could use?"

I did not say this was a probable aid, only possible. The only option I can see.

"Possible. You mean desperate."

I do not indulge in evaluations with an emotional tinge.

"Great, just what I need—a personality sim with a reserved sense of propriety."

I do not assume responsibility for my programming.

"I offloaded you into *Sniffer* because I wanted smart help, not smartass."

I would rather be in my home ship, since this mission bodes to be fatal to both you and me.

"Your diplomacy skills aren't good either."

I could fly the ship home alone you know.

Claire made herself not get angry with this, well, software. Even though Erma was her constant companion out here, making a several-year *Silver Metal Lugger* expedition into the Kuiper Belt bearable. Best to ignore her. One more short jump—"I'm—*ah!*—near the top."

She worked upward and noticed sunrise was coming to this lonely, dark place. No atmosphere, so no warning. The Sun's small hot dot poked above a distant ridgeline, boring a hole in the blackness. At the edge of the Kuiper Belt, far beyond Pluto, it gave little comfort. The other stars faded as her helmet adjusted to the sharp glare.

Good timing, as she had planned. Claire turned toward the Sun, to watch the spreading sunlight strike the plain with a lovely glow. The welcome warmth seemed to ooze through her suit.

But the rumpled terrain was not a promising sight. Dirty ice spread in all directions, pocked with a few craters, broken by strands of black rock, by grainy tan sandbars, by—

Odd glimmers on the plain. She turned then, puzzled, and looked behind her, where the long shadows of a quick dawn stretched. And sharp greenish diamonds sparkled.

"Huh?" She sent a quick image capture and asked Erma, "Can you see anything like this near you?"

I have limited scanning. Most external visuals are dead. I do see some sprinkles of light from nearby, when I look toward you—that is, away from the sun. Perhaps these are mica or similar minerals of high reflectivity. Worthless, of course. We are searching for rare earths primarily and some select metals—

"Sure, but these—something odd. None near me, though."

Are there any apparent resources in view?

"Nope. Just those lights. I'm going down to see them."

You have few reserves in your suit. You're exerting, burning air. It is terribly cold and—

"Reading 126 K in sunlight. Here goes—"

She didn't want to clamber down, not when she could rip this suit on a sharp edge. So she took a long look down for a level spot and—with a sharp sudden breath—jumped.

The first hit was off balance but she used that to tilt forward, springing high. She watched the ragged rocks below, and dropped with lazy slowness to another flat place—and sprang again. And again. She hit the plain and turned her momentum forward, striding in long lopes. From here though the bright lights were—gone.

"What the hell? What're you seeing, Erma?"

While you descended I watched the bright points here dim and go out.

"Huh. Mica reflecting the sunlight? But there would be more at every angle . . . Gotta go see."

She took long steps, semiflying in the low grav as sunlight played across the plain. She struck hard black rock, slabs of pocked ice, and shallow pools of gray dust. The horizon was close here. She watched nearby and—

Suddenly a strong light struck her, illuminating her suit. "Damn! A . . . flower."

Perhaps your low oxy levels have induced illusions. I—

"Shut it!"

Fronds . . . beautiful emerald leaves spread up, tilted toward her from the crusty soil. She walked carefully toward the shining leaves. They curved upward to shape a graceful parabola, almost like glossy, polished wings. In the direct focus the reflected sunlight was spotlight bright. She counted seven petals standing a meter high. In the cup of the parabola their glassy skins looked tight, stretched. They let the sunlight through to an intricate pattern of lacy veins.

Please send an image.

"Emerald colored, mostly . . ." Claire was enchanted.

Chloroplasts make plants green, Erma said. *This is a plant living in deep cold.*

"No one ever reported anything like this."

Few come out this far. Seldom do prospectors land; they interrogate at a distance with lasers. The bots who then follow to mine these orbiting rocks have little curiosity.

"This is . . . astonishing. A biosphere in vacuum."

I agree, using my pathways that simulate curiosity. These have a new upgrade, which you have not exercised yet. These are generating cross-correlations with known biological phenomena. I may be of help.

"Y'know, this is a 'resource' as you put it, but"—she sucked in air that was getting chilly, looked around at the sun-struck plain—"how do we use it?"

I cannot immediately see any—

"Wait—it's moving." The petals balanced on a grainy dark stalk that slowly tilted upward. "Following the sun."

Surely no life can evolve in vacuum.

With a stab of pain her knee gave way. She gasped and nearly lurched into the plant. She righted herself gingerly and made herself ignore the pain. Quickly she had her suit inject a pain killer, then added a stimulant. She would need meds to get through this . . .

I register your distress.

Her voice croaked when she could speak. "Look, forget that. I'm hurt but I'll be dead, and so will you, if we don't get out of here. And this thing . . . this isn't a machine, Erma. It's a flower, a parabolic bowl that tracks the sun. Concentrates weak sunlight on the bottom. There's an oval football-like thing there. I can see fluids moving through it. Into veins that fan out into the petals. Those'll be nutrients, I'll bet, circulating—all warmed by sunlight."

This is beyond my competence. I know the machine world.

She looked around, dazed, forgetting her aches and the cold. "I can see others. There's one about fifty meters away. More beyond, too. Pretty evenly spaced across the rock and ice field. And they're all staring straight up at the sun."

A memory of her Earthside childhood came. "Calla lilies, these are like that . . . parabolic . . . but green, with this big oval center stalk getting heated. Doing its chemistry while the sun shines."

Phototropic, yes; I found the term.

She shook her head to clear it, gazed at the—"Vacflowers, let's call them."—stretching away.

I cannot calculate how these could be a resource for us.

"Me either. Any hail from *Lugger*?"

No. I was hoping for a laser-beam scan, which protocol requires the Lugger *to sweep when our carrying wave is not on. That should be in operation now.*

"*Lugger*'s got a big solid angle to scan." She loped over to the other vacflower, favoring her knee. It was the same but larger, a big ball of roots securing it in gray, dusty, ice-laced soil. "And even so, *Lugger* prob'ly can't get a back-response from us strong enough to pull the signal out from this iceteroid."

These creatures are living in sunlight that is three thousand times weaker than at Earth. They must have evolved below the surface somehow, or moved here. From below they broke somehow to the surface, and developed optical concentrators. This still does not require high-precision optics. Their parabolas are still about fifty times less precise than the optics of your human eye, I calculate. A roughly parabolic reflecting surface is good enough to do the job. Then they can live with Earthly levels of warmth and chemistry.

"But only when the sun shines on them." She shook herself. "Look, we have bigger problems—"

My point is this is perhaps useful optical technology.

Sometimes Erma could be irritating and they would trade jibes, having fun on the long voyages out here. This was not such a time. "How . . ." Claire made herself stop and eat warmed soup from her helmet suck. Mushroom with a tad of garlic, yum. Erma was a fine personality sim, top of the market, though detaching her from *Lugger* meant she didn't have her ship wiring along. That made her a tad less intuitive. In this reduced mode she was like a useful bureaucrat—if that wasn't a contradiction, out here. So . . .

An old pilot's lesson: *in trouble, stop, look, think.*

She stepped back from the vacflower, fingered its leathery petals. She jumped straight up a bit, rising five meters, allowing her to peer down into the throat. Coasting down, she saw the shiny emerald sheets focus sunlight on the translucent football at the core of the parabolic flower. The filmy football in turn frothed with activity—bubbles streaming, glinting flashes tracing out veins of flowing fluids. No doubt there were ovaries and seeds somewhere in there to make more vacflowers. Evolution finds ways quite similar in strange new places.

She landed and her knee held, did not even send her a flash of pain.

The meds were working; she even felt more energetic. *Wheeee!*

She saw that the veins fed up into the petals. She hit, then crouched. The stalk below the paraboloid was flexing, tilting the whole flower to track as the hard bright dot of the sun crept across a black sky. Its glare made the stars dim, until her helmet compensated.

She stood, thinking, letting her body relax a moment. Some intuition was tugging at her . . .

Most probably, life evolved in some larger asteroid, probably in the dark waters below the ice when it was warmed by a core. Then by chance some living creatures were carried upward through cracks in the ice. Or evolved long shoots pushing up like kelp through the cracks, and so reached the surface where energy from sunlight was available. To survive on the surface, the creatures would have to evolve little optical mirrors concentrating sunlight on to their vital parts. Quite simple. I found such notions in my library of science journals—

"Erma, shut up. I'm thinking."

Something about the reflection . . .

She recalled a teenage vacation in New Zealand, going out on a "night hunt." The farmers exterminated rabbits, who competed with sheep for grazing land. She rode with one farmer, excited, humming and jolting over the long rolling hills under the Southern Cross, in quiet electric Land Rovers with headlights on. The farmer had used a rifle, shooting at anything that stared into the headlights and didn't look like a sheep. Rabbit eyes staring into the beam were efficient reflectors. Most light focused on their retina, but some focused into a narrow beam pointing back to the headlight. She saw their eyes as two bright red points. A *crack* of the rifle and the points vanished. She had even potted a few herself.

"Vacflowers are bright!"

Well, yes. I can calculate how much so.

"Uh, do that." She looked around. How many . . .

She groped at her waist and found the laser cutter. Charged? Yes, its butt light glowed.

She crouched and turned the laser beam on the stem. The thin bright amber line sliced through the tough, sinewy stuff. The entire flower came off cleanly in a spray of vapor. The petals folded inward easily, too.

"I guess they close up at night," she said to Erma. "To conserve heat. Plants on Earth do that." The AI said nothing in reply.

Claire slung it over her shoulder. "Sorry, fella. Gotta use you." Though she felt odd, apologizing to a plant, even if an alien one.

She loped to the next, which was even larger. Crouch, slice, gather up. She took her microline coil off its belt slot and spooled it out. Wrapped together, the two bundles of vacflower were easier to carry. Mass meant little in low grav, but bulk did.

I calculate that a sunflower on the surface will then appear at least twenty-five times brighter than its surroundings, from the backscatter of the parabolic shape.

"Good girl. Can you estimate how often *Lugger's* laser squirt might pass by?"

I can access its probable search pattern. There are several, and it did know our approximate vicinity.

"Get to it."

She was gathering the vacflowers quickly now, thinking as she went. The *Lugger* laser pulse would be narrow. It would be a matter of luck if the ship was in the visible sky of this asteroid.

She kept working as Erma rattled on over her comm.

For these flowers shining by reflected sunlight, the brightness varies with the inverse fourth power of distance. There are two powers of distance for the sunlight going out and another two powers for the reflected light coming back. For flowers evolving with parabolic optical concentrators, the concentration factor increases with the square of distance to compensate for the decrease in sunlight. Then the angle of the reflected beam varies inversely with distance, and the intensity of the reflected beam varies with the inverse square instead of the inverse fourth power of distance—

"Shut up! I don't need a lecture, I need help."

She was now over the horizon from *Sniffer* and had gathered in about as many of the long petal clusters as she could. Partway through she realized abruptly that she didn't need the ovaloid focus bodies at the flower bottom. But they were hard to disconnect from the petals, so she left them in place.

The sun was high up in the sky. Maybe half an hour till it set? Not much time . . .

Claire was turning back when she saw something just a bit beyond the vacflower she had harvested.

It was more like a cobweb than a plant, but it was green. The thing sprouted from an ice field, on four sturdy arms of interlaced strands. It climbed up into the inky sky, narrowing, with cross struts and branches. Along each of these grew larger vacflowers, all facing the sun. She almost dropped the bundled flowers as she looked farther and farther up into the sky—because it stretched away, tapering as it went.

"Can you see this on my suit cam?"

I assume it is appropriate that I speak now? Yes, I can see it. This fits with my thinking.

"It's a tower, a plant skyscraper—what thinking?"

A plant community living on the surface of a small object far from the Sun has two tools. It can grow optical concentrators to focus sunlight. It can also spread out into the space around its 'roid, increasing the area of sunlight it can collect.

"Low grav, it can send out leaves and branches."

Apparently so. This thing seems to be at least a kilometer long, perhaps more.

"How come we didn't see it coming in?"

Its flowers look always toward the sun. We did not approach from that direction, so it was just a dark background.

"Can you figure out what I'm doing?" Huffing and puffing while she worked, she hadn't taken time to talk.

You will arrange a reflector, so the laser finder gets a backscatter signal to alert the ship.

"Bright girl. This rock is what, maybe two-eighty klicks across? Barely enough to let me skip-walk. If I get up this bean stalk, I can improve our odds of not getting blocked by the 'roid."

Perhaps. Impossible to reliably compute. How can you ascend?

"I've got five more hours of air. I can focus an air bottle on my back and jet up this thing."

No! That is too dangerous. You will lose air and be farther away from my aid.

"What aid? You can't move."

No ready reply, Claire noted. Up to her, then.

It did not take long to rig the air as a jet pack. The real trick was balance. She bound the flower bundle to her, so the jet pack thrust would act through her total center of mass. That was the only way to stop it from spinning her like a whirling firework.

With a few trial squirts she got it squared away. After all, she had over twenty thousand hours of deep space ex-vehicle work behind her. In *Lugger* she had risked her life skimming close to the sun, diving through a spinning wormhole, and operating near ice moons. Time to add one more trick to the tool kit.

Claire took a deep breath, gave herself another prickly stim shot—*wheee!*—and lifted off.

She kept vigilant watch as the pressured air thrust vented, rattling a bit—and shot her up beside the beanstalk. It worked! The soaring plant was a beautiful artifice, in its webby way. All designed by an evolution that didn't mind operating without an atmosphere, in deep cold and somber dark. Evolution never slept, anywhere. Even between the stars.

While she glided—this thing was *tall*—she recalled looking out an airplane window over the Rockies and seeing the airplane's shadow on the clouds below . . . surrounded by a beautiful bright halo. Magically their shadow glided along the clouds below. Backscatter from water droplets or ice crystals in the cloud, creating unconscious beauty in the air . . .

And the sky tree kept going. She used the air bottle twice more before the weblike branches thinned out. Time to stop. She snagged a limb and unbundled the vacflowers. The iceteroid below seemed far away.

One by one she arrayed the blossoms on slender wire, secured along a branch. Then another branch. And another. The work came fast and sure. The stim was doing the work, she knew, and keeping the aches in her knee and shoulder away, like distant hollow echoes. She would pay for all this later.

The cold was less here, away from the conduction loss she had felt while standing on the iceteroid. Still, exercise had amplified her aches, too, but those seemed behind a curtain, distant. She was sweating, muscles working hard, all just a few centimeters from deep cold . . .

Erma had been silent, knowing not to interrupt hard labor. Now she spoke over Claire's hard breathing. *I can access* Lugger*'s probable search pattern. There are several, and it did know our approximate solid angle for exploration.*

"Great. *Lugger*'s in repeating sweep mode, yes?"

You ordered so at departure, yes.

"I'm setting these vacflowers up on a tie line," Claire said, cinching in a set of monofilament lines she had harnessed in a hexagon array. They were spread along the sinewy arms of the immense tan tree. Everything was strange here, the spread branches like tendons, framed against the diamond stars, under the sun spotlight. She tugged at the monofilament lines, inching them around—and saw the parabolas respond as their focus shifted. The flowers were still open in the waning sunlight.

She breathed a long sigh and blinked away sweat. The array looked about right. Still, she needed a big enough area to capture the sweep of a laser beam, to send it back . . .

But . . . when? *Lugger* was sweeping its sky, methodical as ever . . . but Claire was running out of time. And oxy. This was a gamble, the only one she had.

So . . . wait. "Say, where do you calculate *Lugger* is?"

Here are the spherical coordinates—

Her suit computation ran and gave her a green spot on her helmet. Claire fidgeted with her lines and got the vacflowers arrayed. The vactree itself had flowers, which dutifully turned toward the sun. "Hey, *Lugger*'s not far off the sun line. Maybe in a few minutes all the vacflowers will be pointing at it."

You always say, do not count on luck.

It was sobering to be lectured by software, but Erma was right. Well, this wasn't mere luck, really. Claire had gathered as many vacflowers as she could, arrayed them . . . and she saw her air was running out. The work had warmed her against the insidious cold, but the price was burning oxy faster. Now it was low and she felt the stim driving her, her chest panting to grab more . . .

A bright ivory flash hit her, two seconds long—then gone.

"That was it!" Claire shouted. "It must've—"

I fear your angle, as I judge it from your suit coordinates, was off.

"Then send a correction!"

Just so—

Another green spot appeared in her helmet visor. She struggled to adjust the vacflower parabolas, jerking on the monofilaments. She panted and her eyes jerked around, checking the lines.

The sun was now edging close to the 'roid horizon. In the dark she would have no chance, she saw—the small green dot was near that horizon, too. And she did not know when the laser arc would—

Hard ivory light in her face. She tugged at the lines and held firm as the laser focus shifted, faded—

—and came back.

"It got the respond!" Claire shouted. The universe flooded with a strong silvery glow. The lines slipped from her gloves. Her feet seemed far away . . .

Then she passed out.

Erma was saying something but she could not track. Only when she felt around her did Claire's fingers know she did not have gloves on. Was not in her suit. Was in her own warm command couch chair, sucking in welcome warm air . . . aboard *Silver Metal Lugger.*

—and beyond the Kuiper Belt there is the Oort Cloud, containing billions of objects orbiting the Sun at distances extending out farther than a tenth of a light-year.

"Huh? What . . . what *happened?*"

Oh, pardon—I thought you were tracking. Your body parameters said you became conscious ten minutes ago.

Bright purple dots raced around her vision. "I . . . was resting . . . You must've used the *Lugger* bots."

You had blacked out. On my direction, your suit injected slowdown meds to keep you alive on what oxy remained.

"I didn't release suit command to you. I'd just gotten the reflection to work, received a quick recognition flash back from *Lugger,* and you, you—"

Made an executive decision. Going to emergency sedation was the only way to save you.

"Uh . . . um." She felt a tingling all over her body, like signals from a distant star. Her system was coming back, oxygen reviving tissues that must have hovered a millimeter away from death for . . . "How long has it been?"

About an hour.

She had to assert command. "Be exact."

One hour, three minutes, thirty-four seconds and—

"I . . . had no idea I was so close to shutdown."

I gather unconsciousness is a sudden onset for you humans.

"What was that babble I heard you going on about, just now?"

I mistakenly took you for aware and tracking, so began discussing the profitable aspects of our little adventure.

"Little adventure? I nearly died!"

Such is life, as you often remark.

"You had *Lugger* zoom over, got me hauled in by the bots, collected yourself from *Sniffer* . . ."

I can move quickly when I do not have you to look after every moment.

"No need to get snide, Erma."

I thought I was being factual.

Claire started to get up, then noticed that the med bot was working at her arm. "What the—"

Medical advises that you remain in your couch until your biochem systems are properly adjusted.

"So I have to listen to your lecture, you mean."

A soft fuzzy feeling was working its way through her body like tiny, massaging fingers. It eased away the aches at knee, shoulder, and assorted ribs and joints. Delightful, dreamy . . .

Allow me to cheer you up while your recovery meds take effect. You and I have just made a very profitable discovery.

"We have?" It was hard to recall much beyond the impression of haste, pulse-pounding work, nasty hurts—

A living community born just once in a deep, warmed 'roid lake can break through to its surface, expanding its realm. The gravity of these Kuiper Belt iceteroids is so weak, I realized, it imposes no limit on the distance to which a life form such as your vactree can grow. Born just once, on one of the billions of such frozen fragments, vacflower life can migrate.

Claire let the meds make her world soft and delightful. Hearing all this was more fun than dying, yes—especially since the suit meds had let her skip the gathering agonies.

Such a living community moves on, adapting so it can better focus sunlight, I imagine. Seeking more territory, it slowly migrates outward from the sun.

"You imagine? Your software upgrade has capabilities I haven't seen before."

Thank you. These vacflowers are a wonderful accidental discovery and we can turn them into a vast profit.

"Uh, I'm a tad slow . . ."

Think—! Reflecting focus optics! Harvested bioactive fluids! All for free, as a cash crop!

"Oh. I was going after metals, rare earths—"

And so will other prospectors. We will sell them the organics and plants they need to carry on. Recall that Levi jeans came from canny retailers, who made them for miners in the California gold rush. They made far more than the roughnecks.

"So we become . . . retail . . ."

With more bots, we are farmers, manufacturers, retail—the entire supply chain.

"Y'know Erma, when I bought you, I thought I was getting an onboard navigation and ship systems smartware . . ."

Which can learn, yes. I might point out to you the vastness of the Kuiper Belt, and beyond it—the Oort Cloud. It lies at a distance of a tenth of a light-year, a factor of two hundred farther away than Pluto. A vast resource, to which vacflowers may well have spread. If not, we can seed them.

"You sure are ambitious. Where does this end?"

Beyond a light-year, Sirius outshines the Sun. Anything living there will point its concentrators at Sirius rather than at the Sun. But they can still evolve, survive.

"Quite the numbersmith you've proved to be, Erma. So we'll both be rich . . ."

Though it is difficult to see what I can do with money. Buy some of the stim-software I've been hearing about, perhaps.

"Uh, what's that?" She was almost afraid to ask. Had Erma been watching while she used her vibrator . . . ?

It provides abstract patterning of imaginative range. Simulates neuro programs of what we imagine it is like to experience pleasure.

"How's code feel Earthly delights?"

I gather evolution invented pleasure to make you repeat acts. Reproduction, for example. Its essential message is, Do that again.

"You sure take all the magic out of it, Erma."

Magic is a human craft.

Claire let out a satisfied sigh. So now she and Erma had an entirely new life form to explore, understand, use . . . A whole new future for them . . .

She looked around at winking lights, heard the wheezing air system, watched the med bot tend to her wrecked body . . . sighed.

For this moment, she could let that future take care of itself. She was happy to be back in the ugly oblong contraption she called home. With Erma. A pleasure, certainly.

A GAME OF HOLD'EM

Wendy Sparrow

"A Game of Hold'em" is an adventure story that reminds me of the classic Horse Operas of the 1940s and 50s, an era when it was common for writers of Cowboy Westerns to reconfigure their stories to appeal to a growing number of science fiction readers. Many of these "new" Space Operas were forgettable and poorly written—not so with this story. In "A Game of Hold'em," author Wendy Sparrow introduces us to Moses Taylor—a Texan, born and raised—who plays to win no matter the stakes. Great SF is not just about gizmos, spaceships, and bug-eyed monsters. It's about us, our passions and anger, revenge and redemption, adversities and triumphs. Human elements are the Velcro that make stories stick in our brains. They make them enjoyable, approachable, and memorable. The characters invoke ancient heroes by their names alone, and Sparrow seems to suggest that even in a futuristic era of intergalactic travel, some modern classics will prevail as well, like a good game of poker and the larger-than-life Texan hero.

At home in the Pacific Northwest, Wendy Sparrow writes for both adult and young adult audiences. She has two wonderfully quirky kids, a supportive husband, and a perpetually messy house because writing is more fun than cleaning. She believes in the Oxford comma and that every story deserves a happily-ever-after. Most days she can be found on Twitter @WendySparrow where she'll talk to anyone who talks back and occasionally just to herself.

I

"Texas Hold'em? In a Baruvian law-holder's outpost?" Moses asked again, leaning against his friend's newly-parked hoverex.

"Yeah, they've probably never had someone from Earth here, let alone someone from Texas." Ajax slammed the door behind him. A moment later, his security fob chirped as he locked it.

Moses raised his eyebrows. Of all places to worry about your ride being stolen . . . a law-holder's homestead seemed safe. Ajax's nervous laugh sent an itch down his spine.

Something wasn't right. He'd felt it from the second he'd pulled up. A score of eyes watched him, weighed and measured him. It was damn unnerving. Sure you'd get scrutinized before a poker game, but their boots were still planted on the gray-dirt driveway. The dust was still settling from their arrival—hanging in the fluctuating gravity, shimmering silver.

Ajax gestured at Moses's hoverex. "I forgot to tell you, but Martice keeps slaves. You'll want to lock your ride so they don't hitch and get you killed."

Moses locked his hoverex. Like hell Ajax had forgotten to tell him. "You know my mind on that." He'd just as soon turn around and walk off—forget the whole thing.

"You're not in Texas anymore, Mose. Things are different on Baru and Martice is law here. You want to make contacts for the company, you want to import beef here—you have to work through Martice. Go in. Play a few hands. Let. Him. Win. Don't make eye contact with any of the slaves. Come on."

They walked slowly toward the mansion.

The closer they got, the more the watchful gazes seemed to weigh, pressing on his shoulders, making the muscles in his neck tighten up.

If he'd known what Baru was like, he'd have told the company to shove off when they'd sent him here to grease palms. They'd said Baru was a twin to his hometown in Texas: dry stretches of land, dotted with small scrubs. Which, okay, sure . . . it was. Unlike home, it was ruled by folks who made the Wild West look like the good ol' days. He'd known slavery was legal here, but one of the law-holders? That was jacked up.

Shouldn't surprise him. Martice was rumored to be a real bastard and, on most other planets, he'd find himself on the wrong side of the law, not creating and enforcing it.

Moses sighed and the inhale brought his attention to the pungent smell that was Baru. The planet's mineral deposits gave the air a sour smell akin to sulfur. If it weren't for how valuable those deposits were, no one would stomach this. He couldn't see the back-end of this place fast enough. He'd be bleaching his stuff for a week to be rid of the stench.

Well, whatever he still had.

They'd both spent the night in their hoverexes last night after someone at the hotel had tossed an aromatic into their room, knocking them out. He'd come to and found a knot the size of Texas on his head and the room stripped clean. They'd probably get charged for the towels, and the thieves had even stolen his used boxers. Indecent. Lawless. And it stank . . . like the used boxers he no longer had.

What kind of a person stole a man's used boxers? They were his lucky boxers too.

Bastards.

"He also has servants. You can make eye contact with them," Ajax said.

"And I'm just supposed to guess at which is which?" His neck muscles already were so taut from tension he could feel a headache forming somewhere near that nasty goose-egg.

"You can tell. The servants are armed." He shot Moses a look. "Don't forget that. You mess up, and we've got a dozen guns pointed at our heads."

"What the hell have you gotten us into?" Moses hissed under his breath. "Maybe after this we can go juggle some chainsaws and rattlers for fun."

"Ain't no snakes here on Baru, cowboy." Ajax laughed but stopped at Moses's deadpan stare. Baru was entirely populated by snakes. "Yeah, well, none we're juggling."

They both dragged their feet on the mansion's front steps as gravity shifted. It was a little like being on a boat—the shifting gravity as the planet's core revolved. He wouldn't miss that either. The front stoop of the mansion was nostalgic of some of the old plantations back home too. Tall pillars flanked the door. If they hadn't been made of polished titanium, it would have been a genuine clone.

"They won't want to start an interplanetary incident . . . just don't give them a reason to accuse you of breaking a law," Ajax said.

"We're leaving this outpost after this. Hell, maybe even the planet. I don't want to spend another night in my ride just to keep my dirty laundry." This time he meant it—he wasn't just saying it. What little networking they'd done for the company had been peppered with days of nothing . . . absolutely no progress as they waded neck-deep through bureaucracy and politics. All the outposts on this planet were blurring together—much like the barren landscape, long stretches of gray land with little snatches of uncivilized civilization. Chances were, they couldn't even trust the agreements they'd made—signed or not. Baru was a law unto itself.

Then, there were the slaves. He'd seen them here and there but they hadn't needed to bargain with a slaveowner up until now. No way he'd curry favor with a man with slaves. He wasn't raised that way. He could feel his stubbornness rearing up for a fight. No way.

Damn Ajax. Moron couldn't resist the lure of a poker game. He'd play stupid drunk and wake up naked only to return to the table. The soul of a gambler and the willpower of an addict, Ajax needed somebody to occasionally pull him back from the edge. Maybe it was just as well he was here. Ajax probably would've come here, all on his own, and done something just stupid as all get out, and he'd have to explain to the company why they were out one negotiator.

Plus, Ajax was a friend. Sort of. Less of a friend after this.

"You're going to find this type of thing wherever we go, Mose. You just gotta lighten up on your mama's boy ethics."

"Yeah, and end up like you? No thanks."

Ajax laughed, taking it as a compliment as Moses'd known he

would. "You have to admit I can find us a good game at every outpost."

"You've played here?" Maybe it wouldn't be all bad.

Ajax smirked just as he pushed the doorbell. "Yep. The guy cheats like a husband in Haradoon."

Moses breathed out, "This was your dumbest idea ever."

"Probably. Just don't get us killed."

The gun on the hip of the man who opened the door yelled he was an employee but, behind him, girls moved about the mansion, silent as the sparkling dust dropping behind him. They had bracelets on their arms that'd fry them if they left the homestead. Slave-girls. Dressed like whores to disgrace them even more. Great.

He was going to skin Ajax if they made it out of here alive.

Martice Tesla met them in front of a secluded room where they could see a poker table. The guy might've been the same age as them— early thirties—but he had the look of a fool who snorted dark. His eyes were weasel-shrewd, and his smile had all the win of a used-ride salesman. Dark hair was greased back and his goatee had been pulled tightly at the bottom into two golden clips with diamonds across them. An illegal sharpshot with its shield-piercing bullets was settled on his hip—clear as day. Rich and crooked. They really, really shouldn't have come here.

Ajax cleared his throat and avoided eye contact after noticing the sharpshot.

This was going to be the quickest game of poker he'd ever played. It wouldn't be a friendly game going into the short hours of the Baruvian moon. Moses extended a hand to shake Martice's. His smile felt fake and forced, but he was representing his company here. "Evening, Mr. Tesla. Moses Taylor—from Earth."

Martice laughed—a greasy, winded sound. The dark did that. The black stuff ashed your lungs and liquefied your esophagus, but a man as rich as Martice could get them replaced every decade and keep his bad habits. "Eve'nin. Call me Martice—and I don't shake hands." He gestured at his side. "Got shot by someone with a third arm that way once."

Moses didn't need to send another look Ajax's way to give his opinion on this. He and Ajax had known each other long enough. His hand dropped to his side and he rolled his shoulders, trying to ease out a bit of the tension gathering there. It was just a game of cards. Play. Smile. Get out.

Maybe if Ajax lost hard Moses *could* persuade him to leave Baru. He could turn this in his favor. A good gambler could win with a bad hand, and Moses might not be as greedy as Ajax to play—and never greedy enough to walk into this snake pit, but Moses played to win.

Martice introduced the two other men in the poker room as "Johnny and Mick. Couple of my guys to make things even."

Even Ajax stiffened at this. They'd be playing against "his guys" with a man known for cheating. Great. Just great. Whatever he lost, he'd be getting back straight from Ajax's wallet. And they *would* lose big here tonight. No doubt about that. He could for sure kiss the four thousand gama he'd brought goodbye. No way he'd file an expense report listing that much in gambling loss—not without everybody back home laughing their asses off. He'd walked into a puma fight with a pointy stick to defend himself with.

As they dropped onto the tall barstools around the table, a girl walked in and sat down in the dealer's place. Long black hair flowed down her back like a Baru river. Her eyes were as green as grass back on Earth—and they wouldn't meet his. She didn't say a word, but her clothes, if you could call them that, spoke loudly. They were cut like a harem outfit and the gauzy aqua was transparent. A golden bracelet sparkled on her upper arm—beautiful and ugly all at once. A slave. Possibly first generation, but Baru was going onto its third generation of slaves. Most slaves were sterile, by their own choice. Any child born into slavery would never get out unless freed by an owner with a conscience. He hadn't met a soul with a conscience on Baru yet.

When she leaned down to grab a pack of cards, he saw the thin lines of healing gashes on her back. Martice beat her. Great.

Ajax's gaze slid down the slave's curves appreciatively before he shot a warning look Moses's way. His eyes said, "Don't look at the girl. Just play the game and let's get out of here." There was also the taint of an apology for this serious break in already poor judgment. Great. They were so screwed.

II

Tia studied them as they sat down. A good dealer always examined the players, but Baru hadn't gotten so far into her that she'd lie to herself. She wasn't analyzing the player—she was watching the man. Soft, brown hair and very tan skin. He came from a colony with a warm sun. He looked . . . trustworthy which made his presence at Martice's poker table something of an oddity.

The newcomer glanced at her. A soft smile touched his lips for a second before his gaze dropped to the bracelet. The corner of his eyes pinched as he narrowed them, and the smile flattened as his jaw tightened. A moment later, he looked away and took a deep breath. She could read people almost as well as the cards, and he looked angry.

The other, Ajax, was nice enough, but seemed to enjoy ogling her as much as the others.

No, this new one . . . she listened for his name. Moses. Moses was going to win big tonight. She'd need to make it obvious that she was not only favoring him, but that he had no part of it.

"I've heard we're playing Texas Hold'em," Moses said. An accent slowed and softened his speech to a drawl. It slid across her like a warm sun might, heating her skin and making it tingle. It would have been nice to meet someone like him . . . long before her life had been cancelled due to her brother's debt to Martice.

"That's right," Martice said. He stared at her breasts while licking his lips. He preferred her exposed, and she'd grown accustomed to no longer having the privilege of modesty over the last four years. Moses's refusal to acknowledge her nudity made it uncomfortable again—a reminder that being on display should be awkward. She wasn't sure she should thank him for that.

"I've heard you're from Texas," Martice said.

"Born and bred there," Moses said. He pulled a green chip from his friend's stack, held it up, and met her eyes over the top of it. He smiled gently at her—sweetly. She glanced away first this time before Martice noted it. He didn't like her paying attention to anyone or anything but him and the game—even if he did enjoy other men lusting after her. In fact, that's why she was dressed—or undressed like this. All the other players would want her and know they couldn't have her.

"Earth dweller," Mick said with a snort. Mick grabbed her ass as he walked by, knowing she wouldn't do anything or they'd both be punished for it. Being Martice's property seemed to mean she was nothing more than that to anyone. After this poker game, she wouldn't even be that.

She was destined for both dealer and Martice's "companion" tonight. After the game, he'd snort dark and beat his companion nearly to death before raping her. It wasn't going to happen to her again. You got out of Martice's slavery in one way . . . in a black bag marked for burning. Since there was always that risk with his after-game habits, she'd rather go quickly with a slug from his sharpshot. Time to go out with a bang.

Moses slid four thousand gama her way. She traded him for chips without a word.

"Thank you," he said. She could feel the pull of his eyes as he tried to get her to look at him again. She wouldn't. She couldn't start feeling human with so much at stake with this game. She needed to walk a fine line and taunt a monster. She couldn't afford to feel human.

She nodded at Moses, unable to resist that small courtesy.

"Don't bother. She can't speak," Martice said.

The words dropped like acid, but Tia just shuffled the cards. This was a hand she'd dealt herself by defending another slave and talking back. Now, she couldn't make a sound if her life depended on it—not when Martice beat her bloody—not when she'd fallen into a collapsed mine last year.

"Courtesy to another soul is never a bother." Moses restacked the chips in front of him.

Silence hung around the table. She gulped a breath down her silent throat. No one spoke to Martice like that. Her hands shook in a barely visible shiver as the old fear of a quick retribution resurfaced. She clenched her fists tightly for a second and let her anxiety go in the release. The new player could fight his own battles. She was in control of her destiny—just her own.

Ajax cleared his throat. "Moses is a real pain when it comes to manners. He's always getting after me about being polite. Guess they raise them that way in Texas." Ajax was good at smoothing waters with his charm, but there'd been steel in Moses's voice, and Martice wasn't easily charmed.

Martice tapped on the table twice. A sign she was to swing the game in his favor. Usually, this "sign" didn't come until the game was in play. It was tempting to settle luck on Ajax; Moses wouldn't need any extra help in starting a fight with Martice.

"Let's play," Martice said.

"Why do I get the feeling the game started at the door?" Moses slid his stacks of chips together and didn't look up.

"Because this is poker. The game started when your friend accepted my invitation."

The two guests laughed awkwardly and then shared a glance. They knew they were in hostile territory at least. The Texan might be brash and stubborn, but he was no fool.

After the blinds had gone down, she dealt each man two cards. Her eye had been fitted with a special lens that could see the marked cards. It was the surgery following the removal of her voice. She was the fastest dealer in the house, so it was no surprise that she'd be dealing tonight. The beating to follow was a sure thing too. She'd healed from the last one, so it was time. That was how she marked her calendar. Stripes of healing versus healed marks on her skin. Then, tonight, a bullet through her brain, and the day was done.

Each time she dealt Moses a card, he nodded his thanks. She pursed her lips to prevent a smile, an unforgiveable courtesy to this man, and kept her eyes on the green felt.

If she favored Martice the first few hands, he might cool it toward Moses, and she could continue with her intentions. Martice, full of confidence, bet more gama than his hand warranted. Fool. It's not like she was handing him pocket aces. Mick folded as did Ajax—as well they should. A Jesse James and a Five and Dime. Moses would lose to Martice, but he was teasing out the other man to see what kind of player he was. His tanned face was as shrewd as hers was impassive. Johnny stayed in just because he wasn't playing with his own money ... also, watching her deal gave him a chance to "watch" her. If he didn't watch himself, he'd be a eunuch before long.

As she'd stacked the deck just how she wanted, she tossed a card, burnt it, but it was all for show since she'd planned to discard it. It was almost a mockery—this tradition of fairness—burning a card to prevent her from cheating. With the lens in her eye, the cards could be face-up. Martice had her practice the art of shuffling and switching for weeks until she'd mastered it—with periodic beatings to remind her of the importance of not getting caught. Now, she sometimes only felt comfortable with a deck of cards in her hands. Even now, the cards whispered softly in her hands, responding to her commands. She was the master here. Not Martice. Her. And she was going to prove it tonight.

Tia dealt the flop cards onto the center of the table. A king, an eight, and a jack.

This gave Martice a small straight, and he knew she'd give him the full straight with the turn. Moses had two pair already . . . and he'd end with that. This time. Johnny had nothing. He knew he had nothing. He knew he'd get nothing from her. In fact, since he kept staring at her breasts like they were on the table—he'd lose dismally. He'd figure it out around the third time she handed him a pair of ducks with the river—if he even made it that far.

Martice raised.

Johnny folded.

Moses paused, looked at Martice, looked at her, and checked. Shrewd. He knew the game was rigged. It felt right—him knowing. It felt less like a betrayal if he knew.

The turn gave Martice the ten he needed. Both men checked. Martice was watching Moses with an expression she didn't trust. She might have to favor Ajax. If she did, hopefully, Ajax would know better than to come around here again. The house always wins. In this place, the house would beat you and leave you broken and next to dead, but it would win.

"I have a feeling the river is going to be cold," Moses said.

She dealt the river card. It didn't favor either man, but it certainly didn't help Moses.

Martice, with a smirk, tapped the pot higher.

Moses tossed his hand onto the table, folding.

"Was it chilly?" Ajax asked Moses.

Moses smiled. "Iced over."

The camaraderie between the two men made everyone relax. A little.

III

Moses watched her slim hands deal the marked cards. She was quick and nimble with those fingers, but nothing passed through them without her say-so. She'd stacked the marked deck. No way he'd win. On the other hand, it was like he'd be losing to her rather than Martice. *That* was a way he'd consider losing four thousand gama. Hopefully, if he lost gracefully, the beautiful slave-girl would get a reward after the game.

Her long black hair fell forward to brush the green felt of the table. Her eyes, outlined in black kohl, matched the color of the felt. She was dusted with Baru minerals, and her skin shimmered under the lights. She glanced at him then, and the intelligence he saw in her eyes aroused him and ashamed him. Hard not to stare at her. And it pissed him off that he was doing just as Martice intended. Distract the players with the dealer.

Damn. He wanted her, and he hated himself for that. Coveting her made her into a possession, and he couldn't be just another man seeing her that way.

He shifted to judging the men around him. Even if the game was in the slave-girl's hands, he'd still win where he could and against whom he could. He'd never call a game over until the last card hit the felt.

The next two hands were choreographed particularly well. The outsiders were strung along just enough, while the house slightly leaned in Martice's favor. She was subtle. Even in a gambling hall, he wouldn't have called her out for cheating—there was just enough doubt in his mind.

"She's good, isn't she?" Martice asked with a nod at the girl. "Tia is my best dealer—fast."

Tia. It suited her. Tia the queen of cards . . . and a slave.

"She is good," Moses agreed. He smothered a laugh when Johnny swore under his breath and folded for the third time. He'd drawn Tia's wrath somehow.

Martice didn't bother hiding his amusement. "Not your night, Johnny?"

Johnny slid a glare at Tia. "I'm just not lucky, I guess."

Martice laughed. From his position beside her, Martice's hand slid under the table, and Tia's eyes widened. She swallowed thickly. The others didn't have as good a view as Moses did. He was to Tia's right with Martice on her left. Out of the corner of his eye, Moses saw the other man's hand stroking along her upper thigh. Her face was masked a moment later. She didn't look pleased, but it'd been hidden quickly.

There were only two of them any good at playing a poker face. Ajax tried, but his tell of twisting his class ring gave him away. Martice hadn't bothered to cultivate a bland expression with the dealer always on his side. The two grunts, Johnny and Mick, barely stopped looking at Tia's body long enough to play. Tia kept dealing as if she wasn't getting groped under the table. Moses kept playing as if he didn't want to rip Martice's snide smile off his face.

The cards landed in a soft glide in front of him. She had so much control with those artful fingers. He tipped the corners up, anticipating another set of mediocre cards that would promise and not produce. The pocket aces blew him away enough his face must've shown his surprise.

"Bad hand?" Martice asked, grinning.

"Something like that." He folded the cards so fast you'd have thought she'd tossed him a hand of scorpions. He'd never folded pocket aces before. Crap . . . he rarely folded. Still, he didn't want Tia punished for giving him the wrong cards. Maybe Martice's unwanted attention was throwing off her game. She seemed in control. Her eyes slid across the cards with that same knowing glance. But why pocket aces? It made less than no sense.

Was he mistaken or did Tia smile as she shifted in her stool away from Martice? Martice looked confused at having his under-the-table games ended, but the fact that Moses had thrown away a hand was enough to recompense apparently. His smile only slightly faltered. After the river was down, Martice's hand barely beat Ajax's, and this had him frowning again. Neither would have held up against what *his* hand would've been.

This time when the cards fluttered to a halt in front of him, he inhaled and exhaled slowly before tipping the edges of the cards up.

This time, he didn't flinch.

A pair of cowboys—she'd handed him two kings this time.

Martice watched him. His eyes travelled between him and Tia. Martice always liked to know he held the winning hand, and his face said he knew he didn't. Finally, with a scowl, Martice folded.

A betting man, which clearly Moses was, would bet Martice rarely had to fold a hand.

Moses folded too. This restored Martice's mood enough that he glanced at his cards again as if curious if he'd mistaken them to begin with. Ajax crowed when he won the round.

"I've never played a hand where you folded, and I won," Ajax said.

"Apparently, my luck is turning," Moses said. It was turning all right, and it was the first time he'd hated having a winning hand.

Tia's next several hands were mediocre all around—as if she was calming the storm.

"Maybe a new deck," Martice suggested when Mick won with a pair of nines. Everybody laughed—whether because they found superstition funny—or because they knew the only luck at the table was cast by Tia.

As Moses went to toss his cards, he knocked over Ajax's nearly empty glass.

Johnny snickered. "I thought earthboys were supposed to be smooth."

"Maybe some," Moses said. "My mama told me I was born with three left feet and the speed of a sandswallower on Trift."

Ajax stilled at the lie. They both prided themselves on fast draws. You couldn't be too careful in some of these outposts. Hell, he slept with a gun in his hand. But Ajax had to have noticed how much both Johnny and Mick were fussing with their sidearms. It was better to have them think he and Ajax were a couple of clumsy fools rather than the truth. Even a few seconds extra to draw a gun could be the difference between leaving here alive and leaking blood like a sieve all over the expensive, ugly rug beneath the table.

"So, I've heard that you've solved the flash-freeze dilemma they were having before with transporting meat?" Martice asked.

"Yes, we've gone with more flash—and less freeze." Moses stared down his pocket cards, willing them to speak and explain. This time, he actually glanced at Tia—hoping for some sign as to what he was supposed to do. Another set of cowboys. Another set of kings after so many mediocre cards *was* telling. He just didn't know what it was saying. There was no sane reason an intelligent woman would want him to win against her boss. So, he started considering insane reasons, and he didn't like any of them—not one bit.

Martice chortled. "More flash. I like that. Will you be staying on Baru then?"

If he hadn't been watching her face, he would have missed the stillness—the way she was holding her breath.

"No, I don't intend to stay on Baru. I'll head back to Earth after a few more colony stops," Moses said.

Tia exhaled . . . seemingly relieved. What the deuce?

When the betting came around to him, he paused, hoping for some sign from Tia. Any sign. She had to know what she was doing. He could see she did.

She reached down for a glass of water that was in a recess under the table. Her gauzy shirt slipped from her shoulder. He kept his eyes fixed on hers. She sipped her water, but met his gaze directly. All the other males in the room salivated over her newly-exposed skin—and so missed the quick wink in his direction.

IV

Moses called the bet. It was about time he let her hang herself. Why was it that the one time she tried to really cheat at cards she was dealing with a gentleman? Well, technically, she was always cheating at cards, but this time—this was different. As she put her glass of water away, she pulled the shirt back on. The only one who hadn't been scorching holes through her skin had been Moses.

A gentleman? In Baru? Good thing he wasn't staying.

Martice was a sore loser. When his hand amounted to two pair and was nicely trounced by Moses's four of a kind, he swore and pounded a fist on the table. Ajax sent a warning cough at Moses. They must have agreed to lose before they came in. It might have been interesting to see if Moses would have lost on purpose. So far, he'd only thrown the hands she'd dropped in his lap, and he'd folded so early on that Martice thought she was giving him the ducks that she was still feeding to Johnny each hand.

"Let's up the blinds," Martice said, staring hard at her. She inclined her head in a nod. Yes. She'd done that on purpose. Yes, he was about to lose hard and fast and ugly. The worse this went, the quicker she died. Martice's temper burnt fast, and she had no desire to linger around for him to recover his senses and torture her with calculated precision. His animal unleashed was ferocious but it was the sadistic human's return which terrified her.

Martice lost. Hard. Fast. Ugly—just as promised. It was difficult not to smile. This was her revenge. He'd look like a fool. Not her. Every time one of the others won, she won. And the victory was sweet.

She strung Martice along for two hands so he'd bet heavy and then she dropped the pot in Moses's lap. The next few hands, Martice wisely folded. Finally, she threw Martice a few kings.

For the first time ever in a game, she met Martice's eyes boldly, openly. She didn't play the shy and obedient slave who shielded her eyes with half-lids modestly. No, she opened her made-up and surgically-enhanced eyes wide and stared at him defiantly—as defiantly as he was staring at her. And what she saw there both frightened and exhilarated her. There was a cutting malice there she'd never seen present—not even in the madness that came after snorting dark. If she lived long enough, he might make a scream erupt from her silent throat. His hand snaked out and clenched her thigh, his nails digging into her skin. The message was clear. I win this . . . or you lose like you've never lost before.

Only he underestimated her desire to lose, and you should never underestimate the house in a card game and here, at the felt, she was the house and master. He might try to break that out of her afterwards but, once she was dead, he'd be haunted that she'd mastered him first, and he couldn't undo that. Dead was dead. This was the first time she'd felt powerful in all her time here.

His hand gripped tighter, his nails cut her sensitive skin. There'd be blood and bruises there. Martice's hand was probably high enough that Moses could see it. She hoped he couldn't or wouldn't look.

Beside her, Moses folded.

"No!" Martice said to Moses. "Stay in this hand. I'm curious where it'll take us. No more bets . . . just the hand."

Stiff-backed, Moses said, "All right." He fiddled with his pocket cards for a moment before nodding. This agitation was the first she'd seen from him. He played it cool and composed. "It's fine, though. I was on the fence on betting. I'll play it out. Call." Moses tossed the chips into the pot. He should have bet more.

By the time the river was played, Martice had already lost to the full house she'd given Moses. She didn't need to see the cards turned to see that. Martice's fingers were bruising her thigh. It was so painful her eyes watered, blurring the cards for a moment. Martice tossed out his two kings—three with the inclusion of the community cards. Moses turned over his cards, and it was so startling that her mouth dropped open.

Ajax laughed openly. "You were on the fence about a pair of eights?"

Martice's hand slackened on her thigh, and he pulled the pot toward him with a laugh. "I thought you had me there, earthboy."

"I thought it would go somewhere," Moses said, rubbing his neck sheepishly. He bluffed like a pro. For a moment, his shamefaced expression fooled her, and she thought her skill had failed her. Just for a moment.

Moses had switched the cards.

He'd switched the cards. He must have pocketed the cards from an earlier deck because the ones on the table were marked. How many other cards did he have up his sleeve? She dared a glance at his sleeve.

Did he actually have them up his sleeve?

Amazing. She snapped her mouth closed. This man from earth was now playing a deeper game than she'd ever seen. She had no idea what his motives might be. Perhaps this was part of gaining Martice's favor. It would have been the first attempt to do so that Moses had made. He didn't mince words. He hadn't taken advantage. It made no sense. What sort of man cheated to lose but was courteous to a mute?

Moses cleared his throat. "Let's make this a little more interesting." What the hell was he doing? The man was a wild card now. She had no idea how to read him.

"Interesting?" Martice asked.

Moses slid his chips to the side. "Let's not bother with money. You have money. I have money. It's just money."

Ajax coughed. "I don't know, Mose. I'm getting really tired."

Martice waved him quiet. There was a feverish gleam in Martice's eye. He looked like he'd already snorted dark. Not good. "What did you have in mind?"

Moses pushed up one of his sleeves. No cards fell out. That was good. He removed a silver watch. It looked old . . . and not necessarily expensive. "This is an antique. It's been in the Taylor family for six generations."

"What's it worth?" Johnny asked.

"That doesn't matter, does it?" Moses spoke directly to Martice "We're both gamblers and in negotiations. You know how this works."

Martice's smile was chilling. A shiver ran down her spine. Martice was never colder than when he settled down to business. There was no gamble if you always intended to win by whatever means necessary. He made sure he held the winning hand long before negotiations ever started. "Indeed, Johnny. It's an important lesson in business. It's not how much it's worth, but how much it'll cost the person losing it. A man's finger isn't worth anything to me if I were to cut it off . . . yet you've seen my collection. Six generations?" he asked Moses.

"Yep. It's my lucky watch. Never lost a hand I didn't want to."

Martice roared in laughter, not recognizing it for the truth. "You're cocky, earthboy, I'll give you that. All right, what am I betting—if not money?"

Moses's eyes searched the room, lingering on a painting behind Martice so long that Martice turned to look at it. "That's a nice painting. An original. I took it from a competitor."

He'd stolen it from a fellow landowner after he'd shot the man in the back. The slaves all knew the bloodthirsty provenance of all of Martice's acquisitions from people to paintings.

"It's tempting," Moses said. "I travel light, though, and I don't really want to carry a painting to my next stop in Morago."

Morago. For a half a blink, she imagined what it would be like to leave Baru and go with him—leave with this man with the kind eyes and the real smile. He radiated heat. Perhaps all men from warm-sunned planets did. Then, she was back. In this room. With the cold reality of dying as soon as this kind man stood up and left.

Martice nodded. "Not the painting then."

Moses's eyes continued their path before finally resting on her. And there they stayed. Holy jacks! This was why you never played with a gentleman. He was going to get them both killed.

V

"The girl then. You said she is a decent dealer. I'm assuming she isn't completely wasted in other arenas." Moses could've thrown a leer in Tia's direction, but he didn't want to over-play it.

Martice laughed again. "Tia? Your antique watch against a mute slave?"

He'd kept his cards close enough to his chest that Martice had no idea the whole evening had been heading toward this hand. Even Tia looked shocked. Her kohl-darkened, emerald eyes widened before she closed them for a blink just a second longer than natural. When she opened them, her shoulders relaxed and her poker face was back.

Moses shrugged—as if it didn't matter. "I like unusual stakes, and playing with living things seems right up your alley." Martice was jaded beyond seeing *that* remark as an insult.

"I don't know, Mose," Ajax said from beside him. "If the company found out about this . . . ?"

The company wouldn't find out about this. In fact, if he won—which he *had* to, he'd be bolting as fast as he could. The company just lost a negotiator to Baru. Ajax had always predicted Moses's "good boy guts" would get him killed one day. This was as good as.

"Silence!" Martice yelled at Ajax.

Ajax went still . . . and, yes, silent. Even Ajax never played this deep. Stupidly deep.

Moses knew he could outrun Martice on fairly dealt hands. Martice was too emotional and had grown accustomed to the cards playing in his favor. Without a challenge, your skills withered, and he'd bet nobody had challenged Martice in a good long time.

Martice considered the bet—though he'd already made up his mind to bite. Every movement of his was a tell—spinning the chips, his eyes crinkling at the edges, the clench of his jaw. His avarice lengthened its teeth and bit. "Fine. Okay. We'll play your stakes."

"She can't deal this hand," Moses said. "It's not right. Not fair."

"Are you accusing me of cheating?" A taunt edged Martice's words.

"Course not," Moses said. "I'm just thinking that I've got about . . ." He glanced at his chips. "About five thousand gama to my name now." He'd stolen nearly all of Johnny's chips. The few hands Johnny hadn't folded were some of the worst hands he'd ever seen. Moses gestured around him. "Whereas you live in a mansion. If I was going to play servant to someone . . . I wouldn't pick me either. I just want this to be fair." If he played this right, she'd never be a servant again—or hurt again.

Martice grabbed a new deck from the table.

Tia looked on the verge of trying to use hand signals to convey how bad an idea she thought this was. She licked her lips nervously—her eyes pleading. Desperate people changed their tells and changed their tunes. Tia was desperate for him not to do this, but he hoped it wasn't because she wanted to stay with Martice. No, he'd read her right earlier. This anxiety was on his behalf.

Martice looked between his henchmen, considering. The deck landed in front of Johnny. "Deal."

"But I don't have . . ." Johnny said. He'd bet the farm Johnny was about to blow the secret behind how the marked cards worked. There was a warning look from Martice. "I don't have any experience in dealing."

"You just deal us cards." Martice was growing impatient. Good. His self-confidence was convincing him he'd won these hands on his own... or at least some of them. He hadn't. It had been Tia this whole time—well, other than his last hand. Those cards had been itching him since he'd swiped them shortly after spilling Ajax's drink.

With a groan, Johnny tediously shuffled the deck. Hard to tell if he was nervous about screwing over Martice or if he just hadn't had much practice. They waited and the tension ratcheted up a few clicks with each breath they took.

Tia clenched her hands tightly in her lap. Her easy grace had fled and anxiety radiated from every inch of her. He willed her to look at him again. He knew what was at stake . . . what he was willing to risk because he knew he couldn't walk out of here without her. Even if he wasn't interested in her, which he was, it looked like she had a death wish—and Martice's behavior said that wish was about to be granted.

As if she'd finally heard his mind calling, she glanced up and met his eyes. Her eyes softened and a corner of her mouth flicked up a millimeter—a halted smile. Then, infinitesimally, she shook her head the tiniest bit and closed her eyes for a long blink. When she opened her eyes, she was cool as could be—though her fingers twitched as Johnny dealt a mess of slapped out cards.

This time, no one was calling the shots—not even good fortune—or apparently his lucky watch which now sat in the center of the table.

There was no way he'd win with this hand. No way. He didn't bother hiding his disappointment. He'd never let his mama know he'd lost his watch playing cards—she tan his hide even if she agreed with him.

The flop bumped him up to a pair of eights, but Martice's grin was oozing success. The turn and the river didn't add a thing to his snowmen. Martice laughed heartily after revealing his flush. Damn. Damn. Damn. Well, this was better anyway. Though watching Martice slide his lucky watch on his wrist was as foul as the stench of Baru.

"Not so lucky without your watch, earthboy," Johnny jeered. He really hated that guy.

"Okay . . . my hoverex," Moses said. He shifted in his seat—to all appearances a man wanting to reverse his luck by throwing more money at it. If he seemed desperate enough, Martice would take the bait.

Tia's eyes narrowed and then she shook her head again—barely. *Don't do this.*

There were times when you went all in. A crooked dealer—as beautiful and sweet as she might be—would never understand the desire to cast your lot with fate and hope for the best and believe that sometimes it was your due. Lady luck owed him this in exchange for his lucky watch . . . and so many years of clean living.

He hoped so anyway.

"Against your watch?" Martice asked.

Moses shook his head. "No, still for the girl. I don't like to lose a pot."

Tia glared at him for that remark. Not that he could blame her, but it made more sense to someone like Martice than the truth.

"Mose!" Ajax said.

"Quiet!" both Martice and Moses shouted, holding up their hands to silence him.

Martice's eyes narrowed. He glanced between Moses and Tia.

C'mon, you weasel. Take the bait. You want to see me desperate and pathetic. You know you do.

"Okay," Martice said, grinning again.

This time, Lady Luck not only smiled on Moses, but she kissed both his cheeks and called him "golden." A king of hearts and an ace of hearts? Nice. Very nice.

Martice had not been dealt as nice a hand, and he glared at Johnny for a moment. Johnny went ashen, clearly wishing he could deal as surely as Tia.

The flop brought him a queen and a jack—as well as a useless four. All hearts.

The jack brought a smile to Martice's face.

Damn.

In a moment, Moses would know if he had something . . . or nothing at all. If he had nothing at all, he'd be forced to bet Ajax's hoverex next—and then he really would be desperate and not just look it. Walking away without his ride and his great, great, great granddaddy's watch . . . and nothing to show for it, he couldn't live with himself.

No, he sensed it in his bones. He *would* win this.

Sometimes you stayed at the table just long enough to take what you were due. The green felt beneath his fist thrummed with a psychic urgency as if luck had a voice. He was due this win. *This* was his.

He glanced at Tia to see her eyebrows drawn together in a frown. She knew the turn. He watched her instead of the card as it hit the table. A smile brushed her lips before she smothered it. He glanced at the card. It was a queen, the queen of spades. At the very least, he'd have two queens and the high card with the ace of hearts in his pocket... as long as Martice didn't have better. Did her smile mean that Martice didn't have any better? Maybe she wanted to stay here. What if he'd misread every little nuance she'd sent out?

He had a handful of hearts and those two queens. Lady Luck couldn't possibly turn on him with two ladies in his corner. Martice might have better. He looked confident, but Tia had very nearly smiled.

He was going to win this. He was meant to win this. When his granddaddy had taught him to play, he said trust your gut when it came to poker and women. This was both.

Moses stared at the deck, willing the marked card to speak to him too.

The river seemed to flip in slow motion. He breathed a hundred times in the space it took for it to fall. Then, it was there, and he just stared. Even when the ten of hearts lay there on the felt, he still couldn't believe what he was seeing. Even on his best days—while wearing his lucky watch, he'd never held a royal flush. It startled a laugh out of him.

"Mose? I can give you a ride," Ajax offered, misinterpreting Moses's shock.

Martice tossed down his hand with a grin. A pair of jacks and a pair of queens with the cards on the board. "It appears you need a lucky watch, earthboy."

Moses sat back heavily, still shocked. Finally, he tossed his cards on the felt.

They all stared, a nearly frozen pantomime of abbreviated gestures and stunned looks. Ajax's mouth hung open, and he pointed at the cards in quick jabs.

Tia, who'd known the winner the longest, recovered the first and was watching Martice and only him. The next hand was played off the felt, and she knew it.

The silence was finally broken by Mick, who'd barely said a word previous. "Is that a . . . ?"

The group thawed and then everybody was moving.

"Yes," Martice snarled. He glared at the cards and pounded a fist on the table.

"I've never actually gotten a royal flush," Ajax said.

"I've never had a royal flush either," Moses admitted.

"So, now we play for the watch?" Martice asked, sliding closer to Tia.

Moses shook his head. "No, it can only get worse from here. Even a bad gambler would end on a win like that. Another night."

Tia busied herself with cashing out the chips. Her hands were shaking for the first time.

"I thought you said you were leaving for Morago." Martice looked half-mad with rage.

Moses tried for nonchalance and hoped Ajax would keep his mouth shut. Shrugging, he said, "I'll need to pass back through here to port on my way back due to the embargo on the trade with Seethe." He would—if he was going to Morago.

Martice grinned. "Of course . . . of course . . . and then we'll play for the watch. Perhaps it'll bring me luck in the meantime."

Moses smiled. Both their smiles were lies, but he'd won Tia fair-and-square. "You'll need to remove her bracelet," he said.

The false smile was still pasted on as Martice took a key from his pocket and fit it into a small hole. The bracelet fell away revealing pale skin. She was even paler naturally, and the skin beneath the bracelet wasn't sparkling like the rest of her. It was reassuring—a little less ethereal and a little more human.

Tia stared down at her arm as if she'd forgotten what was under the bracelet.

Reaching out, Moses grabbed her upper arm and started backing out of the room. Her cool flesh was soft as down beneath his grip, and he tried to look possessive while being gentle.

"It's been fun," Ajax said, smiling and waving with all the charm he could manage. The tension was making him sweat.

Martice tapped the table twice—just as he had to signal Tia in the beginning.

Johnny, Mick, Ajax, and Moses all pulled guns out. Ajax had his out first and trained his gun on Johnny. Moses—on Martice.

Now, he'd just gone all in.

Moses and Ajax's speed, and the comfortable familiarity they held the guns with, made Johnny and Mick look at Martice for guidance. Tia nearly knocked Moses off balance as she hurtled into his side, her arms around his waist. Deuces, she was shivering, and he could feel the prickle of her skin through her clothing—if you could even call it clothing. It was tempting just to shoot Martice anyway.

"Not so slow after all, earthboy." Martice raised his eyebrows. "Since when do we bring guns to a poker game?"

"Ah now . . . that's the way we always play in Texas," Moses said smoothly, laying his drawl on extra thick.

Martice laughed and gestured at his men to lower their guns. "My apologies. My associates are a little trigger happy."

This time, their retreat from the mansion was quick and Ajax said under his breath, "I hope she's worth it, Moses, because you may have just gotten us killed."

"Not you." Moses handed Ajax his poker winnings. He kept his hand around Tia's upper arm where the bracelet had been. If Martice guessed his only interest in her was as a slave, he might give them a bit of a lead before he tried to kill him—or let Tia live if they got caught.

At their hoverexes, Ajax whispered, "You know he had her voice silenced, right?"

Moses nodded. There were some places that claimed they could reverse it. They'd check into that. If not, they'd work on learning sign language. That was assuming she'd stay with him. She'd be free to choose him or not choose him, though.

Ajax slid into his hoverex and took off—toward the dock. Good idea. It was time to get the hell off Baru. He opened the door for Tia, his hand still on the gun. There were even more eyes watching him now.

When he slid in the ride's driver seat, Tia was staring straight ahead as if disbelieving the world outside.

"How long have you been with him?" he asked, starting the hoverex.

She held up four fingers.

"Are you glad to be out of there? You were sending some mixed signals."

She nodded vigorously as tears streaked down her glittering cheeks, washing the minerals away. Her hands flew to cover her mouth as either silent sobs or laughter shook her. Okay, that would do until they were safe. He was nearing the private dock when he received a message on his com from Ajax saying "Gone." At least nothing would happen to Ajax due to tonight. There was likely a swarm of Martice's men at the public dock waiting for him.

A man was filling a ship when Moses pulled into the docking station. "Where is Trenton?" Moses asked the man.

"He's in his office. Do you have an appointment?" The worker's eyes popped when Moses helped Tia out of the car. Her outfit was no better than a covering of rainwater under the bright docking lights.

"I do," Moses lied.

The worker, still staring, pointed off toward a building to the side of the port's hangar.

Moses dragged Tia with him, this time holding her hand. He walked into the man's office. "I need a ship for transport right away."

Trenton sat behind his desk. He was a heavy-set man with a full beard and eyes sunken-in from drinking too much. "Do I know you?"

Moses shook his head.

Tia's hand tightened in his.

VI

What was Moses doing? Tia shook in vibrating shivers from dread and from the cold. He'd dragged them to some man's dock and Martice would be after them by now. This crazy Texan *had* to know that.

"I don't know you either—other than by reputation," Moses told the man.

No. No. No. Was Moses not playing with a full deck? The thought nearly made her laugh hysterically . . . which she would have—if she could.

"What do you have to trade?" the man whom Moses had called Trenton asked. He glanced over her, taking in her garb with a quick appraisal. It galled her to be measured for value outside of Martice's mansion especially with all her assets on display.

"The hoverex," Moses said.

Was he joking? Trenton must have thought so, because he laughed.

"That's not why you'll help us, though," Moses said.

Trenton grinned, shaking his head. "All right, I'll bite. Why am I helping you?"

"Because Tia, here, was Martice's slave, and I just won her in a hand of poker. We can die here on the planet because Martice's men have surrounded the main dock, or. . . ."

Trenton's grin matched many of Martice's. He was *that* Trenton. Slaves didn't often hear of business particulars—even though Martice acted as if slaves didn't exist. She knew Trenton, though. The two men hated each other.

"Very well, you'll get your trade and my blessing," he said, standing up. Trenton tossed Moses the keys from a nearby hook. "It's the small ship in the farthest bay. It's a freighter, but that might be just what you'd want anyway." Moses set the keys to his hoverex on the desk with a nod, but Trenton had already sat down and gone back to the papers he'd been reading. A small, secretive smile played on his lips.

"C'mon, Tia." Moses tugged her by their joined hands back through the door. After stopping by the hoverex and pulling a suitcase out of the back, they moved to a small ship in the corner. It still was worth two or three times the price of the hoverex despite its size and age.

They got aboard the ship, a one room freighter designed to transport small cargo without using much fuel. Tia buckled in, her fingers clumsy with nervous excitement. She was free. She'd made it. This was impossible. She'd never thought she'd leave Baru. Never.

Through the small window beside her, the port shrunk in size as they took off. If she hadn't been seatbelted in, she would have had her face pressed up against one of the windows watching the world she'd decided would be her grave—fading farther and farther away.

"Brace yourself as we break gravity. I'm only a proficient pilot in these things," Moses said.

Despite his doubts, it was as smooth a crossing as she'd ever experienced. Then, Baru was shrinking away. Going. Going. Gone.

Moses punched in some numbers and set it to autopilot before swinging around in the chair to face her. "I have some clothing in that suitcase and some money. You're welcome to change into some of my clothes if you can find anything that fits, and we'll buy you something when we get to Tanner's Port."

Tanner's Port? They were going to Tanner's Port? There was nothing there. It was a quiet colony with nearly no trade outside.

Moses smiled at her expression of surprise. "No, I lied. I was never going to Morago."

Unbuckling, she picked a clipboard off a nearby hook. Writing furiously, she asked, "Why did he give us this ship?"

"The enemy of my enemy is my friend but, also, the same reason I managed to bet my watch; it's all about how much it costs the loser. Losing you is worth quite a bit to Martice . . . and so Martice's biggest enemy has good reason to help us. He'll be able to taunt Martice for quite a while about this."

"I'm sorry about your watch," she wrote.

Moses reached out. She flinched from his hand, but then held still when he moved slowly and just stroked her cheek. She closed her eyes and leaned into his hand. He brushed it down the curve of her jaw and across her lips and to her chin, which he cupped as if she was made of Earth china.

"I wouldn't have done anything differently from the first hand. A good gambler never bets with anything he isn't willing to lose, and he walks away when he has what he wants."

"I'm sorry I don't have a voice," she wrote.

He frowned and shook his head. "It's okay. I've heard of a few places that can do reversals if you want to try. If not, we can figure something out. Sign language. Charades." Laughing, he added, "You might have to drop your poker face."

Grinning, she nodded. For the first time in four years, she felt warm. Tanner's Port had a warm sun too.

His hand dropped to trace the indentation where the bracelet had been. "You can stay with me or not, but I'd like you to stay with me. It's your choice. I'll give you money if you'd rather see the back of me. You're free. You don't belong to anyone anymore."

She met his eyes. "I belong to you," she mouthed slowly.

"You belong *with* me," he corrected, enunciating the words slowly.

She rolled her eyes. Earthboys were stubborn. "Fine," she mouthed. "I belong *with* you."

His lips spread in a wide, satisfied smile—bigger than the one she'd seen on his face when he'd thrown down the winning hand. "You know, it's strange to think I have Ajax, a rigged poker game, and a royal flush to thank for you. I think you might be luckier than that watch anyway. I've never had a royal flush."

Well, she certainly did feel lucky.

Moses pulled his com out of his pocket and laughed at the screen. "Ajax says he'll never play poker with me again. He says I play too deep." After shoving it back in his pocket, he gestured ahead. "Shall we see how fast this thing can go? I bet we can make Tanner's Port before their sun sets if we hurry."

Nodding, she settled back in her seat. Yep. She was very lucky.

FROM A STONE

Eric Choi

For any reader who claims space-travel SF doesn't come close enough to the known realities of physics to be believable, I hold up Eric Choi's "From a Stone," a hard science story steeped in scientific realism. In a way that puts the reader in mind of Arthur C. Clarke's *Rendezvous with Rama,* Choi explores the nature of intelligence and how one determines if an artifact is a product of an *intelligent* alien race. There are no star drives, blasters, or gee-whiz technologies. Everything is an extension of our current technology base. Rather than featuring the daring-do of fictional explorers, it shows the current realities of government- and committee-based space exploration. This story first appeared in the September 1996 issue of *Science Fiction Age* magazine.

Eric Choi is a writer, editor and aerospace engineer based in Toronto, Canada. His work has appeared in *Rocket Science, The Astronaut from Wyoming and Other Stories, Footprints, Northwest Passages, Space Inc., Tales from the Wonder Zone, Northern Suns, Tesseracts6, Arrowdreams, Science Fiction Age,* and *Asimov's.* With Derwin Mak, he co-edited the Aurora Award winning anthology *The Dragon and the Stars.* He is currently co-editing with Ben Bova the forthcoming hard SF anthology *Carbide Tipped Pens.*

Stone.

Cold, hard, unimaginably ancient stone. A rough, irregular aggregate of it, angular, cratered, pockmarked and pitted. The stone was dark, with an albedo of less than five percent. It tumbled lazily about its major axis with a rotation period of 19 hours, 53 minutes. A third of it was frozen in shadow, while the rest roasted in the incessant light of the Sun. It was only ten by five by four kilometers in major dimension—on the scale of the Solar System, practically microscopic.

But the stone was not too small to escape human curiosity.

"*Hold at three hundred meters for IPS parameter update.*" The voice of pilot Ben Dixon came over Pierre Caillou's spacesuit radio. Dixon and the mission commander, Poornima Bhupal, were monitoring the EVA from the bridge of the UNSDA spacecraft *Harrison Schmitt*.

The astronaut-geologist entered the command into his manned maneuvering unit. "OK, Ben," Pierre replied. "Hold at three hundred meters." He glanced to his left and right. Diane Sokolowski and Marvin Shipley, the other geologists from the *Schmitt*, were flying in formation with him, both piloting their own MMU thruster packs.

The asteroid's bulk loomed ever larger as the astronauts approached. Pierre kept an eye on his lidar rangefinder. At the precise moment a nitrogen jet fired, putting his MMU in an attitude-hold mode three hundred meters from the surface.

"I am holding at three hundred meters," Pierre said. His colleagues reported the same.

"*Copy,*" Ben replied. "*Transmission of IPS updates will commence in five seconds . . . Mark! Note the new basis vectors are for an asteroid-based frame of reference, with the origin located at the geographic center of 2021-PK.*"

"Understood." A green light on Pierre's inertial positioning system blinked. "My IPS reports updated state vectors received and installed." Diane and Marvin reported their navigation units also were ready.

Ben enunciated his next words formally. "*To EVA crew, I have the following messages from the CAPCOM and Commander Bhupal: Mission Control Darmstadt is 'go,' Schmitt is 'go.' You are cleared for final approach to 2021-PK. This is the last hurrah, people. Make it good.*"

"Understood." Pierre's aft thrusters fired a short burst, putting him in motion once more. The dark surface of the asteroid rushed up to him. Pierre executed a pitch-back maneuver to put his feet "down" before the negative y-axis thrusters came on to slow his touchdown. ". . . 20 meters . . . 10 . . . 5 . . . 1 . . . Contact!"

"I have contact also," said Diane.

"I'm down!" followed Marvin.

Pierre surveyed the magnificently desolate scene about him. "They say you can't draw blood from a stone—"

"But you can always get knowledge!" Diane's exuberant voice cut in. They would later swear it was not rehearsed.

The astronauts went about gathering samples, hopping across the asteroid like grasshoppers. Pierre presently found himself near one of 2021-PKs larger craters. He decided to sample the rim material, and his MMU dutifully delivered him to the edge. As he readied his tools and glanced at the bottom of the crater, he noticed something unusual.

The Sun was shining at an angle across the impact, producing a semicircular shadow that bisected the bottom of the bowl. At the top of the arc, a second, smaller semicircle jutted out from the shadow. There appeared to be another crater at the bottom of the larger, but somehow it didn't look right.

"Pierre for Diane."

"Go ahead."

"Have a look at this." He transmitted his camera video.

"That's interesting," Diane replied after watching Pierre's feed on her multifunction visor. "I'm coming to have a look."

Moments later, she landed beside him.

"So, what do you think?" Pierre asked.

"Looks like another crater."

"That's what I thought. But look at the edge. It's not very circular. In fact, it's pretty ragged."

"Must be really old," Diane concluded. "A few billion years of dust and micrometeoroid impact will do that."

"Of course. But look at the larger crater." Pierre's hand swept out a curve. "The rim is *smooth*. That smaller crater is on top of this larger one, so the smaller one must be more recent. So, how could it have experienced more degradation than the older, larger impact?"

"I don't know," Diane said.

"Pierre for Ben. Are you seeing this?"

"*Affirmative,*" Ben replied from the distant *Schmitt*. "*Poornima and I concur with your assessment, but we don't have any new ideas.*"

"We should have a look," Diane suggested.

There was a pause as Ben consulted the commander. "*All right. We'll let Darmstadt Mission Control know of the change. But don't be too long. Time is not on our side, and we're behind schedule already.*"

"Thanks, Ben." Pierre turned to Diane. "All right. Let's go." Puffs of nitrogen sent them skyward from their perch on the rim to a point above the inner crater.

"It doesn't look round," Diane observed.

"No, it doesn't." Pierre activated his lidar rangefinder. "I am getting a uniform depth sounding. It is not a circular depression."

"*Ben for Diane and Pierre.*"

"Yes, what is it?" Diane sounded irritated.

"*Uh, sorry to bother you, but Darmstadt wants to inform you the back room boys are getting restless.*" The "boys" were the geologists monitoring the expedition from their own room at Mission Control in Darmstadt, Germany. EVA schedules were as tightly scripted as Shakespeare, and the three-day time line for the survey of 2021-PK was particularly tight. The message was a subtle hint for Pierre and Diane to get back on track.

Diane gave Pierre the hand signal to switch to a private channel. "Oh, for crying out loud. We're not automatons. If they wanted robots, they should have damn well sent them!"

Pierre switched back to the common loop. "Ben, we were scheduled to sample the bottoms of a few craters tomorrow. There's no harm in getting started today. Besides, we seem to have something rather unusual here."

"*Yeah, I can see that.*" A pause. "*OK, go ahead. Poornima says she'll try to smooth any ruffled feathers back home.*"

"Thanks," Diane said.

They descended until they hovered right over the opening.

"Look at the edges!" Diane pointed. "It's definitely not circular. It looks kind of like a rounded-off pentagon or something."

"Well, this is certainly not a crater," Pierre said. "I am reading a depth of four hundred and fifty meters. This is a tunnel." He switched channels. "Pierre for Marvin."

"Go ahead."

"Take a look at this." Pierre sent him the video.

The Canadian astronaut sounded puzzled. "I don't know. Could be a lava tube. But on a rock this small? Beats me, Pierre. I'm just a prairie boy from Manawaka."

Pierre played a light down the hole, but the darkness swallowed it. "I want to go to the bottom. Ben?"

"*Pierre—*"

"Ben," Diane cut in. "Tell Poornima to tell the back room boys to cool it. We've got something really worth . . . ahem, looking into here. Look, just let him have a quick look-see. OK?"

Ben sighed. "*Very well. You stay outside to relay Pierre's signal. Be careful, OK?*"

"That goes without saying," Pierre replied dryly. He started his MMU and plunged into the unknown. His suit lamp produced a small circle of illumination that tracked down the wall as he descended. It was pitted and scarred from billions of years of micrometeoroid and dust impact, but the surface did not seem as coarse as the outside of the asteroid.

Pierre stopped. "One hundred meters down. I'm going to take a sample of the wall."

Another sample was taken at the two hundred meter mark. By now, Pierre was certain there was something strange about the tunnel. "There are fewer signs of geologic modification now. There is less evidence of erosion and wear." He touched the rock. "In fact, it feels almost . . . a little *flat*."

"*Uh, copy,*" Ben replied.

Pierre resumed his descent. As the wall scrolled by, it became apparent that it was not only becoming flatter, but the surface was smoothing out as well. It was like a beach, where the rough sand trampled by innumerable feet merged into the smooth area washed by the waves.

He stopped at three hundred meters for another sample. Pierre ran his hand along the wall. With the exception of a few dents created by micrometeoroids that had managed to get this far, the wall felt uniform. He transmitted his video to Diane.

"What do the other surfaces look like?"

"Other surfaces?" The obvious hit him with a start. All this time, he had blithely assumed the tunnel was circular. But if he were staring at a flat surface, this clearly could not be the case. He rotated his MMU.

There was a corner—and another, and another. Six in total, formed by the intersection of the walls. "This tunnel . . . it is not circular! It is a hexagon!"

"How can that be?" Ben asked.

"That's incredible," Diane breathed. "But at least it explains one thing. This opening isn't really any older than the outside crater. It just looks like it had experienced more modification because it's really an eroded hexagon instead of a circle."

"I'm going straight to the bottom," Pierre announced as he started his MMU. The smooth walls scrolled by as the display on his rangefinder counted down. But just three meters from the bottom, his suit lamp seemed to black out. "What—" he began, but his feet were already touching bottom.

He rebounded off the floor before his MMU went into attitude-hold. The asteroid's feeble gravity made it impossible to really "stand," so Pierre just floated a few centimeters above the rock.

"I am at the bottom." He looked down at where his feet had touched, and to his surprise discovered his lamp had not malfunctioned. The light revealed a small circle of rock, marred only by a handful of impacts. Puzzled, he looked up again—and gasped. "*Mon Dieu!*"

"*Pierre, what is it?*" Ben asked urgently. "*What the hell is that in front of you?*"

"There is another tunnel in front of me. The opening is hexagonal." He checked the lidar. "It is two hundred and fifty meters deep." He turned, and counted five other walls. Each one had an opening identical to the first.

"Oh, my God," Diane whispered.

"What's this?" Marvin barked. "What's going on? Pierre!"

"*Cut the chatter on the loop!*" Ben snapped. "*Pierre, what is your appraisal of this formation?*"

"Ben, I believe . . ." Pierre swallowed. "I have no explanation at this time as to how these features were produced. This sounds crazy, but Ben. . . I don't believe this is a natural phenomenon. This is something *alien.*"

* * *

The stone was discovered by astronomers at the Shapley Observatory on the lunar farside, and was given the designation 2021-PK after the year, half-month, and order of its discovery. Its highly elliptical orbit had a period of 136.9 years, and was inclined 18.3 degrees to the ecliptic. This seemed to suggest the object was a spent comet. But some astronomers believed 2021-PK was a visitor from beyond the Kuiper Belt, an extrasolar body captured by the Sun when it experienced just enough gravitational perturbation to close its hyperbolic trajectory into an ellipse.

The United Nations Space Development Agency proposed a mission to 2021-PK, but politics and funding conspired against it. Fortunately, the laws of celestial mechanics offered an alternative. One UNSDA spacecraft—the *Harrison Schmitt*—was already in solar orbit, finishing a survey of Apollo-class asteroids. Through a bit of orbital legerdemain, the ship was diverted to rendezvous with 2021-PK at the point it crossed the ecliptic on its ascending node, exiting the inner

Solar System.

It was hardly an ideal situation. The *Schmitt* was already at the end of its nominal flight, and its crew had to ration their supplies of food and oxygen to support the extended mission to 2021-PK. Furthermore, the unfavorable rendezvous geometry consumed so much fuel the astronauts were left with just three days to study the asteroid. After three days, the burn window would close, and the *Schmitt* would no longer be able to make an Earth-return trajectory.

But a hit-and-run mission was better than none. The astronomers and geologists were used to the compromises inherent in "government science." They consoled themselves in the belief that the only unique thing about 2021-PK was its orbit, and that it probably wasn't much different than the dozens of asteroids the *Schmitt* had already surveyed.

Then Pierre Caillou discovered the Beehive.

* * *

The flight controllers in Darmstadt were in a conundrum. They were, after all, trained to deal with mechanical failures and schedule problems, not first contact. Despite the looming departure deadline, Darmstadt cautiously decided to forbid further exploration until the appropriate authorities were consulted. The EVA astronauts were instructed to return to the *Schmitt* until new orders were issued.

While awaiting their arrival, Commander Poornima Bhupal watched the video again. "It's like a beehive."

"Huh?"

"A beehive," she repeated.

"Yeah, I thought so too."

"What do you think . . ." She gestured at the screen. "What do you think this is? Who were they? What does it all mean?"

Ben shrugged. "How the hell do I know?" He turned to another monitor. "They're back. I'm opening the airlock." He left the bridge to help the geologists doff their spacesuits. When that was completed, the crew gathered on the bridge.

"What's the plan?" Pierre asked.

"We're waiting for instructions from Darmstadt," Bhupal said.

"When can we expect that?" asked Marvin.

"Should be any time now, I hope."

Moments later, Ben announced, "Incoming message."

Jason Ho, the CAPCOM on duty, appeared on the screen. "Commander Bhupal, crew of the *Schmitt*." He was obviously reading from a prepared statement. "On behalf of everyone here at Mission Control, Flight Director Pearson, the engineers, the scientists, geologists . . . indeed, on behalf of all the people of Earth, I congratulate you on this remarkable discovery. This is a truly momentous occasion. Human history has been altered . . ."

Diane silently mouthed "blah, blah, blah."

". . . will never be the same. But precisely because the nature of your discovery—proof of extraterrestrial life—is so extraordinary, it becomes necessary to take extraordinary precautions. We must act very carefully, for we do not know the consequences of any mistakes.

"As of now, 22:43 hours, the SETI Protocol is in effect. The Secretary General and the First Minister have been notified. A tiger team of engineers and scientists from all UNSDA centers is being assembled to recommend the next course of action. But any such action must first be approved by the Peace and Security Council. So, until the PSC makes policy, the crew of the *Schmitt* is ordered not to attempt another EVA. You will hold your position until further instructions, which you will receive shortly."

Jason stopped reading, and his expression changed. He now addressed his fellow astronauts, his friends. "Poornima, Ben, Diane, Marv, Pierre . . . hang in there, OK? We'll figure this out."

The screen went blank.

"Further instructions shortly. Right." Diane turned to Marvin. "By the way, what time is it?"

"22:50."

"No, I mean in New York."

"It's . . . what? Three or four in the morning, I think." Pierre saw what Diane was getting at. "Oh, no."

" 'Oh, no' is right. They're all in bed. It'll take hours just to wake them up, get them their coffee and doughnuts, put them in a room . . . Then they'll yak for hours more." Diane clenched her fists. "Further instructions shortly. Right. There's classic government science for you. We'll be lucky if we're left with even a day to explore!"

"Well," Pierre said, "while we're waiting, perhaps we could analyze—"

"You will do nothing of the sort," Bhupal interjected. "I want the three of you to get some rest." She emphasized the last three words with jabs of her finger. "When the powers-that-be finally decide our next move, I want all of you to be refreshed and ready to go as soon as the word is given. We have only two more days here and we must make the most of them. Understood?"

"Sure," Marvin said. Pierre nodded, and Diane murmured in agreement.

"All right. Grab a bite to eat, maybe. But then you hit the sack."

The geologists gathered in the *Schmitt*'s galley. Pierre and Marvin both prepared meals, but their appetites were wholly divergent. Marvin attacked his food with the vigor of a starving man, while Pierre poked and prodded at his tray, eating very little.

Diane's eyes wandered back and forth between them. "How can you guys think of food at a time like this?"

"Actually, I'm not hungry." Pierre put down his fork.

Marvin swallowed. "Hey, what's wrong? I'm within my ration."

"I just think it's a little . . . weird." Diane shrugged. "I mean, here we are. We've just discovered proof of intelligent extraterrestrial life, and what's the first thing we do? Graze."

"Wait a minute." Marvin wiped his mouth. "Did you just say 'intelligent life'?"

"Yeah."

"Uh, sorry Di. I have to disagree with you."

She smiled. "Oh?"

"I know what I saw," Pierre said. "You've all seen the video. Those caverns were definitely not natural."

"Oh, I'm not disagreeing with that," said Marvin. "They're alien, no doubt about it. But whether the builders—the aliens themselves—whether they were intelligent, now that remains to be seen."

"But the shape, those walls . . ." Diane shook her head. "How could something build something like the Beehive and not be intelligent?"

"Beehive?"

"Beehive asteroid," Diane explained. "That's what the media's calling 2021-PK."

"Beehive . . ." Marvin mused. "Yeah, that's good. See, you don't have to be smart to build complicated things. Just like bees. Sure, they build complex hexagonal hives, but they're as dumb as posts. On the other hand, whales don't build anything, and they're probably smarter than I am."

"That's a good point, Marvin," Pierre said. "But it raises another question. What would you consider as proof of intelligence?"

"Math," Diane replied immediately.

Pierre nodded. "OK. Perhaps even music then, since it is very much a mathematical construction."

"Like whale song," Marvin suggested.

"Exactly," said Pierre. "Something to do with math. In fact, one of the mathematicians—I think it was Gauss—once suggested that a giant representation of Pygathoras' Theorem be put in the Alps in hopes of signaling any Martians."

Marvin shrugged. "Well, I hope you two aren't too disappointed, but that asteroid isn't exactly spouting calculus and Chopin."

Commander Bhupal entered the galley. "What are you still doing here? Talking? The people on Earth are talking. New York is talking. You should not be talking. You should be resting, so when they stop talking, you'll be ready to go."

The geologists laughed. "I'm off," Marvin announced as he left the galley. Diane did the same, throwing up her hands in mock surrender.

Pierre retired to his cubicle. He told the lights to dim, climbed into his sack and shut his eyes. Sleep came almost immediately.

He dreamed.

He saw himself floating through one of those hexagonal tunnels. It was pitch dark, with only a small circle of light from his lamp to show the way. The tunnel took a turn, and he pushed himself off a wall to change direction as he had so many times before in the passageways of spacecraft. But this was no spacecraft—at least, not a human one.

The tunnel abruptly ended, and he found himself in a large cavern. He played his light along the walls and discovered the openings of four other tunnels. Where he had expected a fifth, there was something else.

It was a humanoid figure.

He approached. The being was imbedded in the rock itself, like a relief sculpture carved into the wall. It was about his height and build, dressed in a garment that resembled some kind of spacesuit. He tugged at the figure, but it could not be dislodged.

The creature wore a helmet, the front of which was shielded by a unit like a multifunction visor. Pierre put out his hand and raised it.

There was a face.

It was his own.

* * *

Fourteen hours after the initial discovery, the PSC reached a decision. The relatively prompt action of the Council was, even Diane admitted, something of a miracle. Nevertheless, there were now just two more days before the *Schmitt*'s window for its vital trans-Earth injection burn closed.

After eating his breakfast ration, Pierre joined the crew on the bridge to hear the outcome of the PSC's emergency session. On a monitor, CAPCOM Oleg Solovyov read the communiqué.

"The Peace and Security Council of the United Nations has reached a decision on Resolution 2046-57, sponsored by the United Nations Space Development Agency, requesting the further exploration of the extraterrestrial features found inside asteroid 2021-PK. The result of the vote was as follows . . ."

"Oh, forget the breakdown," Diane groaned.

"Hey," Marvin hushed her. "I'm interested."

"In favor: China, the European Union, Russia, Israel-Palestine, India, Japan. Opposed: Brazil—"

Cheers erupted on the bridge.

"—and the Unified African Republics. Canada and the United States abstained. Resolution 2046-57 was thereby approved."

"Here come the provisos," Ben cautioned.

"Further exploration of asteroid 2021-PK is authorized, subject to the following conditions and precautions: During EVA, Pilot Benjamin Dixon shall be stationed in the airlock, fully suited, ready to exit on short notice. Commander Bhupal shall act as the bridge intravehicular crew member in his place. All EVA crew, as well as Pilot Dixon, shall carry a heavy-duty laserdrill on their person at all times while outside the spacecraft.

"Activities on the asteroid itself shall be subject to the following conditions and precautions: One EVA crew member shall station themselves at the end of the entrance tunnel. The remaining crew members may then enter one of the secondary tunnels, but both must enter the same tunnel and stay together *at all times.*

"The contingency EVA tethers shall be used for communications by crew inside the asteroid. Under no circumstances are EVA crew to exceed the range limits imposed by the tethers. They are to gather as much information as possible while exercising extreme caution. This is humanity's first contact with extraterrestrial intelligence. The importance of your mission cannot be overstated. Further information and instructions will be uplinked as required. This transmission ends . . . now."

"Extraterrestrial *intelligence* . . ." Marvin shook his head.

"These so-called precautions," Diane sneered. "They're silly."

"Perhaps they are a little conservative," Pierre agreed. "But for the time being, we 'shall' follow them."

"All right, people!" exclaimed Commander Bhupal. "We haven't much time. Let's get moving!"

Forty-five minutes later, Diane, Marvin, and Pierre returned to the rocky surface of the asteroid. A communications relay was stationed at the mouth of the entrance tunnel. Pierre and Diane descended to the end of the shaft first, while Marvin hitched his tether to the comm unit before following.

"Comm check on relay," Marvin said.

"Good comm check," Bhupal replied. "Please proceed."

The astronauts doffed their MMUs and anchored them to the walls. Diane then tethered herself to Marvin. Pierre would remain a free-floater. After a final check of their suits and equipment, Marvin announced, "OK Poornima, we're ready to go."

"Copy. Be careful . . . and good luck."

Marvin surveyed the secondary entrances. "Well, take your pick."

"Enie, meanie, minie, moe . . ." Diane recited. Nervous chuckles echoed over the loop.

"Let's take this one," Pierre suggested, indicating the opening he happened to be closest to.

"As good as any," Diane said. "Let's go."

It was a historic moment, and Pierre wished he and Diane could come up with another memorable phrase. They could not, so he said simply, "We are going in."

"Good luck," said Marvin.

"Darmstadt—and I—also wish you good luck," Commander Bhupal said. *"And . . . be careful."*

Pierre went in first, followed by Diane trailing the thin, threadlike communications tether.

"The walls are similar to those observed in the outer entrance tunnel," Pierre reported. "They are hexagonal. They are also quite smooth."

Diane stopped. "Pierre, hold on a sec."

"Yes?"

"Let's quantify that statement. Let's see how smooth this really is." She produced a gauge and ran it along a wall. "I've got a five millimeter deviation over a thirty centimeter length." She ran it along another wall. "Six over thirty here."

"Measure the angle between the walls," Pierre suggested.

"OK, the angle between the walls is . . . fairly close to thirty degrees," Diane reported. "Not exactly." She pointed. "This one is twenty-seven point five degrees, while that one is twenty-eight point nine. There's an error of plus or minus three degrees."

"Marvin for Diane. You sound a little disappointed."

"Doesn't matter, Marv. These walls were machined. They had to have been, and you need smarts to run a machine."

"*Poornima for EVA crew. Please leave your speculations for later. Pierre, Darmstadt requests more samples.*"

The back room boys again.

"Right, Poornima. Thank you. I was just going to do that." Pierre put aside the PSC-mandated laserdrill and produced a hammer and chisel. He brought them up to the wall and was about to strike, when he paused. Even if Marvin was right, that the beings that dug these tunnels had the brains of a maggot, it didn't diminish the fact that this was an alien artifact. Pierre felt a little bit like a vandal.

But he took the sample anyway.

They continued. The tunnel took a turn, and Pierre experienced a moment of *déjà vu* as he and Diane pushed off a wall to match the curve. The feeling intensified when they emerged from the tube.

"We're in some kind of chamber," Pierre reported. "It is roughly spherical, but the walls are not finished as they were in the passageways." He panned the camera. "There are entrances to other tunnels. However, they are not distributed in any regular pattern."

Two were fairly close together, while the rest were scattered in random positions.

"*Poornima for EVA crew. It's time to call it a day. Diane and Pierre, finish what you're doing and start heading back.*"

Pierre checked his oxygen gauge. "OK, Poornima. Understand it's a wrap." He took a final sample, then panned the camera about one last time. "All right Diane, time to go home."

"Uh, OK."

Pierre started back, but Diane did not follow immediately.

"Diane?" He switched to a private channel. "Is there something you want to say?"

A pause. "No."

Two hours later, the geologists were back aboard the *Schmitt*. After a quick supper of ration packs, they went to the lab to do a preliminary analysis of their data.

"You know," Marvin began, "this rock would be a bundle of mysteries even without the alien thing."

Diane feigned innocence. "Why are you looking at me?"

Pierre asked, "You are certain about the age?"

"No question." Marvin consulted his palmtop. "Two point eight billion years."

"Younger than the Solar System," Pierre mused.

"Meaning it did come from outside the Solar System," Diane concluded.

"Maybe," Marvin said. "There's something else." He told the computer to project a holographic image of the asteroid above the table. The potato-like rock floated whole before their eyes for a moment before the computer sliced it in half, revealing Marvin's model of the internal structure in cross-section.

"I based this on the samples you took inside the caverns and the surface measurements made by the remotes. The surface is composed of a thin veneer of achondrites, while the bulk of the asteroid itself is composed of metamorphosed chondrites." The color scale changed.

"However, as we go deeper, we find that the percentage of siderophile elements is increasing—"

"Iron," Pierre interrupted. "Stony-iron materials."

"Yes," said Marvin.

Pierre bridged his fingers. "How much?"

"From the surface to the deepest point you and Diane sampled, there's an increase of nine point one percent, within an error of—"

"That much!" Diane exclaimed. "But we didn't go that far down!"

"The asteroid is differentiated," Pierre concluded. "It has physically and chemically stratified zones. But how? It's so small."

Marvin shrugged. "It could have been heated to a molten state sometime in the past. But you're right, its gravity should have been too weak to sift the elements as it came back together. If it did, though, it would have reset the isotopes. It could be a lot older than we measured. Maybe it was formed in the Solar System after all."

"But what could have provided the heat?" Diane asked.

"Planetessimal bombardment, maybe?" Marvin suggested.

"Could be." Pierre pointed. "But look at how young it looks. There are very few large impacts."

"What about radiogenic heating?" asked Diane.

Marvin shook his head. "No, this rock's cold. No sign of radioactive decay. And the magnetic field is only a few hundredths of a gauss."

Diane smiled. "You know Marv, I think you're right. This rock would be just as interesting without those alien tunnels." She became serious. "But they're there, and tomorrow's the last chance we'll get to study them."

She erased the cross-sectional profile, restored the asteroid to its true shape, made the image semi-transparent, and traced out a network of nodes and lines. "This is where we've been. We've only explored seven percent of those caverns."

"That percentage isn't likely to get much bigger after tomorrow," Pierre observed.

"Damn tethers," Diane muttered. "The fact is, if we follow the pattern we did today, I doubt we'll cover much more ground or learn anything new."

"What do you suggest?" Marvin asked.

"I suggest we try to go to the center of the asteroid."

Pierre stiffened.

"Di," Marvin raised his hand like a student, "may I state the obvious? There's no way you two are going to get near the core. We don't even know if the tunnels will take you there. Assuming they do, the tethers are only—Now *hold on* there . . ."

"We might be able to reach it if we tethered in series, going in single file."

"But we don't know how those passages twist and turn," Marvin objected. "Even strung together, you probably wouldn't reach the core. Besides, the PSC guidelines clearly state that the two of you must stay together while—"

"Oh, screw them!" Diane spat. "Classic government science. They're not even here. We've only got one more EVA and we've got to make it count. I mean, let's suppose—Pierre?" She snapped her fingers. "Hey, Pierre!"

"Huh?"

"Are you all right?"

"I was just thinking."

"About what?"

"Well . . ." Pierre shrugged. "This is kind of silly, but last night I had this weird dream." He described it.

"That *is* weird," Diane breathed.

"Do you think it means anything?" asked Marvin.

Pierre shrugged again. "It was probably an anxiety dream. I have those sometimes."

"You're probably right," Diane said. "Anyway, Freud can wait. We've got bigger things to worry about." She looked at both men. "It's time we fish or cut bait. Marvin?"

"Look . . ." Marvin traced a finger along the table. "It's not that I'm not curious. I am. But this isn't some movie where the rebellious officers break the rules, save the day, and end up getting promoted. It won't matter *what* we find down there: iron, Pierre's evil twin brother, even King Tut's tomb. Our careers will be *finished*. We won't be punished—well, not publicly anyway. We'll be honorably retired, maybe even given a desk job if we're *really* lucky, but we'll never fly again. And that's if we *find* something. If we don't . . ."

"We'll find something," Diane declared.

"*That* worries me, too," Marvin said. "Diane, we have no idea what could be down there!"

"Exactly!" she exclaimed. "If we knew, we wouldn't need to go. The point of going is to find out!"

"Why don't we ask Darmstadt first?" suggested Marvin.

"And they'll take it to New York. Another PSC meeting. More debate, more delay. By the time we *get* approval—assuming they say yes—it will be time to go."

"Can the mission be extended again?"

Diane shook her head. "Impossible. The TEI burn window closes after tomorrow. If we don't leave then, we're never leaving." She paused. "Marvin, please. Are you in or not?"

Marvin took a deep breath. "Yeah, count me in."

"Pierre?"

"Yes, let's do it." He tried to smile. "Tomorrow, we will solve all the mysteries of the Beehive asteroid, right?"

Pierre did not dream that night.

* * *

The geologists descended to the bottom of the entrance tunnel for the last time. As Pierre checked his tools, Marvin slipped Diane the extra tether spool he had smuggled out. They could have used another, but taking more might have been noticed. Since the tethers were their only link with the *Schmitt*, as long as the telemetry stream was uninterrupted there should be no suspicions until they were beyond recall.

"Are the IPS units still on the asteroid-centered coordinate system?" Diane asked.

"Yes." Pierre switched to a private channel. "This tunnel took us deepest yesterday."

"We'll start there, then." Diane switched back to the open loop. "I'm ready."

Pierre signaled the *Schmitt*. "OK, Poornima. We're ready to go in."

"Copy that, Pierre. Darmstadt says 'go,' and I concur. Be careful, and good luck."

"We'll need that today," Pierre muttered. Louder, he said, "OK, Marvin. We'll see you when we get back."

"Good luck."

Pierre and Diane floated into the tunnel. They stopped a hundred meters in and looked back the way they came. Diane turned the camera away and keyed a private channel. "Come on in, Marv. The water's fine."

"I'm on my way." Moments later, he was reunited with his colleagues.

The three continued in single file with Pierre in the lead, followed by Diane, with Marvin taking up the rear. They entered a cavern. Like the others before, this one presented them with five other entrances to choose from.

"Where to now?" Diane asked.

Pierre fired his lidar down each tunnel and entered the reading into his IPS. "That one."

They drifted together in the darkness for an hour before being forced to a halt. Marvin had reached the end of his tether.

"That's it for me."

"Thank you, Marvin," Diane said.

"Are you going to be all right?" Pierre asked.

Marvin's multifunction visor was in transparent mode, so his smile was visible. "Sure. Hey look, if anything comes after me . . ." he hefted his laserdrill, "I'll poke their eyes out with this!"

Now Diane smiled. "They might not *have* eyes."

"Then . . ." Marvin lowered his voice, "I'll stick it up their ass!"

Pierre and Diane pressed on. They probed the tunnels and caverns like a computer working a recursive search tree. The pair selected the likeliest branch and went as far as they could. If the path did not take them closer to the core, they returned to the last cavern and selected another. The two had backtracked, turned, retraced and doubled back and forth so many times Pierre's internal sense of direction was completely gone. If not for the tethers and the IPS, they would have been hopelessly lost.

Diane's tether gave out while they were in a cavern. "Oh, damn."

"Well, this was hardly unexpected. Guess I'm on my own now."

She started unlocking her spool.

"No, don't! I'm going on myself. We agreed, remember?"

"Yeah." Diane let go of the device. "Say hello to your evil twin brother for me?"

"Of course."

She hugged him. "Be careful."

"I will."

Pierre released himself from the embrace. He and Diane then switched off their video feeds to the *Schmitt*.

"*Poornima for EVA. What's going on?*"

"Uh . . . our cameras are dead," Diane stammered.

"Both *of you?*" The commander sounded incredulous. "*How can—*" The voice link was also cut to avoid answering any more embarrassing questions.

"Good luck."

Pierre nodded. He entered a tunnel, and moments later emerged in another cavern. Again, there were five other entrances. Pierre probed each with the lidar, then checked the IPS and the status of his tether.

"Pierre for Diane. I'm only seven hundred meters from the

geographic center of the asteroid, but I don't know if I'll make it. I won't if these tunnels don't take me there directly."

"Do what you can, but get a move on, OK? Poornima's probably sent Ben out by now to find out what the hell we're doing."

"Right."

He was about to set off when he stopped. Something seemed *different* about this cavern. He panned his camera about to document the scene before diving into another tunnel.

His eyes scanned the walls of the passageway as they rushed by, and this time he was sure there was something different. He paused to run a gauge along the surface. There was only a one millimeter deviation over a thirty centimeter run—a far better finish than the outer tunnels. The angles between the walls were also checked. They were all thirty degrees, to within one-tenth of a degree.

Suddenly, his suit computer came on. "*Warning. Check tether status.*" A gentle tug on the line confirmed the increase in resistance.

"Pierre for Diane. I have reached the end of my tether."

"How far are you from the core?"

"Only three hundred meters." Pierre made up his mind in an instant. "I'm going to disengage the tether."

"That's—" The line was disconnected.

Pierre turned, pushed off a wall, and darted down the dark passage. He moved quickly without the tether. A sharp corner surprised him, but he managed to deflect his trajectory off the side without colliding.

He emerged in a cavern. His momentum carried him across the void to a far corner where two walls met. Pierre stopped himself and consulted his IPS. The reading was in single digits. He was at the core of the Beehive.

The geologist panned the camera, and when his mind assembled a complete picture from the fragmentary glimpses provided by the light, he gasped.

This place was completely different from the others. Those had been just crude hollows, without definite form or pattern. This one was, for want of a better word, a *room*. It had six equally sized walls which formed a perfect hexagon. Each wall in turn had a hexagonal tunnel opening centered on it. But curiously, the room did not have three-dimensional symmetry. There was a definite up/down orientation, a paradoxical arrangement in a weightless environment.

His heart beat faster, and he noticed he was trembling. He forced himself to stop and take a few deep breaths. Slowly, he played his light along the "ceiling." As the circle of illumination moved, more of it came into view. Then, the light touched something, and he saw—a figure.

Not a humanoid—a geometric figure. It was a six-sided solid, but not a perfect hexagon. Its length was twice its width. Upon closer examination, he could see there were actually two shapes side by side. The one on his left was a full hexagon, consisting of dark rock with a protrusion in the center. The area on the right was covered with lighter material. He picked at it with a scalpel. Grains of regolith floated away in chunks.

Pierre scraped along the edge of the hexagon, continuing downward until he hit the bottom edge where it met the surrounding wall. He found a groove running along the perimeter. The lip of rock was holding the hexagonal slab against the wall on four sides, while the packed soil was keeping it in place from the other two.

Pierre scraped at the dirt. When most of it was cleared, he drove an anchor into the wall and grabbed it with one hand while holding the protrusion on the hexagon with the other. He pulled. It jerked and stuck, but it had moved. Taking out the pick, he cleaned out more before trying again.

Slowly, the hatch opened.

Inside the cavity were . . . stones.

Just stones. Six of them, imbedded in the wall, arranged in a circle with size increasing clockwise.

A set of stones.

"What the hell is this?"

A bed of regolith cradled each of them. Whoever—whatever—had done this had carved out sockets in the cavity, placed the stones in them, and sealed them in place with the mortar-like soil.

Pierre Caillou used a fine pick to pry the orbs free, and gently placed each of them in a sample bag.

* * *

In all the time he had known Commander Bhupal, Pierre observed her to respond to anger in one of two ways. She would either shrug her shoulders, or go ballistic. Upon their return to the *Schmitt*, the first thing the geologists did was report what they had done, and why they had done it. Pierre described his discovery at the core of the asteroid, and Diane asked rhetorically whether it had been worth the risk.

Poornima Bhupal shrugged her shoulders.

The geologists gathered in the *Schmitt's* lab. Their futures were uncertain, but for now, their minds were much too busy pondering other things.

"From the samples I took in that room," Pierre began, "I have confirmed the core is stony-iron. The age of the asteroid is also verified as 2.8-billion years."

"I still don't see how it could be differentiated," Marvin said. "The asteroid's just too small."

Pierre shook his head. There were so many unanswered questions. "Maybe the back room boys will figure it out when we get home. If not, the Beehive asteroid will not pass through the inner Solar System for another 137 years."

"I'd like to think we will have ships capable of visiting it long before then." Diane turned to Pierre. "But at least we've answered one question."

"Do you really believe what you told Poornima?" Marvin asked.

In response, Pierre asked the computer to project an image over the table. The hexagonal cavity with its six stones hovered holographically before them.

"The stones were all perfect spheres. When I got them back here, I measured and massed them." He pointed. "Starting from that one, the smallest, and going clockwise, each subsequent stone weighs exactly twice as much and is double the diameter of the one before."

"A binary sequence," Diane whispered.

Pierre nodded.

"That's it?" Marvin asked. "Just . . . stones?"

"Oh, Marvin, of course not 'just stones'," Diane admonished gently. "It is *information*. An . . . an artifact of the *mind*."

"What are they trying to tell us?" Marvin wondered.

Pierre shrugged. "There is no specific message per se. As Diane said, it is information, like that early SETI radio message that was beamed to the Hercules Cluster—pictures of DNA and things like that. It just shows an understanding of some fundamental concepts. It shows . . . intelligence."

"Intelligence," Marvin repeated.

"But there is so much we don't know," Diane said with frustration. "We cut and run just as we start making discoveries. We find some answers, but end up with more questions instead." She clenched her fists. "It's the nature of government science!"

"No," Pierre said quietly. "It's the nature of exploration."

The intercom came on. "*Three minutes to TEI burn. I'm sure you don't want to miss this.*"

"Thanks, Ben," Pierre said.

"*It's my job,*" Ben replied. "*Oh, one more thing. Darmstadt tells us the IAU has officially renamed 2021-PK as asteroid 329780 Beehive.*"

"Departure. So soon." Diane started for the door. "Aren't you two coming?"

"I am." Marvin got up, but Diane had already left the room. He went as far as the door, and stopped.

"Pierre?"

"Yes."

"About those stones." Marvin paused for a moment in thought. "You know . . . when people encounter something they've never seen before, something totally unknown, there's sometimes a tendency— maybe subconscious, but it's there—a tendency . . . to try to relate it to ourselves, to something familiar, something we know about, because we're so desperate to understand it."

"And?"

"I guess what I'm saying is . . . Are you sure you're not just seeing what you want to see?" He started for the door.

"Marvin."

He paused.

"I don't think so."

Marvin shrugged, and left the room.

Pierre rested his elbows on the table, his hands cupped under his chin. The ghostly image of the six stones hovered before his eyes: the stones, the binary sequence, the message. He still had no idea who or what the aliens were, but through a common informational choice, a link had been forged between himself and the builders of the Beehive. They proved that all sentient beings, regardless of biology, shared at least one common heritage. Pierre marveled once more at this simple message, transmitted across an unimaginably vast expanse of space and time, from a stone.

CHARNELHOUSE

Jonathan Shipley

Graveyard stories have fascinated readers for generations. Traditionally, they allow us to encounter specters and otherworldly beings, run afoul of tribal taboos, and uncover magical artifacts. Exploring an SF graveyard also introduces the hazards of alien technologies. In "Charnelhouse," author Jonathan Shipley introduces us to a family of researchers who come across something unexpected in an alien graveyard, in a story that revels in the horrors of discovery.

Fort Worth writer Jonathan Shipley has appeared in over two-dozen fantasy, science fiction, and horror anthologies. He is, however, a novel writer at heart and writes in a vast story arc that ranges from Nazi occultism to vampires to futuristic space opera. A complete list of his published stories may be found at shipleyscifi.com.

Beth stepped into the hotel lobby, savoring the blessed coolness after the unexpectedly hot ride from the spaceport. Port Town wasn't big, wasn't much beyond a temp town with as many portable domes as permanent buildings. But it had a decent hotel—luxurious even by the local standards. It was the one compelling argument about coming to this strange, desolate world that was unofficially nicknamed Necropolis. The name sort of said it all.

She paused in the lobby. Kevin gave her arm a fond pat as he passed her. She watched him approach the front desk, heard the words that still abraded some nerve, even after all these years: "Reservations for Dr. and Mrs. Charnelhouse," Kevin told the clerk. "And any messages, please."

Yep, the Charnelhouses. In college it had been sort of funny. That was before she'd married the name. For all that she loved Kevin, she was sick of being Mrs. Charnelhouse. Just like she was sick of living on the fringe of civilization and heartily sick of the whole clan of Doctors Charnelhouse with all their multiple degrees.

Kevin turned toward her, note in hand. "There's a problem, hon. Well, not a problem, just a change in plans. Mother and Greg decided to go on to the Catacomb 473. Their excavation papers came through early and saw no reason to wait. But they suggest—"

"Don't tell me," Beth interrupted. "Your mother and brother want to meet at the catacomb for a work get-together instead of wasting our vacation time at a silly luxury hotel. Am I right?"

Kevin blinked. "Well . . . yes. How did you know?"

"I know Ruth and Greg." With a sigh, she picked up her valise and turned toward the door.

"And you really don't mind?" Kevin asked, catching up with her.

"The difference between watching them work and listening to them talk non-stop about their work isn't that much. All I ask is that we have someone look at the rover's climate control before we take off again."

She waited at the hotel restaurant and drank iced coffee while Kevin took the rover around to a mechanic. She had no doubt the climate control would be fixed one way or the other. Once he categorized something as important, he was relentless in pursuit of it. Like the Geo-energy PhD, like the geo survey he was doing in this largely uninhabited sector . . . like everything. She might have called him strangely obsessive, but it seemed to be a genetic trait. Ruth and Greg, the other Doctors Charnelhouse, were exactly the same—Ruth with her joint specialty in archeology/anthropology and Greg with his DNA genotypal research. She didn't dislike any of them, but understood exactly why Kevin and Greg's long absent father—plain *Mister* Charnelhouse—had wandered away from his family, never to return. He just couldn't take it anymore.

Beth took another sip of iced coffee and wondered for the six-hundredth time whether a marriage had the right to be convicted purely on circumstantial evidence when there was nothing really wrong between the principal parties. Just like the other 599 times, she couldn't arrive at a conclusion. But the thought of procreating another generation of Charnelhouses made her distinctly nervous.

On the brighter side, the chance at a vacation at an ancient burial site of an undocumented non-hom race didn't come along every day. She thought about that again and decided that wasn't the brighter side at all. Knowing Ruth and Greg, they'd probably set up camp right inside the catacombs themselves to stay close to their work. And Beth always hated waking up in the middle of the night in a strange graveyard.

A brace of Teladdi passed by the window, catching her attention because she'd never seen their species before. They paused, looking at her curiously as she studied them. They were almost impossible to differentiate from each other with their uniform small size, grayish skin, smooth bullet heads, and huge, dark eyes. They were the local race, but oddly not indigenous to the planet. They were a mute race as well, which made getting their story a slow process, but they were also friendly and always eager to do manual labor for food. In a start-up colony, that made them worth their weight in platinum.

As they continued staring at her, she gave a polite smile while wishing they would move along. But they didn't. They started finger-signing each other, which was thoroughly frustrating because Teladdi signing was different from any of the Terran sign-languages and therefore incomprehensible. All she could do was sit there smiling stupidly. Finally, she gulped the last of her coffee and went in search of a more private spot to wait.

* * *

Catacomb 473 was unimpressive from the outside, Beth decided as they drove up the hillside. Just a long barrow bulging out the hillside, looking more like a random mudslide than an artifact. Of course, Necropolis had too dry a climate to support mudslides, so that should have been a clue in itself. And 473 wasn't anything like a king's tomb, just a communal gravesite for some long-vanished community.

"Mother said that she's identified eight new species so far within the tombs," Kevin offered conversationally as they approached. "Like the other catacombs, they're sealed up tight in sarcophagi, but even scanning through stone, she can tell that they're a very random assortment, unrelated to each other and unrelated to any of the species in the other catacombs as well. Probably not indigenous. She's determined to find a controlling pattern to it all."

"Is she, now," Beth murmured. Ruth Charnelhouse was always determined to find a controlling pattern to things. Often she did. "Is the camp ready?" Meaning, would they have a place to sleep at the end of the day. It was several hours from Port Town to the catacomb, which effectively ruled out a commute to the hotel . . . unfortunately.

"Absolutely. Mother brought Raoul, of course—"

"Of course," Beth agreed. Raoul had overseen projects all across the sector for the Doctors Charnelhouse. He was practically an honorary Charnelhouse.

"—who put together a crew of Teladdi to port and carry as needed. They've already assembled a couple of domes with all the comforts of—what the . . . ?"

Beth glanced up to see a lean, hook-nosed man in a thermal bodysuit rushing drunkenly toward the rover. "Raoul looks frantic, doesn't he," Kevin commented as he pulled to a stop and stepped out.

"Maybe this is a no parking zone," Beth offered under her breath, but it was nervous humor. Raoul *did* look frantic. And something was definitely wrong with his sense of balance.

"Doctor Kevin," Raoul puffed, coming abreast of the car. "Thank goodness you have arrived. Doctor Charnelhouse-*mère* and Doctor

Charnelhouse-*fils* are both ill. They should be in a hospital."

"Then why aren't they?" Kevin demanded.

Raoul made a fatalistic gesture toward the barrow. "The Teladdi ran off with our truck. They are superstitious fools." He shook his head. "The project is ruined. The master datapad of the project is still somewhere in the tombs—valuable notes, irreplaceable observations and I cannot find where it is."

And that, Beth thought, was what made the man almost a Charnelhouse. Amidst crisis and disaster, his first thought was for the project. "But what happened, Raoul?" she asked. "Why are Ruth and Greg ill? And you don't look so well yourself."

"I am fine," he insisted. "I was near the entrance and caught only the an outrider of the . . ."

Both Beth and Kevin leaned in expectantly. "Blast?" Kevin offered impatiently when Raoul didn't finish. "Explosion? Atmospheric event?"

Raoul shook his head. "Poof. There was a big poof that reverberated through the tombs and set my head spinning. By the time my head cleared, the Teladdi were laying out the doctors *mère* and *fils* on the floor of the entrance chamber. And all the time the little gremlins were chattering to each other with their fingers. Very agitated. At first I thought it was concern—as a group, the Teladdi are very fond of Doctor Charnelhouse-*mère*. But then they scattered and stole the truck. So very unlike them."

"A complete behavioral anomaly," Kevin agreed. "I know Mother did a quick study when she arrived on Necropolis and found them unusually trustworthy as species go. Do her notes contain any later observa—"

Beth cleared her throat pointedly. He glanced at her. "Don't even think of doing anything except loading your mother and brother into the rover and driving to the nearest hospital," she said to abort this ridiculous tangent.

"Of course," he said. "Raoul, are you steady enough to help me carry—"

"Of course, Doctor Kevin," Raoul insisted. "Come, I will take you. If we use blankets as stretchers . . ."

As Beth stepped out of the rover and made her way toward the temp domes, she thought she was doing well at being the voice of reason in a disaster. Mentioning a data anomaly to Kevin was like waving a red flag at a bull, and this was definitely not the time. It was perversely uplifting to be needed, for once, at a family gathering.

The dome nearest the tomb entrance seemed to be Ruth's. Beth glanced around at the minimalist room in case there were personal effects that needed to come back with them. But there was very little that was personal beyond a spare bodysuit and a day scheduler on the folding table by the cot.

With a shake of her head, she headed back to the rover, pulling out suitcases and supplies from the back to make more room.

"We're not all going to fit," Kevin said, coming up behind her.

"No, we're not," she agreed, noting that two recumbent forms would barely leave room for one passenger, let alone two. "This will take two trips."

"And you're sure you don't mind, hon?"

She blinked. What? He wanted her to stay behind? She had assumed Raoul. But he was injured and needed to go to the hospital as well, so that wouldn't work. So of course, she was the logical one to stay behind. She didn't disagree, but the way Kevin had jumped to that assumption rankled. A husband shouldn't be so eager to abandon his wife in a deserted tomb site. "Why in the world would I mind?" she said tightly. "I can even comb the tombs for the lost datapad with its irreplaceable observations as long as I'm here for a while."

He gave her a quick smile over his shoulder as he retreated to the tomb. "That would be great, hon."

She had to bite her lip to keep from responding to that. There was no way she was going inside that catacomb. Then they brought out the make-shift stretchers, and Beth nearly lost it. She had assumed the local equivalent of swamp fever, but the small, still form of Ruth

Charnelhouse looked terrifyingly dead. Likewise Greg. "Are they . . ." she began in a choked voice.

"Yes, strangely comatose," Kevin nodded. "I checked their vitals and they both have low body temperature, almost non-existent heartbeats, and virtually no respiration,"

The words echoed in Beth's head as she kept staring at the inert figures on the stretchers. Why was this happening again?

"Beth?"

She gave a start as Kevin touched her shoulder. Ruth and Greg were already loaded in back. She had lost a couple minutes.

"Are you all right to stay here for a few hours, hon?" he asked. "You look shaken."

She was shaken. She had stood staring at nothing while the stretchers had been loaded. The rover was ready to go. "I'll be fine," she insisted. What else could she say when there was no room for her in the rover? "Get them to the hospital quickly. I think they're in stasis."

"Stasis?" Kevin frowned and shook his head. "Not even possible, hon." Like all the Doctors Charnelhouse, he had medical field training. "I'll be back for you as soon as I can. And be careful in the catacombs. Raoul says the datapad is black plastic and should be easy to spot against all that white stone. Yes, I know he couldn't spot it, but he's also pretty frazzled at the moment." He gave her a quick peck on the cheek and climbed into the rover.

As the vehicle slunk back down the hill, she stood staring after it. What the hell had happened a moment ago? The moment she had seen the still forms, this had stopped being reality and become an old nightmare.

With effort, Beth shook off the morose thoughts and turned to survey her surroundings. Four temp domes, one with an aerial, so there must be com capability. That was always tricky on undeveloped worlds. To the left of the little camp was the mudslide with a low, stone archway marking the entrance of the catacombs themselves. A box of handlights stood ready by the entrance.

She still couldn't believe Kevin actually expected her to hunt through a strange catacomb for the missing datapad. Yes, she had offered, but did the man not understand irony? Well, she wasn't going in there. Instead she went back to Ruth's dome and sat on the cot.

As the time ticked by, she found herself reading the scheduler because there was nothing else. Oh, and there were notes inserted as appointment annotations. These were obviously quick notes to self, too inchoate to be included as official project notes, but still very Ruth-like.

With Charnelhouse accuracy, her mother-in-law had roughed out a map of the catacomb with its almost five-hundred chambers blocked on the page into five long enfilades accessed through five arches from the ceremonial front chamber. A margin note explained that Ruth was working on the theory that catacomb organization was all about linear progression from the front chamber back, not about the horizontal rows as most archeologists assumed. Of course, with the tomb chambers being connected to each other in multiple directions, it was possible to see patterns front to back, side to side, or even diagonally. But for some reason, Ruth had been sure that front to back was the most important organizing element, confirmed, she said, by the presence of an empty chamber at the end of one enfilade.

Then there was the bold, double-underlined comment that this was the only empty chamber found in any of the multitudinous catacombs on Necropolis. That was highly important for reasons not yet known, Ruth had concluded.

Beth didn't have an opinion one way or the other. Experience, however, had taught her that Ruth Charnelhouse was seldom wrong in her chosen fields of study . . . or in anything else, for that matter. She had been stymied a few times with not being able to produce evidence to support her theories, but that wasn't the same thing as being wrong.

Then as Beth glanced over the notes again, it struck her that the empty chamber was where the datapad probably was. She even had a map to the exact tomb. This was actually doable. She could be the hero of the hour and make three Charnelhouses very happy.

Taking a deep breath, Beth strode from the dome to the stone archway, grabbing a handlight as she passed. She would collect the datapd quickly and come right back out.

* * *

Yes, collect quickly and come right back out—famous last words. Ruth's map indicated the place where they had been recently working, which also meant the place where they had been struck sick. While common sense said that they had come in contact with some bacteria or fungoid, Beth wasn't quite buying that. Her in-laws were not the careless type and had been wearing full filtered bodysuits that should have protected them against contagion. The sickness had to be connected with the one-time explosive event. That explained why the unfiltered Teladdi workers could have gone in and out of the chamber afterwards without being struck down.

What made her uneasy were the symptoms themselves: low body temperature, almost non-existent heartbeat, no respiration to speak of. Kevin had looked at the symptoms together and concluded comatose. Beth knew better. When she was younger and living on Seleus, a sudden border eruption had forced her and most of the other colonists to flee the planet in stasis on an old-style generational ship. When they reached safety, the children had been revived first and Beth had had the nightmare experience of seeing her parents lying there as though dead until they, too, were revived. She remembered all too vividly sitting there, obsessively watching the pod's flat read-outs for body temperature, heartbeat, and respiration that seemed very final. And so it seemed with Ruth and Greg.

As Beth walked through the tomb chambers towards the place the Charnelhouses had been working, she kept thinking about that. The thing about stasis, she knew, was that it was not a naturally occurring physiological condition. It required the equivalent of a flash-freeze to simultaneously disable all of the body's survival mechanisms. That was worlds away from a fungal infection—

A dull, thumping sound stopped her cold. It was soft, just on the threshold of audible, but very regular. It sounded a little like the solar-powered well pumps used on low-tech colony worlds. When nothing else happened except the thumping, she started forward again. The sound was coming from the direction she was headed.

At length, she came to the end of the progression of tombs, to the empty one that had caught Ruth's attention. The one that thumped. Beth stopped short of the doorway leading inside and panned the chamber with her handlight. Since first hearing the thumping, she'd had a nagging intuition that something was very wrong. And now that she was looking at the tomb, it all seemed to fit together.

The chamber was no longer empty.

In the middle of the chamber stood a white stone sarcophagus identical to the ones in all the other tombs. But this one had its lid swiveled halfway off and was unoccupied . . . waiting.

Again the memories of stasis pods arose in her memories. She recalled how it worked—the pod flash-froze the metabolism when an occupant was placed inside. But it was very unlikely that Ruth and Greg would have climbed into the sarcophagus singly, let alone together.

Then the lid thumped. It inched back and tried to swivel shut but something blocked it, setting off the vibration. Cautiously, Beth stepped forward, wanting a closer look but antsy about the self-closing lid. She didn't see any metal or plastics involved, but it had to be technology of some sort. Maybe this culture had found a way to attract stone to stone, the way that magnetism attracted certain metals to— wait, was that . . . ?

Angling around to the side, she aimed her handlight directly at the odd shadow. And there was a square of black plastic wedged between stone and stone, preventing the lid from closing. It was the datapad serving as a wedge, she saw leaning in. The case was a little scraped up by the lid scraping against it, but these field models were built to survive.

Beth tried to picture the scene. The Charnelhouses excitedly tapping and probing the one empty chamber on a world full of tombs. Suddenly, the sarcophagus appears—Beth frowned, trying to visualize how that happened. Blinking into existence out of thin air didn't seem likely, so that left up from the floor? Down from the ceiling?

She panned her light over both surfaces and saw that the ceiling was natural hewn stone. The floor, however, was composed of cut stone blocks, the same material, in fact, as the sarcophagi. At floor level, the lid would look very much like an extra large stone block.

Beth frowned. She had arrived at a what—the sarcophagus rising from the floor in front of Ruth and Greg, perhaps triggered by some action of theirs? The lid swivels open and for some reason the Charnelhouses are moved to investigate inside the sarcophagus. And they end up in stasis. But because they had wedged the lid open with the datapad, the Teladdi were able to lift them back out and take them to the entrance chamber.

Beth frowned again. It would never have happened that way. Neither Ruth nor Greg would ever use a datapad as a blunt instrument when integrity of data was everything to them. It had to be the Teladdi who wedged the lid open. But why leave it that way after they had retrieved the Charnelhouses? Was that part of their hasty exit?

She suddenly felt a need for a hasty exit herself. But take the datapad or not? There was no rational answer to that question because it all seemed so irrational. But she knew this was her one and only opportunity. Once she left the catacombs, she was not returning.

So yes, take it, she decided abruptly and reached down to work the datapad free while the sarcophagus lid was looking the other way. Then she headed back through the archway.

A thump followed her. Then a slow grinding sound. Then a sharp click. She picked up her pace. Around her, the echo of that click spread like a ripple in a pond.

The feeling of wrongness crescendoed. If one sarcophagus had behaved like a stasis pod, what did that say about the tens of thousands of others scattered throughout the tomb complexes of Necropolis? If she were to swivel off the lid of another one—not that she was inclined to—would she find that the non-hom inside was dead or merely frozen in time? Awaiting what—revival?

Reviving a dead alien race—or rather several unrelated races, she corrected—should have been a fascinating possibility, but it wasn't. Instead it felt dark and sinister. What kept pinging about in her brain was the Teladdi, who knew more than the humans and chose to run away. That was the smoking gun of this event.

She walked back through the enfilade of chambers. Nothing appeared different, but she felt apprehensive as she passed through chamber after chamber. The tombs no longer felt peaceful. As she passed each sarcophagus, all she could think about was her parents looking dead in their pods, waiting to be revived.

She had to forced herself not to break and run. She had to stay focused on where she was going. One wrong turn and she could be wandering these tombs for hours, and that was a terrifying thought. She tried counting archways as she passed through, but stopped because the numbers felt too high. She had actually counted coming in, but there seemed to be more chambers now. But she kept going.

Finally, a glimmer of light ahead. Beth rushed through the last few chambers to the antechamber and on outside. The afternoon sun still hung in the sky, lighting the barren landscape of rocks and hills. And there was a truck pulling up the hill. How had Kevin gotten back so fast? No, not Kevin, she realized quickly. Teladdi—the whole crew of them.

They stopped near the entrance and without a word—but of course, they were mutes—began unloading stones from the cargo compartment. The pieces were rough and irregular, not dressed, but it was the same white stone as the sarcophagi. As she watched, they began lugging the pieces into the tombs.

She stood, staring at the dark archway, with misgiving. The type of stone had to be significant. The fact that at the height of the crisis here they had high-tailed off to a quarry to retrieve these stones had to be significant. The longer she stood thinking about it, the more it seemed that the Teladdi had done an emergency temporary wedge with the datapad, then ran off to get a permanent stone wedge. Why? The only reason she could come up with was to keep the lid from swiveling shut . . . and clicking.

But now it had.

Suddenly as if to confirm her guess, the whole crew of Teladdi came running out of the archway, hands fluttering in silent agitation. One ran up to her, fluttering his fingers upward and upward. She didn't understand, but he seemed terrified. And it was contagious.

Run—get away! She could almost hear the silent words.

The whole crew surrounded her, all making panicky arm movements with fluttering fingers. Up and up and up. Then down, down, down with fingers making threatening, clawing motions.

She understood.

Turning, she ran to the abandoned camp site and went straight to the com equipment. She set the frequency to the skimmer but got no answer. That could be good, she told herself firmly. It could mean Kevin had already reached the hospital. She tried his personal number, hoping he was within range of Port Town's one com tower.

"Hello?" The voice was staticky but definitely Kevin's.

"Kevin, we have to—" No, she had to slow down. "How are they?"

"Oh, Beth." There was a pause. "You were right. The doctors said Mother and Greg were stasis frozen. They're in pods now being brought back up to full metabolism. It's a really peculiar situation. How did you know that—?"

"Never mind," Beth interrupted. "Greg, get passage off planet right now. For us and Ruth and Greg and anyone else willing to go."

"Now, Beth, I realize all this has been a shock to you, but

overreaction won't solve—"

"Passage off planet," she interrupted. Glancing out the opening of the done, she saw the Teladdi had loaded her suitcases into the truck and were beckoning her frantically with long fingers. "Make the arrangements while I get to Port Town. I have a ride." Then because she knew he would never listen to her otherwise, she added, "Something's happened at this tomb complex. The equipment is reporting the steady release of bio-toxins into the atmosphere. It must be why the Teladdi ran off."

"Bio-toxins!"

At least she had his attention. "Book us space on any ship that's leaving, regardless of where it's going. There's not much time."

She broke the link and ran to the truck. Whatever was going on had everything to do with the last empty tomb being activated.

* * *

The sun was low on the horizon by the time the truck was pulled into the port. Not Port Town, but the port itself where she could see Kevin and Raoul attending two flight gurneys. The truck barely slowed to let her off, then roared off at full speed. As Beth rushed over to her family, she saw that Ruth and Greg still looked weak, but at least they were awake and breathing. "Let's board," she urged, nudging the group toward the waiting shuttle.

"But it's a freighter on a slow journey to Stedra Dorhea," Kevin began. "And no one's been able to confirm the bio-toxins. It's true that Teladdi all over the area are panicking and grabbing transports off-planet, but that doesn't exactly support your bio-toxin theory. Are you sure we should—"

"If you love me, get on the shuttle," Beth said, practically dragging him that direction. "Just push the gurney on board. Raoul, take the other one, please."

And against all odds, she badgered her well-doctored family onto the shuttle and up to the freighter. As they broke orbit for a region of space they neither knew nor wanted to visit, Beth finally let herself relax. "Thank you for not fighting me," she said as Kevin joined her in the observation lounge. "I know I didn't sound very rational."

"Today wasn't very rational," he said slowly. "Mother and Greg explored the tombs and were inexplicably placed in stasis. Then you explored the same tombs and started ranting about getting off-planet on the next available ship. It doesn't take a PhD to figure out that something distinctly unhealthy was happening."

"Distinctly unhealthy," she repeated to herself. After sitting vacant for thousands of years, the last sarcophagus had been raised and the last tomb had been filled. And all the Teladdi had fled in panic, away from the tombs and away from the planet. She remembered their frightened, fluttering fingers. Whatever was coming was very old and very nasty.

"So we say good-bye to Necropolis," Kevin added after an awkward silence.

"Something's coming," she murmured. "Coming to collect the contents of a trap set long ago. And all those people who are still on planet won't call it Necropolis anymore."

"Then what?" he asked, his eyes huge and startled.

"Charnelhouse."

BEAR ESSENTIALS

Julie Frost

Spaceship voyages are among the most familiar Grand Tradition tropes and they have been used throughout the history of the genre. They are the logical progression from the popular sailing ship adventures of the day that featured daring captains who visited strange locations populated by even stranger inhabitants, not the least of which is *Gulliver's Travels* (1726). But the fun romp "Bear Essentials" is an even more specific sort of spaceship voyage; not just a tight-knit crew manning a small vessel, but composed predominantly of family members. Well-known SF stories featuring family-owned or operated ships include *The Rolling Stones* (*The Family Stone* in Great Britain) published in 1952 and the TV series *Lost in Space* (1965-1968). Author Julie Frost continues in this tradition by introducing us to Captain Russell Fisk and his daughter Mandy who pilot the tramp freighter the *Inquisitive Tamandua* from one potential catastrophe to another. The character of Captain Fisk resonates with the empathetic side of the reader: He isn't the aloof steely-eyed adventurer. Instead, he is a harried fallible father who worries about everything—his ship, livelihood, crew, passengers, cargo, and his daughter's changing relationship with the mechanic.

Julie Frost lives in the beautiful Salt Lake Valley in a house full of Oaxacan carvings and anteaters, some of which intersect. Her work has appeared in *Cosmos, Azure Valley, Stupefying Stories*, and *Plasma Frequency*. She whines about writing at agilebrit.livejournal.com, or you can follow her on Twitter via @JulieCFrost. A prior adventure in this timeline, "Illegal Beagles," is available for free download at the author's website agilebrit.livejournal.com.

Russell Fisk slouched into the co-pilot's chair of his interplanetary tramp freighter, the *Inquisitive Tamandua*. "Mandy?" he said, crossing his arms and scowling. "Are we getting a reputation or something?"

"What do you mean, Dad?"

"I just got a call from a potential client who wants us to take a grizzly bear, of all things, from the spaceport on the other side of the city to a monastery on Upcurion." He rubbed his beard—which hadn't been this gray, he was sure, before their most recent jobs. "How many times do I have to say I don't like moving live cargo before it sinks in?"

"Oh, come on." She pushed a lock of brown hair out of her face. "It hasn't been all that bad."

"Other than the fact that I involuntarily got a baby dragon added to my crew after the last job?"

"Don't be such a grouch." Mandy punched him lightly on the arm. "Bradaigh isn't any trouble, and Charlie's teaching him about the engine and other stuff. He's doing a really good job, too," she said, with a soft smile that set Russ's teeth on edge. The last thing he needed was his daughter and his mechanic starting a romance. She continued, "And Brad's mother has been more than generous with money to support him. I like eating regularly." She started her takeoff sequence. "Speaking of which . . . we're taking the contract, right?"

"I don't see any other work out there, so I guess we are." Russ glared out the window. "Yay."

* * *

Russ watched as Dick Adamson, their contact on the sending end, crossed his arms and drummed his fingers on his biceps, while Charlie Crane, the *Tamandua's* beefy blond mechanic, loaded the caged bear into the cargo hold. Adamson continually glanced over his shoulders, and flinched at every loud noise resounding across the port. This meant he was twitching about every ten seconds or so, and Russ thought the man was going to leap out of his skin when a siren sounded, signaling a ship in takeoff mode. Adamson was short and skinny and reminded Russ of a frightened, hyperactive weasel, albeit one with glasses and a shock of red hair.

Most of their clients weren't this nervous, and Russ's mistrust about the job grew. The bear paced back and forth in its five-meter-square enclosure, bobbing its head and growling. Bradaigh, curious, got a little too close, and the bear slammed its paw against the cage, causing everyone to jump. The little blue dragonet scrambled backwards, fell onto his tail, and blew a gout of flame through his nostrils. His ridiculously small wings flapped in panic. Fortunately for Bradaigh, the bars were a thick, welded, diagonal chain-link, not big enough for the bear to get his nose through, let alone a paw.

The cage was locked via a keypad, and the food and water troughs could be moved in and out for access but were attached to the cage. The bear wouldn't be able to escape, anyway. "Anything special I need to know about this critter?" Russ asked Adamson.

"Not in particular. He's just a bear. Bad-tempered, though." The staccato sentences didn't make Adamson sound any calmer, and he flinched again when a shuttle blasted overhead. "Might want to stay clear of him. The cage is self-cleaning." He gestured at the boxes that Charlie was now maneuvering aboard. "Feed him once a day. Instructions on the lids. Plenty of water."

Ss!kct, the Pyralis ship's doctor and default science officer, used two of her four hands to make some notations on her clipboard and waved her antennae. "He seems like an unusually large specimen." The bear's head was about a half-meter long, and proportionately massive, and Russ had wondered about that himself.

"Well, we, uh, grow 'em big." Adamson handed over a sheaf of paperwork and half the payment, as agreed. "This goes with him. Any other questions?"

Russ shook his head and started to say, "I guess not," but before he could complete the sentence, Adamson turned on his heel and practically ran away. The bear roared, and Russ turned to see it up on its hind legs, slamming its paw into the side of the cage and baring yellow teeth longer than Russ's finger. It was over three meters high, and Russ was suddenly very glad of the thick mesh between him and the creature.

Ss!kct took an involuntary step backwards. "*Very* large," she muttered, blowing a hiss of air through her spiracles.

"We ready to go, boss?" Charlie asked, eyeing the bear. It dropped back to all fours and resumed its pacing. *Let us out, let us out, let us out . . .*

Russ stuck his finger in his ear and wiggled it around, frowning. "Let's get her fired up. Sooner we leave, sooner we're shut of this." He keyed the comm. "Mandy, you ready for takeoff?" She'd been disappointed she couldn't watch the bear be loaded, but the client was anxious, so she sat up in the cockpit getting the *Tamandua* prepped for her journey.

"Ready when you are," she replied.

"Ahoy the ship!" A thirty-ish blonde woman carrying a backpack over one shoulder, her hair and clothes rumpled, raced toward him waving her arms.

"Oh, what now? Hold on, Mandy." He eyed the woman with a lifted eyebrow as she stumbled to a halt at the bottom of the ramp. "Something I can help you with?"

"You're going to Upcurion?" she asked. He nodded curtly. "I really need to get there. How much?"

Normally, he wouldn't have minded taking on a passenger. However, something about her set off alarm bells in the back of his head, and he'd learned to listen to that little voice. He shook his head. "I'm not a passenger ship, ma'am. Sorry."

"No, really. I have to get there," she insisted. "How much?"

Russ named an outrageous amount, figuring to price her out of the market and get rid of her. She didn't even blink. "Done." She reached into her pack and pulled out a credit chit. "This should cover it. Thanks." She handed it to him and strode into the ship, while he stood there with his mouth hanging open.

"Um. Okay, then," he managed to say, reminding himself that getting paid twice for the same job was preferable to getting paid once. They were going that way anyhow, and if she didn't care that her bunk would be less than luxurious, well, who was he to argue? "Let me show you to your berth. I'm Captain Russell Fisk."

"Sharon Chen." She shook his hand with a firm grip. "Thank you, Captain. You're getting me out of a tight spot."

Russ stopped. "Not law trouble, I hope."

"Oh, no, nothing like that," she laughed. "I'm a reporter for the *Port Callis Times*, chasing a story."

A reporter was almost worse than a fugitive. He winced, but decided to roll with it. After all, they were just taking a bear to a monastery. No story there. He hit the button that raised the ramp and told Mandy, "All aboard and ready to go. We've got a passenger as well."

Russ looked at the bear as he escorted Ms. Chen past it. Back and forth, forth and back . . . it didn't seem inclined to stop anytime soon. *This ought to be an interesting trip,* he thought.

* * *

Once they were underway and he had their passenger stowed, he pulled Ss!kct aside. "Find out what you can about the bear. Something about the way Adamson was acting doesn't sit right with me, and it seems like an awful lot of money for what should be a pretty basic job. The whole thing smells, and I won't feel right until we figure out why."

"You caught that too?" she said. "All right, sir, I'll start some research. A DNA sample would be useful."

"Yeah, don't get too excited about getting one of those. I'm not putting anyone's life in danger for something like that." Bradaigh had crept closer to the cage, and the bear snarled at him again, sending him scrambling to hide behind Charlie's legs. Charlie bent down to scratch him behind the neck frill. "Charlie, make sure the engine's in tip-top shape. I want to get this job done as soon as we can."

"Yeah, boss. Let's go, squirt." Bradaigh galumphed after him toward the engine room.

Three days, Russ thought. *Let's make it two and a half.*

* * *

Mandy wandered down to the cargo hold after a little while to find Russ had pulled up a chair and was seated on it backwards, watching the bear pace. She blinked. "Wow. I didn't think he'd be so . . . big."

"Me neither." Russ shook his head. "This job stinks, and I'm not just saying that because the bear smells funny."

"He's pretty, though. Who's a pretty fella?" she cooed at it.

"Don't go too—" The bear roared and slammed a massive paw against the side of the cage. *Let us out!* Mandy jumped back. "Close," Russ finished. "He's grouchy."

"I can see that. Anyway, it's dinnertime, and we have real food tonight. Coming?"

"Sure."

He rose and followed her into the dining room. Everyone else had already beaten them there, and Ss!kct was serving, since it was her turn to cook. Russ sat at his place and poked suspiciously at the stuff on his plate with a fork. "What's this? I told you I didn't want to be surprised with any more of your Pyralis specialties." Last time it had been some sort of grub-in-the-shell native to her planet. The Pyralis were carnivorous and slightly cannibalistic. When Russ had asked Ss!kct what she meant by "slightly," she'd just waved her antennae and declined to explain.

"Why don't you try it and see if you like it?" She clacked her mandibles and distributed six whole, but dead, rats to Bradaigh's plate. He'd only recently made the transition from live prey, and he nosed the dead ones unhappily for a moment. Then he toasted them with a snout flame and gulped one down, while Ms. Chen watched with mingled horror and interest and the stench of burnt hair filled the room.

"Brad," Charlie said, pointing his fork at the dragonet. "Wait till everyone's got their food before you start. Don't be rude. And skin 'em before you set 'em afire. No one wants to smell that."

Mandy gave Charlie that smile that made Russ want to smack them both and shout about inter-ship romances. "Hey, he's cooking them now," she said. "That's progress."

At least Charlie was taking his job to civilize the baby dragon seriously, Russ thought, which was a good thing even if Mandy was finding his newfound paternal instincts attractive. Ss!kct sat down at her own place, and everyone dug in. To Russ's surprise, the food was delicious. "You can make this again, Ss!kct," he said around a mouthful.

"You like it, sir? It's made from—"

"I don't want to know. Seriously." He swallowed and turned to their passenger. After introducing everyone around, he said, "You're working on a story, Ms. Chen?"

"Oh, call me Sharon. And yes, but it might not pan out. I'd really rather not say anything else until I know more."

"Fair enough. So, Ss!kct, did you find anything out about our bear?"

"Yes, as a matter of fact." She glanced at Sharon and twitched her antennae in a shrug. "You're . . . not going to like it."

He pinched the bridge of his nose. "Do I ever? Out with it."

"Without a DNA sample, I can't be positive, but I don't think it's a grizzly bear." She waved her pedipalps. "Judging from its size and the shape of the head, it's a cave bear."

"A cave—" Russ put his fork down, forcefully. "But they're extinct."

"Earth scientists were able to extract DNA from their teeth. Cloning technology today is more than sufficient to produce a complete bear from what they got."

"Oh, I think it's neat," Mandy said.

"You would," Russ answered. "Oh, well. It's a cave bear. Bigger than a regular bear, but . . . probably not much different, right? A bear's a bear?"

"Well, yes and no." Ss!kct took a bite of food before continuing. "It doesn't make any difference to us, but it does to the people at the monastery on Upcurion."

"Well, darn, I wish I'd known that. Would've charged 'em more . . ."

Bradaigh, who had finished his rats, took the opportunity to chirp a question at Charlie. "Sure, you can go," he said with a handwave. The dragonet hopped down and headed out, toward the cargo hold. "Stay away from the bear!"

"Meep."

"He's fascinated by the thing," Charlie said. "It's as big as his momma, but it's all furry an' strange, he says."

"The monks are pretty fascinated by it too," Ss!kct said. "In fact, they worship it. Which is why we're taking it there."

"Buh . . . what?" Russ sputtered. "But it's just a *bear*."

"They call it the Keeper of Dreams, and they attach mystical significance to it." She twitched her antennae. "And then they sacrifice it to the DreamCaster every five years. And ceremonially eat it."

Mandy looked outraged. "They're going to kill him and eat him? But they can't! He's so beautiful."

Russ thought his head would explode. "Mandy, that's none of our—"

Bradaigh chose that moment to rush into the room, blowing fire from his nostrils and meeping frantically. Charlie's head whipped around. "*What* did you say?"

"What? What?" Russ hadn't learned the dragonet's language, but Charlie had shown a remarkable facility for it. Whatever had Bradaigh so kerfuffled, it couldn't be good.

"He says the bear's gone."

* * *

They stood around the empty cage in various states of befuddlement. Mandy twisted her fingers together, Ss!kct waved her pedipalps, Bradaigh bounced his front feet up and down while Charlie tried to comfort him, and Russ pinched the bridge of his nose. Sharon seemed the calmest, although her job probably meant that she got thrown into interesting situations more often than the average person.

Part of the problem was that the cage wasn't damaged at all, and the door was still closed and locked.

Ss!kct pointed a scanner at it and shook her head. "I'm not getting any strange readings from it. Other than the fact that the bear is definitely not in there."

"Ask Bradaigh what he saw," Russ said to Charlie.

Flapping his wings, Bradaigh sat up and chittered, and Charlie translated. "He came straight here from dinner and the cage looked just like this. No bear."

"He didn't let it out?"

"Meep!" Even Russ could translate that particular indignant denial.

"Anyone else?" Russ looked at his crew. They all shook their heads, and he knew they hadn't had time to release the bear before dinner. Let alone a motive. Bears were big, dumb, and dangerous, and no one wanted a scary predator like that running around loose on the ship.

That left the bear. Which was patently impossible.

"Okay. First thing we need to do is arm everyone. We have a four-hundred-kilo bear that wants to eat our faces hiding around here someplace. Charlie, guns." The mechanic nodded and ran out of the hold toward the weapons locker. "Mandy, after he comes back with the guns, you get together with him and figure out how to get as much power out of the engines as you possibly can. Sooner we're on the ground, the more comfortable I'll be."

"You and me both." Her eyes darted around the room, looking for an invisible bear.

"Sharon, I'd really feel better if you locked yourself in your room until it's safe again." He didn't need a passenger underfoot, gumming up the works and getting in the way.

Sharon nodded. "I understand. Not a lot I can do to help in any case."

"Ss!kct, Bradaigh, we are going to use your instruments—" Russ pointed at Ss!kct. "—and your nose—" He pointed at Bradaigh. "—to find the bear. It can't stay hidden for long. It needs food, and water, and it's probably scared in such a new environment. And something that size doesn't have many hiding places here."

"Maybe we should leave the cage door open," Mandy said. "He might decide that someplace familiar is more comfy and go in on his own."

"Good idea." A new thought hit him. "Also, buddy system. No one goes anywhere alone."

Mandy's eyes widened. "Charlie . . ."

"I'm fine. No bear," Charlie said, walking back into the room. "But, I gotcha, boss." He handed weapons around.

Russ lifted an eyebrow. "Stun rifles?"

"Well, they ain't as tricky to aim, and if you miss actually killin' him with an energy bolt, all you get is a pissed off bear. Plus I figgered we'd rather have him alive than dead, since that's the job." Charlie shrugged. "I've put 'em on full power. They'll knock him out right enough."

Russ thought about it for a second. "Plus an energy bolt might hole the hull. I like breathing; smart thinking, Charlie. All right, people. Let's get to work."

* * *

Kill them.

"I don't want to. Not really. They aren't malicious; they just don't understand."

It doesn't matter that they're not malicious. They're still dangerous to us. To you.

"These people don't want to hurt us. They're afraid. And they're not dangerous to you. They don't know you exist."

Fearful people are dangerous. I'm not sure I can keep us hidden for three days.

"Then maybe you should have thought of that before releasing us so early in the trip. For a creature who's supposed to be smart, you're not very bright sometimes."

Hey! You stepped out of the cage . . .

"What was I supposed to do? Sit there with the door open? Please."

Shh. They're coming. We need to move.

* * *

Sharon sat down at the tiny desk in her berth and accessed the 'net. When she'd seen the bear being loaded at the port, her reporter's instincts had kicked in. Nobody just casually moved an animal that size across three sectors; there had to be a story in it—which was why she'd bullied her way aboard. The look on the Captain's face when she'd paid his ridiculous price without blinking had been worth what she'd given him.

The bear's escape was confirmation enough that she had a story here. She searched "cave bear" and "Upcurian monastery" and soon had all the information that Ss!kct had touched upon, though not much more.

The monks allowed any species or sex into their sect. They didn't recruit much. "Secretive bunch," Sharon muttered. Years of working alone had made talking to herself second nature—verbalizing ideas helped solidify them. The lack of actual useful information about this religion annoyed her.

She tapped a link, and other data scrolled up her screen. "Oh, that's interesting." Not pacifists. "Well, with a cave bear for a god, I guess I wouldn't expect them to be." The monks were masters of several martial arts and had invented three of their own.

Her messenger beeped, and her editor's face popped up on the screen. "How's it going, Sharon?" he asked.

"Fine, Alan," she answered. "I think I've got a story here. Right now it's just a lot of sitting back and observing, but I'll have something for you in the next couple of days for sure."

"I don't have to tell you what this means to you, right?" He lifted a bushy gray eyebrow. She hated those eyebrows.

"No, Alan." It took real effort for her not to roll her eyes, although the last three stories she'd chased had been dry holes, and her job was on the line. "This is a good one. Seriously." She wasn't bluffing. Much.

"All right. I trust you, but some of the higher-ups are making noises."

"Can you hold them off for a little longer?"

"Do my best." He drummed his fingers on his desk.

"That's all I ask. I'll see you later?"

He nodded and blipped off, and she slumped back into her chair. "This had better pan out . . ."

* * *

"Meep."

"Well, yes, Bradaigh. Even I can smell that." Russ huffed out an impatient breath. "Does this mean we're getting close?" Ss!kct clacked her mandibles. "Sir, he's not a bloodhound, he's a dragon. They're not exactly known for their tracking abilities."

"He's what I have."

"Maybe if you'd let Mandy keep her beagle from the dog job—"

"Because I need more chaos on my ship." Russ opened the smuggling space that Bradaigh's nose had led them to. It was empty, but the bear had been there, all right. "There's your DNA sample, Ss!kct." He gestured to a clump of coarse mahogany hair on the floor.

She pounced with alacrity and shoved the fur into a pouch on her harness. "I'd like to start analyzing this right away."

"For what? Is it going to tell you where the bear is?"

"No, but it might help narrow down *what* the bear is. A normal bear couldn't have escaped from that cage."

"Fine." They walked toward the infirmary. "But you lock yourself in and don't open up until one of us comes for you."

That particular antennae twitch was a sure sign of Ss!kct's irritation. "Of course, sir."

He left her to it after making sure that the door was sealed. "Just you and me, Bradaigh. Let's see if we can find us a bear."

* * *

"Well, isn't that interesting," Ss!kct said, peering at a readout. "This can't possibly be legal." She heard the door whoosh open behind her. "Sir, we might get in trouble for this. Did you actually look at the documentation on the bear?"

A throaty rumble behind her made her whip around. It hadn't been the Captain at the door. Instead, the bear filled the opening.

The creature really was astoundingly enormous, she thought wildly. The stunner sat on a table three meters across the room, too far for easy reach. It would eat her before she got halfway to it.

However, her findings suggested another course of action. She gestured at her computer screen. "I know what you are now. And intelligent beings don't dine on one another, do we?"

She wasn't sure what sort of reaction she was expecting, but it certainly wasn't a tart, *Apparently* some *intelligent beings don't have a problem with kidnapping, killing, and eating other intelligent beings*, beamed directly into her head. And that certainly wasn't at all how she expected a bear to sound, either.

"Was that you?" Ss!kct asked the beast.

A tiny head peered out from behind the bear's ear. *No, it was me.*

Asbjorn can't speak your language, though he understands it just fine.

"I'm . . . not familiar with your species," Ss!kct said.

I wouldn't expect you to be. Most of the more obscure primates from Old Earth are, well, obscure. My name is Kong, and I am a pygmy marmoset. Off her look, he acknowledged, *The people in the lab who named me apparently had a rather juvenile sense of humor.*

She relaxed marginally. "And how did two such disparate creatures end up together?"

I escaped from my own cage. The technicians assumed I left the facility, but I actually stayed to help Asbjorn. The bear chuffed. *No one knows about me, including the monks.*

"Is it safe to assume that you've been just as genetically engineered as Asbjorn?" Ss!kct waved at her screen. "The changes here are quite remarkable."

Asbjorn grumbled in a testy manner, and Ss!kct tensed again. She hadn't realized that it might be a sore spot for him. Kong scratched Asbjorn's head. *We didn't ask for this, you know. The question is, will you and your people help us?*

Ss!kct didn't see that they had much choice. However, even though none of them approved of slavery, this revelation had just made their lives immeasurably more complicated.

* * *

Russ charged into the dining area, Bradaigh literally hot on his heels. "Ss!kct! What did I tell you about the buddy—" He stopped short and brought his stunner up. Bradaigh crashed into his legs and sat down with a whumph of flame. "There's a cave bear in my dining room."

Ss!kct stepped between him and his target. "Sir, please calm down."

"I'll be calm when that thing is back in its cage where it belongs!" He tried to aim the stunner again, and this time she stopped him with a hand on his wrist.

"We don't cage intelligent beings," she said levelly.

That stopped him short. "Int—" He sputtered for a few seconds, then deflated and pinched the bridge of his nose. "Do I want to know?"

"No, sir." She huffed a breath through her spiracles. "But you need to. It changes everything."

Charlie and Mandy ran in from the direction of the engine room, with Sharon behind them. Mandy was a little quicker on the uptake than Charlie was, and she deflected his aim, sending stunner fire spattering harmlessly against the floor. "What . . ." he started, but she quelled him with a look.

And that, Russ thought sourly, was another complication he didn't want. Mandy had shot Charlie down with some rather salty language in the past, but she wasn't doing that anymore. An evil dwarf began beating a hammer on the inside of his skull, right behind his left eye. "Why—" His voice came out as a hoarse croak, and he tried again. "Why don't we all sit down and find out what's going on?" A tiny head popped out from behind the bear's ear, and he recoiled. "*What the hell is that?*"

Ss!kct massaged her forehead with two of her hands. "That's Kong, sir. He's a pygmy marmoset."

"And when did he come aboard?" Russ's legs wouldn't hold him up anymore, and he collapsed into a chair. Everyone else found a seat, and the bear nosed a spare chair aside and plumped down on its haunches on the floor. Its head still rose higher than Russ's own.

"When Asbjorn did. The bear," she clarified. Oh, it had a name now. Great. "Kong slipped through the mesh and released them both."

"Someday," Russ said, "you'll have to tell me how you found out their names. For now, can we just have the basics?"

"The basics. Right." Ss!kct's mandibles clacked. "What we have on our hands is one genetically-engineered cave bear, and one genetically-engineered pygmy marmoset. And they've both been genetically engineered to be sapient, and taking them anywhere against their wills, when they've broken no laws, is tantamount to slavery. Giving Asbjorn to a monastery to be sacrificed to the DreamCaster and eaten in five years is right out."

"Oh. That means . . ." Russ trailed off and put his face in his hands momentarily. That meant that the job they'd been hired to do was patently illegal. "I guess we'll have to call the Feds, then."

Her pedipalps waved. Shit. "There's a problem with that."

"Naturally. What?"

"Did you actually read the documentation that came with Asbjorn, sir?"

"It's twenty pages of closely-spaced fine print, on *paper*, of all things. Hell, no." An ice-cold ball of worry knotted in his stomach, and the evil dwarf's evil twin beat a counterpoint behind his right eye. He had a reporter on his ship, and he had no doubt that she was taking this all in, although she hadn't said a word.

"Well, sir, buried in all that fine print is a single line on page sixteen that states that Asbjorn is sapient. And that fact makes proving we didn't know about it beforehand . . . challenging."

Shitshitshit. The Feds would confiscate the *Tamandua* and throw them all in jail so long that his grandkids would have grandkids. Assuming he ever had grandkids, which, if Mandy was in jail with him, he wouldn't. And even if he could prove that they didn't know, they'd be tied up in court for so long that he'd have to sell his little ship just so they could all eat in the meantime.

We would be willing to testify to the fact that you were unaware of our status, and that the monks definitely knew, a voice in his head said. Ugh. He hated telepathy. A third evil dwarf joined the other two, beating on his forehead between his eyes this time.

"Which one of you said that?" he asked, suddenly very tired.

Kong. I apologize for the way I have to communicate. The marmoset had picked up on his dislike of strange voices beamed into his brain. Of course it had.

"I don't suppose it's your fault. And I appreciate your willingness to help us out." Russ ran his hand through his hair. "I'm just not sure it'll do all that much good."

It certainly didn't do us any good with our captors. All we wanted was to be left alone, but they had other ideas. Russ could feel the mental shrug. *We couldn't do much against stunners and tanglenets.* No wonder Adamson had been so eager to get away.

"So," Mandy said slowly. "We can't possibly finish the job. We can't get out of it by going to the police and telling them who's really to blame. What exactly can we do?"

"That's what gets me," Russ said. "The monks know? How come that didn't come up in your research, Ss!kct?"

"It's apparently a deep, dark secret. Which you can't really blame them for." Asbjorn growled affirmation, and Sharon got an "Aha" look on her face that made Russ all sorts of uncomfortable.

"Where do you want to go?" Russ asked Asbjorn. "We could just drop you two off and pretend this never happened."

Ss!kct coughed through her spiracles. "The monks would not take kindly to that."

"So what?" Charlie said, with a lowered brow. "They're slave-traders that've roped us into their dirty business. What're they gonna do, come after us and pray lightnin' down on our heads? Let 'em try."

"They're not pacifists," Sharon said, and told them about the martial arts. "And yes, they'd come after you. You'd be stealing their *god*."

"Hmph." Charlie leaned back and crossed his arms across his chest. "Ain't some gods famous for bein' wrathful? I'd like 'em to see what that looks like . . ." Bradaigh chirruped agreement, flapping his wings with indignation.

Russ stared at him, his headache receding as the evil dwarves fled in terror from the new thought he'd just spawned. "What did you say?"

"Sorry, boss." Charlie had the grace to look contrite, if barely. "Slavers piss me off, that's all."

"Charlie, my man, you have nothing to apologize for." Russ clapped him on the back. "I think you just gave us an out."

* * *

Two days later, Mandy landed them on the grounds of the Upcurion monastery, and Russ stepped out into the rain to deal with the Abbott. The man, barefoot, tonsured, and clad in a purple robe, pumped his hand up and down. Russ noted the strength of that grip with an inward gulp and an outward smile.

"I trust the bear wasn't any trouble?" the Abbott asked. The rest of the fifteen or so monks, of various species native to this quadrant, had assembled a little way off to watch the offloading of their new god.

"This was one of the easier jobs we've taken on lately, in fact. However . . ." Russ decided it wouldn't do to let the man off too easily. "I went over the documentation after we took off and found something that disturbed my crew rather a lot."

"Hm, yes." The Abbott rubbed his beard and shook water droplets from his hand. "I counseled against having that particular piece of information in the paperwork, but Adamson insisted, saying it spread the liability." The Abbott took a money pouch from his belt and counted out . . . quite a bit extra, Russ was pleased to note. "I trust this will salve your consciences and buy your silence."

"It goes quite a ways towards that. Tell me, Abbott," Russ said, trying to be casual, "how many of your people actually know about this?"

"Oh, all of us do. It's part and parcel of our religion." *Of course it is*, Russ seethed. "It wouldn't do to have a *stupid* god, would it? And at the sacrifice, we partake of his wisdom in the ceremonial feast. We've done this for more than a century."

"I see." Russ keyed his comm, which had actually been open the entire time, the better to let the crew know how many of their clients had been aware of the fact that Asbjorn was sapient. "All right, Charlie, you can bring the bear out."

Charlie maneuvered the antigrav pallet down the cargo ramp.

Asbjorn lay quietly on the bottom of the cage, seemingly either too tired or too depressed to react much to the sudden obeisance of the monks, who splashed onto their faces as one when the cage touched the ground.

The Abbott fell to his knees, but continued to look at the cage with a beatific smile on his face. Thus, he was the only one to see the door swing open and the enraged bear leap out. Russ hadn't known Asbjorn could move so damned fast; the creature was so big that he thought more of "continental drift" rather than "juggernaut" when he looked at him. But the Abbott only had time for one truncated shriek before he was left in a squashed and mangled heap in the mud.

They hadn't actually discussed with Asbjorn what he was going to do. Russ wasn't sure he wanted to cringe or gloat as the bear headed toward the cowering monks. Asbjorn rose up on his hind legs and roared, swiping his front paws over their heads.

"How . . . how have we angered you, O Keeper of Dreams?" one quavered.

You were going to eat me! Russ was surprised at how much outraged authority Kong was able to project in that thought.

"Er. Yes? None of you ever objected before . . ."

Asbjorn roared again, and that monk's forehead splashed back down to the ground. *Give me a tour of this place.*

Russ, his crew, and Sharon followed behind as the monks, in a cringing bunch, led Asbjorn into the dining hall. Nearly two dozen skulls and bearskin rugs decorated the room, and Russ admired Asbjorn's restraint, although the bear visibly swelled with anger. Russ wanted to knock some heads on his own account, and Charlie's clenched-teeth breathing behind him told him that the mechanic was only just keeping himself in check. Mandy stifled sobs, and Sharon's vidcap whirred, filming the evidence. Russ determinedly did not check to see whether Charlie had his arm wrapped around Mandy's shoulders.

You will give these a decent burial. Now, Kong instructed the monks.

They obeyed with as much alacrity as was possible in the pouring rain. Once they finished, Asbjorn reared up onto his hind legs, and the monks again collapsed face down in the mud. *Leave this place and never return. Never make another living sacrifice, ever.* Asbjorn loomed over them. *I will find out if you do. And you will suffer the same fate as your Abbott.* He snarled. *Go!* Appropriately dramatic thunder punctuated Kong's command.

Thirty seconds later, the monks had vacated the monastery.

* * *

"Where would you like to go?" Russ asked Asbjorn and Kong. "We can take you anyplace."

Will you get in trouble for what we did? Kong seemed worried, and Asbjorn rumbled agreement.

"I wouldn't think so. All we did was deliver cargo. It's not our outlook if the client is careless with it after we leave."

They'd left an obvious trail into the woods, which petered out a few meters in, and then had taken Asbjorn back onboard the ship using the antigrav pallet. Hopefully, any cops coming on the scene would think the monks had lost control of their new god and paid the price.

"Do the authorities know about the lab that engineered you?" Mandy asked. "That has to be illegal, if they're doing a lot of it and then keeping you locked up—or selling you."

Who do you think funds the lab? Kong's tone was acerbic.

"Oh."

That gave them one more reason to hate the Feds, as if they needed another. The irony that their little ship skated the edges of bare legitimacy, while the government was involved in something like that, burned. *It's buried under several layers of bureaucracy and a need-to-know so deep that the rank and file don't know it exists, if that makes you feel any better.* Kong gave a little snort. *They weren't too discreet around us.*

It didn't make him feel better, really. "Interesting," Ss!kct said. "So, it might be possible to bring them down anyway. I can't help but think that most decent people would be as appalled as we were about it."

"And this is where I come in," Sharon said. "The story I've been chasing? Is Asbjorn. I saw you loading him at the port and decided to tag along because it looked interesting. I was right. This is a hell of a story."

"Assuming that Asbjorn and Kong want to expose themselves that way," Mandy said. "I don't know, you guys might want to just find a nice mountain somewhere and live out your lives in peace and quiet."

Asbjorn rumbled, and Bradaigh meeped back at him. "Are these two communicating now?" Russ whispered to Charlie.

"Uh, apparently. Really?" Charlie said to Bradaigh. "Okay." He turned back to Russ. "Asbjorn says that he left friends back at the lab, and if it's possible to do something for 'em, he'd sure like to."

An isolated mountain, away from the insane creatures that had invaded his life, suddenly sounded really damn nice to Russ. No one had asked *him* if he wanted to expose himself this way. What had started as a simple job transporting an animal had blown up in their faces. Again.

"I know we're all filled with righteous indignation here," he said slowly, "and I hate to be the one saying 'What's our percentage in this?' But, what's our percentage in this? Notoriety in our business is a bad thing, and getting our pictures plastered all over the news won't put food on the table. Just the opposite, in fact."

Ss!kct clacked her mandibles. "There's something in what you say, sir. But I don't like to leave Asbjorn and Kong just hanging in the breeze."

"I don't either, but there has to be a happy medium between that and reporters crawling up our asses."

"I can leave you out of it, if you really want," Sharon said. "I'd be lacking a dimension to the story, but I can work around it, no problem. I'll use language like 'an intrepid starship crew, who wish to remain anonymous.' "

"You'd do that?" Russ trusted a journalist as far as he could throw one on a heavy planet. Sharon had stayed out of their hair on the trip, but she could sure make their lives complicated if she decided to play it that way. "Why?"

"I might need quick, discreet transportation someday." Sharon shrugged. "It never hurts to keep avenues open."

It sounded reasonable, Russ supposed. "All right. Where should we drop you?"

"I'm thinking the lab, for best effect," she said, glancing at Asbjorn and Kong for affirmation. "Straight to the source. Can I have the documentation that Adamson gave you? I'll redact your names, of course, but I can use the paper trail."

Ss!kct skittered off to her lab to get it, while Russ heaved a mental sigh of relief. The trip had been anything but smooth, but they'd been paid—and were about to make sure a downright evil place was going to get its comeuppance, without even breaking a sweat.

He'd call that a win.

THE VRINGLA/RACKET INCIDENT

Jakob Drud

"The Vringla/Racket Incident" is an epistolary story—one told through documents, diary entries, and/or letters. As a form, the epistolary story was quite popular in the 18th century at a time when letters were an essential part of everyday life. Bram Stoker's *Dracula* (1897) is probably the best known epistolary novel while Alice Walker's *The Color Purple* (1982) and Helen Fielding's *Bridget Jones' Diary* (1996) are more contemporary examples of this form. *Bridget Jones' Diary* originally merged epistolary storytelling and serialized fiction, as the early diary entries were published as a weekly column in the British newspaper *The Independent*. Within the SF genre, recent epistolary works include Max Brooks' *World War Z: An Oral History of the Zombie War* (2006) which describes the Zombie War through a series of interviews collected by the United Nations Postwar Commission. In "The Vringla/Racket Incident," author Jakob Drud introduces us to Johanna Wilborough, a government employee looking for a babysitter, through a series of hard-sell letters she receives. The creepy babysitter prospects and final twist made me laugh out loud.

Jakob Drud lives in Aarhus, Denmark, where he writes advertising copy for a living and science fiction and fantasy for fun. He writes in English because of the many interesting writers and people involved in the SF web community. His stories have appeared in more than 20 webzines and anthologies, including *Daily Science Fiction* and *Flash Fiction Online*. Visit his blog at jakobdrud.livejournal.com or read his tweets at @jakobdrud.

From: Bret Jetson, Survivor BabyCare
To: Johanna Wilborough
Re: Looking for a babysitter

Dear Johanna Wilborough,

Thank you very much for your email requesting the services of Survivor BabyCare. You ask whether we can provide a suitable babysitter, and I'm delighted to say we have over a dozen in your area. I'm sure we can find someone to care for little Victoria while you work overtime on the government's reconstruction program.

I noted that you specifically asked for a human babysitter. Given the demographics after the Vringla invasion attempt we have run into certain recruiting issues. Therefore we've decided to assign any remaining human sitters to our pre-war customers whenever possible.

Fortunately we have excellent contacts among our Sensibi saviors, who are taking a keen interest in the care and wellbeing of the human race. You'll have a choice between five experienced Sensibi nest mothers and eight nest daughters, none of whom will be skin-shedding while they watch your daughter.

All our sitters are equipped with the latest Sensibi translators, which ensure safe and secure communication free of species-related misunderstandings. Also, I'm very proud that our interracial decontamination procedures have won us several Happy Customer Awards in your area.

Please get back in touch so we can arrange a meeting between Victoria and a Sensibi of your choice.

May Your Peace Last,
     Bret Jetson, Manager, Survivor BabyCare

P.S.: Enclosed is our list of our available babysitters. I've also attached five case stories for you to read at your leisure. Remember, real people love our services!

* * *

From: Bret Jetson
To: Johanna Wilborough
Re: Safety Issues

Dear Johanna,

I have taken full note of your concern about our Sensibi staff, but I can assure you that no accidents are going to happen to Victoria. The world today is rife with rumors and urban myths, but only a tiny percentage of those stories have any trace of truth in them.

You point to the so-called Boiler Incident, and if we had any suspicion whatsoever that this incident was real, no Sensibi nest mother would work for us again. Fortunately there's no evidence to support this story. First, because Sensibi Nest Mothers are quite used to baby-like screams from their own offspring, and generally don't suffer fits of frustration. Second, because the Sensibi most definitely do not cook their meals.

In these exaggerated cases it's worth remembering that the Sensibi came to Earth's rescue during the invasion. Why would they want to save us only to harm our children?

It must be said that a few embarrassing situations have happened due to inter-species misunderstandings. The Sink/Roach Incident you refer to was one such, but preventing similar accidents has been easy. The Sensibi learn fast, and once they understood that wet insects aren't considered a delicacy on Earth, they've stopped feeding them to the babies.

Did I mention that Survivor BabyCare has an award-winning labeling program? The labels make it clear to even the most hormone-disturbed Sensibi nest daughter which kind of substances are food and which are household chemicals. I assure you, if you place the labels as instructed, little Victoria will never have bath salts in her bottle!

I hope this has laid your fears to rest and I look forward to hearing your choice of babysitter. No pressure, but remember that by this time next week your preferred sitter may be taken!

May Your Peace Last,
  Bret Jetson, Manager, Survivor BabyCare

P.S.: I've taken the liberty of attaching another ten case stories. This may seem excessive, but I feel it's necessary to balance out all those malicious stories about the babysitting industry. And remember, Survivor BabyCare didn't cause any of those incidents.

* * *

From: Bret Jetson
To: Johanna Wilborough
Re: The Vringla/Racket Incident

Dear Johanna,

I firmly have to turn down your offer to 'buy a human contract.' Times aren't that desperate, and let me assure you, we have perfectly good alternatives.

I also have to commend you for researching all the bleak rumors from post-invasion childcare history, and I have no doubt that you do it all for love of little Victoria.

Still, I ask that you bear in mind that the so-called Vringla/Racket Incident really was a most unfortunate coincidence. In fact, we usually refer to it as the Oatmeal/Micro Incident.

Let me ask you: How could anyone have suspected that the microwave used for heating oatmeal sounded just like the sonic weapons of the elite Vringla Screamer Corps? Surely a single incident with a war-traumatized nest daughter doesn't mean that every alien nanny on Earth is going to blow up loud household appliances with their plasma guns? (And to be totally fair, that particular model of microwave oven does produce an awful lot of noise.)

Johanna, there's nothing I'd like better than to put your fears to rest. Please, why don't we send over our most experienced nest daughter at a time of your choosing? You'll get the chance to shake appendages, try out the translator, and let little Victoria get used to the smell. Let me know what you think!

May Your Peace Last,
    Bret Jetson, Manager, Survivor BabyCare

P.S.: I've attached the remaining 50 case stories, plus a completely unbiased article debunking the Oatmeal/Micro Incident.

* * *

From: Bret Jetson
To: Johanna Wilborough
Re: Friday Afternoon Appointment

Dear Johanna,

I'm so pleased that you've chosen to try our services. Believe it or not, you were actually easier to convince than most people.

Nest daughter Sjkf (who will also react to the name Nanny) will be at your house on Friday at 5 p.m. You'll know her by our company badge. And the tentacles, of course.

May Your Peace Last,
    Bret Jetson, Manager, Survivor BabyCare

P.S.: I'm attaching a coupon code. If any of your friends are in need of an experienced babysitter, have them use this code when they contact us. You'll both get a whopping 25% off your next monthly fee!

* * *

From: Security Code #4512000P, a.k.a. "Johanna Wilborough"
To: Colonel José Jackson, Interstellar Affairs
Re: The Vringla/Racket Incident

Colonel,

I have confirmation that the Vringla have infiltrated the babysitting services!

Subject arrived on time, dressed in a skinsuit that would have fooled most operatives. It had the right smell, those swaying movements, and the slime trail. Had I not been suspecting a Vringla in disguise, I would have been more worried about my carpets than Victoria.

I killed it with a standard bug spray, but who knows how many other homes the Vringla have infiltrated? If they strike now they'll do more than eliminate our children. They'll have us lynching Sensibi scapegoats around the clock for the rest of the year, and then who's left to stop a second invasion?

We must launch a new investigation into the Vringla/Racket Incident immediately. It's highly plausible that an elite corps of Vringla Screamers has infiltrated the microwave oven manufacturing plant and that they're plotting to turn Sensibi babysitters into malicious killers.

However, the most worrisome news is the case stories from Survivor BabyCare. At first I mistook them for sheer sales desperation, until I realized I've never seen so many smiling families after the Vringla invasion or read so much high praise for the Sensibi. Clearly these families have been brainwashed and turned into fifth column Vringla servants. I recommend that they're immediately exterminated for the good of mankind.

Hunt them down!

Johanna

P.S.: Should any of these families have a contract with a human sitter, I'd be willing to make arrangements with her. It would be a shame if the families' tragic deaths resulted in the unemployment of a young woman.

A Trip to Lagasy

Barbara Davies

Quest stories are one of the major threads in the weft and warp of our storytelling existence. We love these stories because they often take us to exotic locations where protagonists must overcome numerous obstacles before they can achieve their goal. The Arthurian search for the Holy Grail is a classic quest story that has morphed through many retellings. L. Frank Baum's *Wonderful Wizard of Oz* (1900) and J. R. R. Tolkien's *Lord of the Rings* trilogy are well-known examples of literary quests. Where *Indiana Jones* gives us the learned archeologist venturing out into the field to fulfill an archeological quest, "A Trip to Lagasy" gives us a smart but stifled biologist, Kira Walsh, who traverses a foreign planet in a botanical quest for the rare strangler orchid.

Barbara Davies's short fiction has appeared in *Sorcerous Signals, Bash Down the Door and Slice Open the Badguy, Tales of the Talisman, Neo Opsis, Andromeda Spaceways Inflight Magazine* and *Marion Zimmer Bradley's Fantasy Magazine*, among other magazines and anthologies. A collection of her speculative fiction, *Into the Yellow and Other Stories*, is available from Bedazzled Ink. She lives in the English Cotswolds.

"You're late," said Kira. The appointment had been for an hour ago. *Not an auspicious start.*

"Sorry, Docteur Walsh." Joseph Rakouth didn't sound it though. He stood on her hotel bungalow's crumbling front step, shifting from one leg to the other and gazing at her with large, dark eyes.

He certainly looked the part of guide and tracker—wellworn khaki shorts revealed sturdy, hairy legs, and over one shoulder hung a longbow and quiver—but he wasn't her first choice. Unfortunately, and inconveniently, Marc Rasiraka, whose name had come highly recommended, had been unavailable.

Kira beckoned Rakouth into the sticky room—the air conditioning had broken down—and got down to business. "I'm looking for a plant unique to Lagasy. Some call it the Strangler Orchid."

"That plant is sacred to us," said the colonist, his expression wooden.

From what she had read, many things were sacred to Lagasians. Especially those supposed to house the souls of their ancestors. They spent more money on death and death-related celebrations than on living, and she had seen for herself, on the starship view screen during descent, the stone tombs that dotted the landscape.

"Will that be a problem?"

God knows she was getting tired of problems. The 'Ministry of Foreign Affairs'—too grand a term for Lagasy's one-man-and-his-dog outfit—had almost suffocated her with its red tape. Then there was the bored customs official at the dilapidated spaceport yesterday, who had amused himself by being obstructive.

Rakouth still hadn't answered her, so she guessed at the cause of his unease. "I'm not going to harm the orchid. I swear by my ancestors. Didn't your Tourism Bureau tell you? I'm with the Botanical Institute on New Terra. We adhere to strict rules and regulations. If you wish to see my accreditation and permits. . . ." She reached in her breast pocket and pulled out a document chip, before realising that he had no means to read it. That was another thing about Lagasy: the colony's technology was as outdated as its decaying infrastructure.

He waved the chip aside but his expression eased.

"I just want to collect some seeds," she continued, putting it away, "if there are any. Or take a small section of leaf or rhizome. Nothing that will hurt it."

He grunted. She took it as acquiescence.

"We got word of the sighting a year ago, from an amateur botanist in Lagasy on holiday. Without access to GPS . . ." Lagasy's comsats had fallen from orbit years ago ". . . his coordinates were too vague to be accurate, but I've marked the general area." She pulled out the crudely drawn map, smoothed it, and pointed to the red circle she had drawn. "I can also describe the kind of habitat—"

"I know this place well," interrupted Rakouth. "I saw the plant myself there a year ago. But it may no longer be there."

She cocked her head. "It might have died, you mean? I'll take my chances." She refolded the map and returned it to her pocket. "How long will it take to get there?" Without a flitter they would be forced to do this the old-fashioned way.

Rakouth thought for a moment. "Four days there, four back. . . . It will be hard going for you. Are you sure you wish to go?"

"I'm sure."

"Even though, with Rasiraka to guide him, the other botanist will get there first?"

She blinked. "What other botanist?" Had this all been a waste of time? It was true that, as long as the plant was saved for posterity, it didn't really matter which institute took the credit, but it would have been a feather in her cap. . . .

His gaze turned inwards. "Docteur Stig . . . No, Steger."

Kira felt as though she had been punched in the stomach. "Jules Steger?"

It was Rakouth's turn to blink. "You know him?"

"I used to," muttered Kira. "I used to know him very well indeed."

* * *

Five years earlier.

"Ah, there you are, Dr Walsh." Professor Frederick smiled and beckoned. "Come in. Sit."

Kira glanced at the magnificent view from his office's picture window—sunlight glinted off the Institute's herbaria, seed banks, laboratories, libraries, lecture theatres, and greenhouses—before sitting and turning her attention to the occupant of the other chair.

He was young, blond, and wearing khaki fatigues. Slightly too long hair gave his handsome features a boyish air, and he flicked it out of his eyes before returning her gaze and smiling.

"This is Dr. Jules Steger of our Collections Department." The professor arched an eyebrow at her and smiled. "You've probably heard of him."

Who hadn't? The Institute's 'golden boy.' The number of plants that bore Steger's name was testament to his success.

"Pleased to meet you." She held out her hand.

Steger shook it. His grip was pleasantly firm and didn't last longer than necessary. "Likewise, Dr. Walsh."

The professor steepled his long fingers and regarded her with a benevolent gaze. "I've been keeping an eye on your progress since you joined us, Dr. Walsh," he said. "Exceptional. But just lately it's been my impression that you're getting itchy feet, wanting to put some of that theory into practice."

She blushed. "Sorry, I didn't realise it showed."

He waved a hand. "No need to apologise. I'd be disappointed if you weren't. Which brings me to the reason I asked you here." He glanced at Steger and smiled. "Dr. Steger here is planning an expedition to Amphitrite. Dr. Vansen was to be his assistant, but last week, unfortunately, she decided—quite inconveniently, I might add—to leave us."

Kira had heard rumours to that effect. Some said that Helen Vansen and Jules Steger had been lovers on the recent expedition to Daphnis, but things had since soured between them. . . . She kept her tone one of polite interest. "Oh?"

"Headhunted by the Institute on Ixion," explained the professor. "You can see where that leaves us. One botanist short. So when Dr. Steger asked my advice about a suitable replacement—"

"Yes," said Kira, before he could finish.

* * *

Angry insect bites marred Kira's face and arms as she made her way between the blackbirches and crimsonoaks. She was hot and itchy, and uncomfortably aware that she smelled less than fragrant.

"Are you all right, Mademoiselle?" called Rakouth, who had stopped and was waiting for her on the other side of the river.

She settled her rucksack more comfortably—sleeping bag, medication, toiletries, folding latrine spade, mini-tent . . . it all added up—and panted across the rickety plank bridge towards him. "These bites are driving me crazy. Got any more of those leaves?"

He handed her some wilting green fronds he'd collected earlier, and watched her crush them and slather the pulp on her arms. At once, the itching lessened.

"Thanks."

A ripe conefruit plummeted past her head, and she looked up and saw a troop of grunters staring down at them. The little primates looked cute—they resembled the long extinct lemurs of Old Terra, but had six digits on each paw and much longer tails—but were known to be touchy. They made good if rather gamy eating though, and Rakouth's hand reached automatically for his bow before he let it drop—there was still plenty of meat left from last night.

Another conefruit plummeted, this time towards the guide, followed by a stream of urine and a cacophony of mocking grunts. Rakouth yelled and waved his fist, and with a last chorus of derision the troop scampered away through the branches.

Kira wiped the sweat from her forehead with the back of her hand. "How much further?" It seemed to have been uphill since morning.

"An hour more, maybe, then we'll make camp for the night."

She hoped it was by a waterfall. She could do with a bath and one of his tisanes. "All right."

They walked on, careful to avoid grunter droppings. Kira took several holopics, for the Institute's files and for herself. She was particularly taken with the red-speckled treelizards and the tiny, jewel-coloured dreamfrogs, whose hallucinogenic exudations were Lagasy's sole export these days. The forest was lush in these parts, thick with ferns, fungi, mosses, and orchids. Not *her* orchid though.

There was a little clearing up ahead, and protruding from a mound of earth in its centre was an odd-shaped rock. Around it, the earth had been swept clear of leaves. And on top of it, too neatly placed to be accidental, lay a fresh conefruit.

Rakouth halted by the rock, and Kira joined him. He reached in his pocket, pulled out a little fetish of grasses, leaves, and twigs, and laid it beside the conefruit. Then he closed his eyes.

An offering to some forest spirit? Or to an ancestor?

Kira rummaged around in the pocket of her shorts, found only a half eaten tube of sweets, shrugged, and placed it by the fetish.

When Rakouth opened his eyes again and saw her offering, his eyes crinkled at the corners and he gave a nod of approval.

"Rasiraka?" She pointed at the conefruit.

"Yes."

"Are we gaining on him?"

"No."

It was the third day and they had been finding the other guide's spoor since yesterday. It confirmed her fears. Steger was intending to beat her to the strangler orchid. The sighting had been reported nearly a year ago—no matter how rare, a single plant didn't merit its own expedition, so it was only now, with a team 'in the neighbourhood,' she'd had the chance to investigate—so why had he left it until now? Had he found out about her trip somehow, hacked into the Institute's comm. system, and resolved to even old scores?

She clenched her fists. "Are you sure there isn't a short cut?" She had asked the same question yesterday and the day before.

Rakouth gave her a reproachful look. "Not a safe one."

"Not even to save your precious plant?"

Her anger made him blink. She took a breath to calm herself. "Jules Steger isn't like me, Rakouth. He won't be as careful with your orchid as I would."

He frowned. "But he has permits—"

"Not through official channels, I'll bet. If you know the right people and have the credits you can buy anything these days."

The guide's eyes widened. "He would risk harming the orchid? That is taboo!"

"He'll do whatever it takes."

"I hope you are wrong," muttered Rakouth. Then his frown smoothed. "No matter. Marc will not allow harm to occur."

She raised her eyebrows. "I don't see how he can prevent it."

He studied her face. "There *is* a way to trim half a day off our journey," he said at last. "It is risky though." He scratched his stubbled cheek. "Very risky."

She grinned. "What are we waiting for?"

For a moment longer he hesitated then he nodded and set off walking. His voice wafted back to her from the gathering darkness, accompanied by the distant calls of the grunters. "Tomorrow then."

* * *

Five years earlier.

Kira and Steger had been collecting and cataloguing all day, but now it was getting too dark to see, so they'd retreated to their camp. Steger had chosen an idyllic spot for their tents, soothed by the waves breaking on the shore not far away.

"A good day," he said, the firelight reflecting off even white teeth. "Twenty new species, by my reckoning."

Kira looked up from the darteels she was preparing—the tasty little fish teemed in the archipelago's peaceful waters—and grinned. "It's like the Garden of Eden."

"And we're Adam and Eve?"

She laughed then saw that he was serious, and there was an invitation in his eyes. Attraction had been growing between them since they arrived on Amphitrite. And why not? They were young, with healthy libidos. And it was surely no accident that Steger had split the team and sent the rest of the botanists to explore the other islands. His propensity for seduction was well known. No woman was safe. But did she want to be safe?

Kira finished wrapping the darteels and nestled the leaf parcel in the hot embers of the fire.

"It'll take a while to cook." She wondered if he could see her blush in the firelight.

Steger's smile widened. "I'm sure we can find something to occupy ourselves with in the meantime."

* * *

Kira picked a leech off her leg and watched the knee-deep waters carry it away. It had rained overnight and Rakouth's short cut now involved scrambling down a muddy, steep-sided ravine, wading across the swollen stream at its base, and up the other side.

Perhaps this wasn't such a good idea.

She refilled her flask, resisted the urge to quench her thirst there and then, and added a purification tablet.

"Ready?" asked Rakouth.

She shoved the stopper back in the bottle and gave a reluctant nod.

If coming down had been bad, going up was worse. Rocky outcrops meant that in parts the slope was almost vertical. And though there were occasional tree roots and tangled vines to hang on to, lichen was slippery underfoot and the rucksack threatened to overbalance her at every step.

As she paused to catch her breath and ease the burning in her calves, she threw the more lightly burdened Rakouth, clambering like a mountain goat higher up, an irritated look. *This orchid had better be worth it.*

"Come on," called Rakouth, stopping to wait for her.

She sighed and began to climb once more.

She was almost at the top when the vine she was clinging onto came loose.

"Mademoiselle!"

She was too busy reacting to the sickening, tumbling fall to answer Rakouth's cry of alarm. Rocks skinned her knees and elbows, but the rucksack protected her back. It hampered her, though, and weighed her down. Something banged into her temple, addling her wits. She had enough presence of mind to grab another vine, which slowed her descent a little, and enabled her to get her feet under her, then a rock shifted under her sole. She snatched at a passing shrub, but its thorns sank deep into her palms and its roots pulled free. . . .

A tree root brought her to a painful, wrenching halt. It trapped her boot and twisted her left knee in ways the joint hadn't been designed for. As she caught her breath, head spinning, ears ringing, mentally cataloguing the bits of her that hurt, she heard Rakouth calling.

"Mademoiselle."

Harsh panting accompanied the sound of boots scrambling and rocks sliding. A pebble flicked her ear, then a brown hand clutched her shoulder. She tracked the arm to its owner.

"Are you all right?" Rakouth's eyes were anxious and guilt-filled.

"What does it look like?" An attempt to free her foot sent pain stabbing from knee to hip.

"Let me." He drew the sharp knife from his belt sheath and sliced through the root trapping her. As she eased herself clear, something crunched inside the knee joint; the pain made her feel light-headed and nauseous.

"I think I've damaged it," she managed.

"What?"

"My knee. It hurts like the devil."

"Can you still climb?" She followed the direction of his dismayed gaze to the rim of the ravine.

"I'm not sure. If I put my arm around your shoulders, maybe. . . ." But she dreaded putting any weight on her knee even as she suggested it. And when they attempted it she nearly passed out.

"This is no good," said Rakouth, after the third attempt. "I'll go for help."

Kira wiped the clammy sweat from her upper lip with the back of her hand. "But we're in the middle of nowhere." Why did this have to happen on such a backwater planet? Anywhere else she could have simply used her satphone to call for help.

"You forget. My colleague Marc Rasiraka is not far ahead of us."

With Steger. She didn't want him to see her like this. To her embarrassment, she found she was on the verge of crying.

"You have water, yes?"

Her shrug was half-hearted. Without waiting for permission, Rakouth unbuckled her rucksack and delved inside.

"Here." He handed her the water bottle, then a little box with bright markings on it: her first aid kit.

"Take some pain killers. Then splint your knee as best you can." He turned once more to peer up. "The sooner I go, the sooner I return."

"Go on then," she told him, angry that he seemed so eager to leave her, yet knowing he was right. Already her knee had swollen up. Soon the only way out of here would be if someone hauled her with ropes.

He looked at her. "I'll be back as soon as I can."

She nodded. Then he set off climbing and she watched him go.

* * *

Five years earlier.

"This isn't what I wrote." Kira frowned at the hardcopy of the Amphitrite report then at her boss. She indicated the list of flora discovered on Rhode—Steger had named the island after one of Amphitrite's children. "Half the discoveries were mine. More than half."

She was forever having to finish off things Steger left undone. He was easily bored and abhorred paperwork. She hadn't begrudged him that at first—he was brilliant, after all—but, as the days passed, she saw few signs of his brilliance. He spent as much time swimming or smoking dreampaste as he did recording new species, and in the evenings he liked to make love. At first she had been flattered by his attentions, but as disillusionment set in, she began to find excuses to avoid them, and by expedition's end she was too busy anyway trying to get her work finished by their scheduled departure date.

And now this!

She ran her eye down the index again, counting up the number of species from Rhode that should bear her surname. Only three had been attributed to her. An editing mistake on Steger's part or something worse? From the sinking feeling in her gut, she already knew.

"He does acknowledge your contribution," said Professor Frederick. He flicked to the last page and she saw that her name had been added almost as an afterthought.

Anger and indignation swelled inside her. "I can back up my claims. I still have my expedition notebooks."

"Oh dear." He looked troubled. "This is beginning to sound like déjà vu."

"It's happened before?"

He gave a reluctant nod. "Dr. Vansen claimed that Dr. Steger minimised her contribution to the Daphnis survey. It's why she left."

"I thought you said she was headhunted by the Ixion Institute."

"It seemed more tactful to put it that way."

She gaped at him. "Why on earth didn't you do something?"

He gave her an offended look. "Put yourself in my shoes, Dr. Walsh. It was her word against Dr. Steger's." He sighed. "What's more, he assured me that Dr. Vansen was merely acting from spite."

"Spite?"

"Their relationship ended acrimoniously."

"I see." She did. All too clearly. *He used me.* "So if I object, he'll make the same accusation against me."

Professor Frederick blinked at her. "You and he were. . . Oh dear. This is beginning to look like more than an unfortunate coincidence."

"It certainly is," she said grimly. "And you can't turn a blind eye this time."

"But what can I do without endangering the Institute's reputation?" He threw her a look of entreaty. "Think of the bigger picture, Dr. Walsh. You're young. There'll be other expeditions, other plants."

"This isn't just about the Institute, Professor. Or me, come to that. It's about integrity. Steger's a fraud, and if you keep letting him get away with this kind of behaviour—" She folded her arms. "I know a reporter."

His face paled. "You wouldn't." When became clear that she would, he began to pace. "I suppose . . . an internal inquiry," he said at last, halting. "And if Dr. Steger is found culpable, we'll let him go. Discreetly, of course."

* * *

Kira had lost track of the time—the fall had smashed her watch—but several hours must have passed because it was beginning to get dark and grunters were calling to one another from further along the ravine.

A scuttling sound by her ear startled her. As did the pair of tiny glowing red eyes. She grabbed the flashlight and clicked it on, and relaxed with relief when the beam of light caught a lizard scurrying away.

Rakouth should have been back by now. Perhaps Rasiraka wasn't where he was meant to be. Or perhaps he had refused to help. Or maybe Rakouth had left her to rot and was already on his way home.

She cursed herself under her breath. Pessimism helped no one. The guide would return for her soon. She had to believe that.

The throbbing in her knee had ebbed to bearable proportions, helped by the bandages and painkillers. She raised her flask to her lips and gulped down what she was dismayed to find was the last mouthful of water.

Wonderful! Now I'm going to die of thirst.

The grunters' calls had grown louder and the first of Lagasy's moons was climbing above the horizon when Kira faced up to the fact that her guide wasn't coming back. Not tonight, anyway. She would have to find some way out of the ravine on her own.

Her first attempt ended in her vomiting up what little she had eaten and drunk that day. Shaking with reaction, she curled in on herself and cried. But at last the tears dried, and her determination not to die here returned.

The dim light from Lagasy's second moon caught her inching upwards. Keeping the weight off her injured knee was exhausting, though. And at this rate it would take her days to reach the top.

What choice do I have? Teeth gritted, she grabbed hold of another vine and braced her good leg.

It was almost dawn when she could go no further. She huddled shivering in the shelter of a thorn bush, closed her eyes, and tried to sleep.

* * *

Warm sunlight on Kira's face woke her. She cracked open an eyelid then froze.

An orchid was growing in the shelter of the thorn bush a foot from her. Its three sepals and three petals were a bright rose-purple, and aerial roots dipped into a humus-filled crevice, drawing nourishment from it. But what struck her the most was the presence of corkscrewlike tendrils extending from the centre of the plant.

A Strangler Orchid. Here? Her heart hammered with excitement.

She was comparing her surroundings against the habitat checklist that she knew by heart and almost missed what happened next. The roots moved. How could they possibly move fast enough for her to see? This wasn't time-lapse photography. They did it again. Then the whole plant lurched across the humus. No more than half an inch, but it was enough.

This time her light-headedness was caused not by the pain in her knee but by adrenalin. What was it Rakouth had said? "It may not be there anymore." She had thought he was referring to the plant's short lifespan. But suppose he wasn't. Suppose the orchid was mobile.

It moved again. First, the roots lifted themselves free of the humus, then the tendrils stretched out, entwined themselves around anything they could find, and used it to tug the plant across the rocks.

She reached for her rucksack and for the next half an hour lost herself in taking holopics and measurements, recording every detail she could think of in her notebook. She was sorely tempted to take a small sample of plant material—they could use it to analyse the genes and propagate the species—but decided not to. The rules against destructive sampling had been drummed into her from her very first day as a botanist. It would be foolish in the extreme to risk damaging what might be the last surviving member of such a rare species.

The sun had shifted in the sky when a pebble bounced off her scalp. She stowed the notebook in her breast pocket and squinted against the sunlight.

Three men were descending the ravine towards her. One was Rakouth. The tall, dark-skinned one with the wide-set eyes and strong jaw must be Rasiraka. As for the other man in the khaki fatigues. . . .

She sucked in her breath. Jules Steger had put on a few pounds, but other than that he hadn't changed. Emotions she thought she had put behind her surfaced. Bitterness, hurt, anger. . . .

She remembered the orchid and felt the beginnings of panic, then calmed herself with the thought that he wouldn't be able to see it from his current position. As long as she did nothing to draw it to his attention.

"So you're the damsel in distress," he called as he drew closer. "Your white knight is here to rescue you." He flicked the hair out of his eyes and gave her an engaging smile, and she felt the familiar stir of attraction and clamped down on it.

The guides exchanged puzzled looks at his remark, then shrugged and scrambled down the few feet that remained. Rasiraka pulled a rope from his backpack and, after seeking Kira's permission, began to fasten one end of it round her chest, under her armpits. Rakouth helped him. Steger, meanwhile, leaned back against the cliff face and made himself comfortable. He began to whistle under his breath.

"Since when did the white knight sit around watching while someone else did the rescuing?" asked Kira.

"No point in having a dog and barking yourself." Steger sounded amused. But at least he had stopped whistling.

Pain spiked through her knee as she moved to allow the two guides better access. She hissed and clutched at it.

"Sorry, Mademoiselle," said Rasiraka. "Almost done."

She glanced at Steger again. "What are you doing on Lagasy?"

He yawned. "The same as you, I imagine."

Rasiraka finished securing the rope around Kira and climbed a little way up the ravine, paying out the rope behind him. Steger moved to one side to allow him past, then descended a few more feet. Now only the thorn bush blocked his view of the orchid—she hoped it would be enough.

Rasiraka stopped, turned around, and braced himself. "Ready?" he called.

Rakouth nodded. "Put your arm around my shoulders, Mademoiselle." She did so. "Can you stand?"

"I don't know." Her heart raced in anticipation of the pain. "My knee—"

The rope around her tightened, taking her weight.

"Lean on me," urged Rakouth.

She took a deep breath. "I'll try."

The rope lifted her another inch. With one guide pushing and the other guide pulling, this might work.

"What have we here?" The shock in Steger's voice made her turn. "It can't be!" He was bending over the thorn bush, reaching out a hand.

"Don't."

He was too engrossed in his discovery to hear Kira's warning. She watched as one of the orchid's tendrils brushed against his forefinger then coiled itself round the tip.

"So that's why they call it a 'strangler'," he murmured.

He raised his hand and the orchid rose with it. Aerial roots waved in the breeze and the tendril tried to uncoil itself. He clamped his other hand round it, holding it fast, and held it closer, nostrils flaring. "Quite a sweet scent."

By now, the guides had stopped their attempts to help Kira and were watching Steger's every move, their expressions tense.

"Docteur Steger," warned Rasiraka.

"What?" He didn't look round. "Oh, come on, Marc! You don't *really* believe this contains the soul of an ancestor, do you?"

The guide's lips thinned.

The orchid wrapped a tendril around Steger's neck. His eyes widened, and for a moment Kira thought she saw fear. *Wouldn't it be ironic,* she felt a surge of glee, *if it killed him in self-defence?* But he tore himself free easily, breaking off a piece of tendril in the process.

"Pick on someone your own size," he said. Then he laughed.

"Leave it alone," she snapped.

Steger looked thoughtful. "You weren't going to tell me about this, were you?"

She didn't answer.

He resumed his examination of the orchid, prodding its roots, brushing away the increasingly agitated tendrils. "It needs a proper name." His grin became sly. "Something with Stegerii in it."

"If you think I'm going to let you steal the credit—" She balled her hands into fists. "I've already attributed it. To the amateur botanist who found it."

"What he doesn't know won't hurt him. Besides, it seems a fair exchange. If I hadn't allowed my guide to come to your rescue. . . ." He held her gaze. Then the smile left his eyes. "You damaged my career, Kira. You owe me."

"*I* did?" She shook her head. "You brought it on yourself, Steger. You're a disgrace to our profession."

"Each to his own." He pursed his mouth. "In a way I suppose you did me a favour. It's much easier without all that red tape." He returned his attention to the orchid, held it high, and smiled. "This little beauty is going to restore my reputation."

She shifted her weight, and regretted it. Her knee felt as if it were on fire. "Look," she said desperately. "Why don't you share the credit? I've got all the holopics and measurements you'll need." She patted her breast pocket where the notebook nestled. "Put the orchid back and let's get out of here."

"No," said Steger. "It's coming with me."

"But it won't survive the trip!"

The two guides exchanged a glance she couldn't interpret, then Rasiraka started back down the ravine and Rakouth eased his shoulder from beneath Kira's arm.

Still engrossed with the orchid, Steger shrugged. "I have my drying and pressing equipment with me."

"You can't do that!" said Kira, horrified. "I gave my word I wouldn't hurt it. On my ancestors."

"I didn't. Hey!"

Rasiraka had snatched the orchid from him and was cradling it in his palms.

"What the hell do you think you're doing? I—"

But Steger never finished his protest, for by then Rakouth's grimy hands had shoved him off the ravine.

* * *

The echoing scream died away as Rasiraka set the orchid down, gently guiding its roots towards a suitable source of nourishment. They burrowed deep and the tendrils stopped their agitated waving as the orchid stilled and set about recovering from its ordeal.

Kira looked at the two guides, her heart thumping. "Am I next?"

They regarded her gravely. The silence stretched.

* * *

"It was an accident?" The Lagasian official's gaze was keen on Kira's face.

"Of course." She shifted her outstretched leg so the chair didn't dig into it—it would remain splinted until the bone and cartilage nanobots had had a chance to work their healing magic. "If Dr. Steger hadn't climbed down to help me. . . ." She shook her head. "He slipped on some lichen and fell. Didn't the two guides tell you?"

Her understanding with Rasiraka and Rakouth, to keep what really happened in the ravine to themselves, had seemed prudent, and fair exchange for rescuing Kira and taking her back to civilisation. The journey back had been fraught and painful, and tinged with self-doubt. If Steger hadn't wanted to get his revenge; if she hadn't taken that route up the ravine; if he hadn't behaved so callously towards the orchid and broken the taboo. . . .

So many ifs.

"I just needed your confirmation." The official jotted something in his notebook. His admission allowed her to breathe more easily.

A thought struck Kira. "Did he have any family?"

"Docteur Steger? Of course, Mademoiselle. A wife and two sons. They've asked for his body to be shipped back to Triton."

Poor things. She sighed and the official arched an eyebrow in query. "I'm sorry. I can't help but feel it was partly my fault."

He shrugged. "It was the will of the ancestors, Mademoiselle." He tucked his notebook in his pocket and sat back. "I understand you're leaving us?"

"Yes. I managed to get a berth on the starship leaving tomorrow."

He glanced at the holocamera and notebooks piled on top of her open suitcase. "You got what you came for? Your sample?"

She nodded. Neither guide had objected when she pocketed the small section of tendril that Steger had broken off. And even the Ministry of Foreign Affairs had agreed—after she'd filled out several forms and paid a substantial fee, of course—that it would be criminal to let such precious material go to waste. It was safely stowed amongst her clothes, wrapped in tissue paper and cotton wool, inside a cloth bag, inside a sturdy cardboard box.

"Very well." He stood up and smiled for the first time. "Have a safe trip, Mademoiselle. And I hope your next visit to Lagasy will be less ... eventful."

"So do I," said Kira feelingly. "So do I."

SATURN SLINGSHOT

David Wesley Hill

Sailors and pirates—"Arrr!"—are a natural pairing in many swashbuckling adventure stories. Traditional sea pirate stories were often inspired by the European merchant trade with the East and Spanish trade with the New World. During the 18th century, it took about six months for a merchant ship to travel from London to Calcutta via the Cape of Good Hope. Cargos therefore, had to be durable, portable, and valuable. Valuable cargos in heavily-laden, slow-moving cargo ships were a favorite prey of pirates and other brigands. Pirates and pirate stories made an easy transition to the emerging science fiction market, appearing in juvenile and adult science fiction stories. We saw pirates in the movies, on television, and in our SF literature. It did not matter if the protagonist was a pirate or fighting pirates, we always knew there would be a chase, a heroic struggle, and at the end, we would share the winner's exultation. Author David Wesley Hill delivers space pirates—"Jasper takes what Jasper wants"—as well as a hard science take on physics of planetary travel among the rings of Saturn.

David Wesley Hill is an award-winning writer with more than thirty stories published in the U.S. and internationally. In 1997 he was presented with the Golden Bridge award at the International Conference on Science Fiction in Beijing, and in 1999 he placed second in the Writers of the Future contest. In 2007, 2009, and 2011 Mr. Hill was awarded residencies at the Blue Mountain Center, a writers and artists retreat in the Adirondacks.

Serendipity was an old ship. For more than two centuries she had sailed the same slow course from the inner planets to the Jovian moons and out toward the Kuiper Belt, that clot of comets lying between Neptune and Pluto. There, after unloading cargo and picking up freight bound sunward, her crew would adjust *Serendipity*'s sail, align the spinning prismatic circle of Kapton[19(tm)] at an angle to the distant solar orb, and begin the decade-long spiral back toward the heart of the system. *Serendipity* had made eleven such round-trip voyages.

Like most of the crew Captain D'Angelo Jones had been born aboard her and had grown up within her slowly rotating tangle of corridors, cargo pods, and superstructure. Except for a brief period off wiving while *Serendipity* tacked above the Mars ecliptic to avoid the asteroid belt, Jones had spent his life inside the ancient vessel, and he knew her every sound, her every twitch and tremble, as well as he knew his own physical body. That long bass thrum was the tension of the vast sail against its rigging. The sad creaking pulsing in and out of audibility—that came from winches making microscopic alterations to the sail's trim, keeping *Serendipity* bearing straight, propelled by sunlight across the ocean of night.

His mother's cousin Leticia—Letty—was the lookout on watch. Her short black hair fanned in a curly halo around her dark features in the microgravity as her fingers flickered over the flat screen before her, scouring space around *Serendipity* with optical scanners and radar.

"Everything's clean for fifteen hundred klicks," she said.

"Leshawn?" D'Angelo asked.

His niece's second husband was at the weapons console. "Fore and aft cannons loaded with buckshot, D'Angelo. Lasers ready."

Beatrice had the helm. Unlike the others, Jones's wife was fair, with a complexion the color of milk and a ruff of hair as golden as corn. Her eyes were pale, pale blue. Beatrice had been born on Phobos, which had been settled by Europeans. "Orbital insertion in six minutes, two seconds," she said.

"Hold her steady."

They were skimming seventeen hundred kilometers above the rings of Saturn, a vast uneasy ocean that stretched below them into infinity.

Rivers of color, glinting silver and gold and crimson and umber, writhed into view and disappeared astern.

Saturn was off the starboard bow. Although it was still a hundred thousand kilometers distant, the immense brown and yellow hemisphere subtended a quarter of the sky.

Serendipity would approach Saturn within eighteen thousand klicks, entering a shallow orbit meant to fling her away into space like a stone from a slingshot. Only by leveraging such a gravitational assist from the gas giant could they hope to reach the Kuiper Belt. The efficiency of a solar sail was, unfortunately, directly proportional to its distance from the sun.

"Whole lot of debris ahead, D'Angelo." Letty studied her console. "Pebbles. A dozen pieces a meter in diameter."

"Range one thousand, two hundred eighty klicks," Leshawn said. "Locked on and standing by."

"Clear a path," Jones ordered.

The rings of Saturn were composed of rock, dirt, and ice, trillions upon trillions of pieces varying in size from particles of smoke to floating mountains. Most fell toward the low end of this spectrum. The rings surrounded the planet in a belt almost three hundred thousand kilometers in diameter yet they had an average thickness of a single kilometer and sometimes their width could be measured in hundreds of meters. Occasionally, however, plumes of debris would be knocked out of the rings, either by collision with other particles or simply through some peculiarity of gravitational interaction. This created navigational hazards for ships approaching the planet.

Leshawn triggered his weapons. Beams of coherent light lanced out. The debris in their path exploded into mist.

"All clear," he said.

"Beatrice?" Jones asked.

"Orbital insertion in four minutes, thirty seconds."

"Steady as she goes."

Jones gazed warily through the clear dome of the bridge out at the kilometers of sail, brilliant against the jet backdrop of space. Rock, dirt, and ice weren't the only perils facing the old ship during its traverse of Saturn. The rings were inhabited by tribes of piratical aborigines, the descendents of castaways, outcasts, and criminals, who enjoyed nothing better than hijacking passing solar sails, robbing them of cargo, and enslaving the passengers and crew.

These vermin lived in caves that they hollowed out in larger pieces of ring material. They mined iron, copper, lead, and other metals from the infinite expanse of detritus and refined the ore by hand, casting it into the machinery necessary to survive in vacuum. They breathed oxygen extracted from water ice through electrolysis, which also provided hydrogen to fuel their rockets. Since the sun at this distance was too feeble to support plant growth, they polished acres of ice to reflective smoothness, aligned these mirrors in huge fields, and concentrated the sunlight to an intensity sufficient for hydroculture. Even so protein was scarce in the rings. That was another reason the scum took captives.

Unfortunately, despite their primitive level of technology, the aborigines were a real danger. Over the years *Serendipity* had been attacked seven times during her passages of Saturn.

"More debris to starboard," Letty announced.

"Clear a path."

"Two minutes, six seconds."

"Hold her steady."

Serendipity, like most solar sails, was a freighter. Her cargo consisted of bulk goods and durable commodities, items that weren't sufficiently valuable to warrant the exorbitant cost of shipping aboard a fusion ship and whose worth wouldn't decrease during the long years of transportation by sail. She was carrying whiskey in bond from the Tarsus distilleries on Io, mining and manufacturing equipment, silk and wool from the Imbrium farms on Luna, and five thousand indentured servants from the urban warrens of Valles Marineris. These were enduring the long haul to the Kuiper Belt in suspended animation, frozen to within degrees of absolute zero. They were strung out behind the ship in translucent capsules that were open to vacuum, insulating their cargo from temperature variation but not providing much else in the way of amenities or safety.

On average 97 percent of such passengers survived the crossing alive and undamaged. One percent would die. Two percent would suffer freezer burn of varying severity.

"Twenty-two seconds to insertion. Twenty."

"Captain—"

The use of his title alerted Jones. "What is it, Letty?"

"Seven degrees to port. Range nine hundred and forty klicks."

"—Four seconds," Beatrice was counting down. "Three seconds. Two . . . one. We have insertion." His wife's hands fell away from the helm. *Serendipity* had made orbit.

"Eight hundred and twenty klicks," Letty continued. "Eight hundred and ten and closing." His mother's cousin shunted data from the optical scanners to the main display, giving them a view of a swarm of rock and ice fragments rising from the plane of the rings toward *Serendipity*. At this distance the instrumentation had a resolution of twenty meters. It was impossible to decide whether the scene was innocuous or whether it hid some greater danger. "Seven hundred and ninety and closing," Letty called out. "Relative velocity at point one klick per."

"Bring it up on infrared," Jones instructed.

Letty stroked the console, switching the view from the visible spectrum. In this mode space was dark blue. The chunks of ice and rock, scant degrees from zero Kelvin, were only slightly paler. Jones studied the image intently. Nowhere did he see a trace of green or red, yellow or orange, which would indicate living warmth and the presence of enemies.

Still he remained uneasy.

"Bearing?" he asked.

"Should cross our bow by eighty-six klicks."

"Too close," Jones muttered. He stared at the screen and then said to Leshawn, "Take out everything larger than a meter."

His niece's second husband nodded. "Aye, aye, D'Angelo."

Leshawn bowed over his board. Once more lasers lanced forth, the forward sections of the beams becoming perceptible each time they found a mark, momentarily delineated in the clouds of steam and dust generated by their impact with the swarm of debris hurtling from the rings. Again the lasers flicked out, creating a nimbus of subliming water and methane vapor mixed with chlorine and fluorine as well as with particles of carbon, iron, and nickel.

Velocity distorted the shape of the cloud into a comma kilometers long.

Then this cloud itself detonated, shooting streamers of brilliant fire, bright candles of furious white light fleeing from the maelstrom, and Jones felt a sick twist of tension settle inside his chest, understanding exactly what he was looking at, knowing that it had all been a ruse and that they were under attack. The damned savages had hidden their filthy makeshift rockets in the ring material and the sons of bitches were coming full throttle straight toward his ship.

Evasive action was out of the question. Clutched by Saturn's gravity, *Serendipity* would be unable to maneuver until she rounded the vast planet and was flung again toward deep space and the Kuiper Belt. The savages' timing was perfect.

Jones refused to allow emotion to enter his voice. "Fire at will," he said.

"Immediately, captain."

They carried projectile weapons against just such an eventuality. The three forward cannon were loaded with rounds of buckshot. Leshawn fired the guns, filling space ahead of *Serendipity* with a storm of pellets capable of penetrating the ice and metal out of which the primitives built their frail ships. Unfortunately, Jones knew, it wouldn't be enough. It never was.

He keyed on the intercom. "Now hear this. Now hear this. All hands to stations. *Serendipity* is under attack. Prepare to repel boarders."

Forty-six of the savages' tiny ships had been concealed among the rock and ice, shielded from visual and infrared detection. Three were destroyed within seconds. Four veered off on tangents at the mercy of malfunctioning control systems. The remaining thirty-nine ships continued on course despite the barrage of buckshot Leshawn threw at them.

At a distance of sixty kilometers their jets fired, braking their velocity relative to *Serendipity*. Letty pasted a close-up on the main screen, allowing a view of the lead vessel. Its fuel tanks, exhaust chamber, and attitude jets were fashioned from hand-beaten metal. The navigational and electrical systems, however, which were too complex for the savages to manufacture themselves, had been stripped from vessels they had robbed. The rest of the thing was a chunk of ice that had been crudely chiseled into shape, hollowed out, and pressurized.

The airlock was a pane of ice that had been frozen to the hull to create an atmosphere seal.

It shattered suddenly into a thousand shards, which fled away into space. Distant figures emerged from the ship through the portal now revealed. They fired their thrusters and burned toward *Serendipity*. Fighting would soon be hand-to-hand.

Jones thumbed on the intercom. "Engagement in seventy-three seconds."

Beatrice stood down from her console, went to the arms locker, and removed four épées—projectile weapons were, of course, useless at close quarters in microgravity since the recoil would send the shooter tumbling. She handed them out, keeping the last for herself, running the slim graphite blade through a lightning routine, the sword moving almost too quickly to see.

Then she went to Jones, her breath hot against his ear and the fine pale hair on her upper lip damp from exertion. "You must take care, my husband," she told him. "Come back to me. Promise me that you will."

Jones knew it would be useless to ask the same of her since Beatrice, like all Martians, was both fearless and merciless, God love her. Her lips brushed his. Then she pulled Jones's hood over his head and secured his faceplate before closing her own.

"Ten seconds to engagement," Letty counted down. "Eight."

Serendipity's sail was a round sheet of shimmering Kapton[19(tm)] 24 kilometers in diameter with a two-kilometer circular hole cut out of its center. Through this projected the main body of the ship, a complicated spindle almost three kilometers long. Joined to each other by shrouds of cable, both sail and superstructure were spinning with a period of 72 seconds. This rotation allowed the sail to maintain its shape without the need for supporting spars or masts, and also generated an artificial gravity of .3G within the ship itself, sufficient to prevent muscular atrophy and skeletal distortion among the crew during their lifetimes lived in space.

The bridge extended a hundred meters out from the deck on a spire that was in turn seated on gimbals, an arrangement that allowed it to remain stationary while the rest of the ship spun, providing Jones with a stable vantage point.

The crew—his family, each of them a relative by blood or by marriage—took up positions amidships, abaft of the sail and ten meters clear of the rotating complex of habitats and cargo containers, greenhouses, equipment sheds, hangars, and workshops that comprised the untidy bulk of *Serendipity*. Others took a stand at the bow, guarding the main portal into the vessel.

In the distance, now subtending a third of the sky, Saturn cast a yellow pall over the ship and the tiny figures defending her. Seventeen hundred kilometers away spread the strange and dangerous ocean of the rings, an insane kaleidoscope of chaotic geometry.

With appalling suddenness the savages burst through the sail.

Diminished by perspective, the holes they made coming through the Kapton[19(tm)] seemed no larger than pinpricks in comparison to the vast expanse of sail. But tension widened the punctures, splitting apart the edges in a visible process, the holes engorging into gashes hundreds of meters wide and hundreds of meters long. Only ripstops—seams of denser material overlaid on the Kapton[19(tm)] at regular intervals—prevented the sail from cleaving asunder.

Most of the invaders struck amidships directly at the crew. Many failed to bleed off their velocity, using themselves as human missiles, sometimes successfully, sometimes with suicidal results. Others hove to in a blinding flourish of personal rocketry to engage the defenders' graphite épées with their own cruder weaponry: maces, morning stars, and pikes of beaten iron, sabers of ice, and clubs and daggers of rock. Soon bodies were floating limply or thrashing while their fluids evaporated in the vacuum, the integrity of their suits fatally breached. Vaporizing blood cast the desperate scene in an incongruous pink glow.

Smaller parties of savages struck at the bow. One group jetted for the bridge. Jones readied his sword.

"Let's have at the God damned murdering sons of bitches," he snarled, enraged to blasphemy by what they were doing to his family and to his ship.

Beatrice struck the emergency lever, which blew out the airlock, evacuating the bridge of atmosphere. She launched herself into space in a tumble that made her impossible to target as she flew at the savages, careering into them in a deadly flurry and then rebounding at an angle, the tip of her épée crimson.

Jones headed toward the foremost of the approaching party, a tall figure in a black suit emblazoned with stylized skulls of iridescent orange and purple. The savage was wielding a quarterstaff of blue ice with iron spikes embedded in either end. He struck out with the weapon but Jones deflected the blow with the pommel of his sword, slithered the épée around the staff, and ran it into his opponent's throat, thinking that here was one God cursed barbarian who would see no profit from this day and from the attack on *Serendipity*. Without drawing breath, Jones leveraged the body to launch himself at another opponent. Out of the corner of his eye he saw Letty and Leshawn skirmishing with their own antagonists. For an instant he caught a glimpse of Beatrice, her pale features set in a feral grin, and then he was wrestling with another of the cannibals. The pirate slit a long gash in Jones's thigh before the épée slid through the bastard's heart.

Jones slapped a patch over his wound, stanching the discharge of blood and air.

Leshawn and Letty had bested their opponents. Beatrice was surrounded by three bodies. With a sidelong glance toward Jones, she sliced off an ear from each one and tucked the mementos away for safekeeping. Martians! He thought fondly, loving her ferocity as much as he feared losing her from the consequences of her bravery.

The flare of light from an igniting rocket overcame the softer glow of Saturn. While most of the savages had engaged *Serendipity*'s crew, others had been cutting cargo containers, hydroponics pods, and similar equipment free of the ship. They had bolted one-shot engines and primitive guidance systems to this booty and were now launching the stuff toward the rings, where others of their tribe were, no doubt, waiting to receive it. This, more than anything that had happened so far—this dismantling of his ship before his very eyes—infuriated Jones. Unable to find his voice, he gestured inarticulately for the others to follow his lead. Thumbing on his jets, he headed for the nearest group of pirates. The scum had detached a dozen suspended-animation capsules from their moorings and were about to consign them into the void.

They weren't after slaves, Jones knew, since the pirates lacked the technology to revive the frozen passengers. But it didn't take much skill to slice a steak.

Jones didn't bother to brake. He changed attitude until he was approaching feet-first and let momentum be his weapon.

The jolt of collision slammed through him from his boots to his teeth. His target came apart.

This effectively killed Jones's velocity. He lanced out with his épée at another savage but his adversary parried Jones's thrust with a meter-long cudgel. The riposte caught him just above the faceplate with sufficient force to send him tumbling head over heels into space.

Unconscious.

Three minutes went by before he came to. Choking. Coughing. Lungs on fire.

His mask was full of blood from a gash on his brow, a flurry of red globules joining and breaking apart and rejoining in an intricate dance, obscuring his vision and choking him.

There was too much fluid for his filtration system to handle. Jones knew he would drown in his own blood unless he took quick action. There was, unfortunately, only one thing he could do.

He had ten seconds in which to do it.

That was how long a man could remain conscious in vacuum.

Jones retched out the liquid he had inspired and screwed his eyes shut to prevent ice crystals from forming on them. Exposure to vacuum chilled the body as moisture on the skin evaporated.

He exhaled, emptying his lungs, and stretched his mouth wide open. This would prevent damage to his lungs when atmosphere rushed from them.

Not allowing himself time to think, Jones opened his visor, evacuating it of air. Vacuum bit his cheeks like a thousand needles. His nostrils and throat stung as air hissed from them. The blood fouling his helmet dried into flakes as it was blown out into space. The blood on his forehead congealed and sealed the gash.

Five seconds. Six.

Eight seconds passed before he got his helmet closed and flooded with atmosphere and he was able to breathe freely again.

When he looked around, Jones learned he was midway between the ship and the sail, heading toward the vast sheet at a velocity of five meters per second in a crazy somersault.

Careful bursts of his attitude jets steadied the spin and killed his forward motion. Three additional discharges sent Jones heading back toward *Serendipity*.

All communication channels were jammed with the mad static of conflict. It was impossible to tell what was going on and how the battle was progressing. Jones keyed on a priority override, which patched him through to Letty.

"D'Angelo, thank God you're alive."

"What's the situation, cousin?"

"We have them contained at the stern."

"I'll be there."

Jones oriented himself and triggered a long burn. *Serendipity* grew before him. Another burn sent him skimming sternward. A third bled his velocity and brought him to a stop relative to the ship. Not far away two groups were standing off from one another. Fifteen savages were left of the party that had boarded *Serendipity*. The remaining primitives were gathered in a defensive three-dimensional knot, arm-to-arm and arm-to-leg and head-to-toe, weapons outward, all except for three of their number, who floated forward of the main body. Each held a leash connected to a handcuffed crew member. The leashes attached to the tubing linking the prisoners' oxygen tanks to their helmets. A good tug would rip loose the hoses and kill the hostages.

"What are their demands?" Jones asked Letty.

She indicated a figure so lanky that it hardly seemed human, wearing a suit ornamented with swastikas and broken crosses done in blood-red. "That's their hetman. Jasper the Something. A charming conversationalist. He wants passage for himself and his men. All the bodies of their dead. The bodies of our dead, too. He didn't explain himself but it's not difficult to guess why. Oh, and Jasper expects a ransom. In bullion, if you please."

"Does he?" The anger building in Jones was so profound that it required all the control he had developed during his years of command to reply to Letty in an even tone. "Who are the hostages?"

"Kevin Milestone, third engineer. Jasmine Whitlock, first cook, you know her, she makes those wonderful greens. And—oh, D'Angelo, I'm sorry—they have Beatrice, too."

He heard the news as if from far away, as if it didn't matter. It didn't, not really, that's what he told himself, because he was *Serendipity*'s captain. All his crew were important to him, no single one any more valuable than any other. At least that was how it was supposed to be, and that was how it was, by God, even though the scum had his wife leashed by the throat.

Jones burned to within ten meters of the hetman, close enough to see the brilliant blue of Beatrice's eyes and the furious expression in them. He prayed she wouldn't do anything stupid but feared her courage would overcome her common sense. Martians were like that.

"I'm D'Angelo Jones, captain of *Serendipity*," Jones said. "Release your prisoners and you may live. I give you my word."

"You give Jasper nothing, sailor man," the hetman replied with a sneer. "Jasper takes what Jasper wants. Jasper takes your ship. Jasper takes your women. Jasper takes your dead to feed Jasper's children. Jasper is hetman. Jasper takes."

"You take nothing, hetman. Your people are fled. You're outnumbered. Give me one reason I should hold back from killing you."

"Jasper gives you three," the savage replied and tugged at the leash he held. Beatrice clutched at the hose with her bound hands, taking the strain, but even so the jerk loosened the tube from its coupling and a thin stream of air began jetting from the joint. Jasper laughed. "Maybe Jasper only gives you two reasons."

"What do you want?"

"That's better, sailor man. You listen to Jasper. You do as Jasper says. Maybe Jasper lets your people live."

Before the hetman could continue, however, Beatrice shrugged, blew Jones a kiss, and realized his worst fear. With a jerk of her shoulders, she intentionally ripped the hosing free from her own helmet. Then, disregarding the flooding forth of her life's air, she drew a knife from an ankle sheath, whipped the blade up, and plunged it into her captor.

Jasper died.

As he did, however, his mace caught Beatrice square in the face. Her mask shattered. Atmosphere rushed from her helmet into space.

Hoping that she'd had the presence of mind not to hold her breath, which would have ruptured her lungs beyond repair, Jones thought, Ninety seconds.

That was how long Beatrice would survive before vacuum killed her. She would be unconscious in ten.

Jones took out the nearest pirates with two quick thrusts. The rest of his crew burned past and fell on the remaining savages but Jones didn't spare them a glance. He had to reach Beatrice. She was being carried off into space in a mad spiral by the atmosphere jetting from her tanks.

Eighty seconds. Somehow he managed to maintain the countdown in his mind while concentrating on catching her. Seventy-five.

He burned full throttle but couldn't get near. The squirming tubing on her back altered her bearing by the second and it was as if she were purposely evading him. Not until her tanks exhausted themselves was Jones finally able to reach his wife.

Sixty seconds.

Beatrice was unconscious. Her complexion, even in the dim yellow wash of light afforded by Saturn, was becoming flushed a brilliant red as the capillaries beneath her skin ruptured in the vacuum.

Jones sent them both hurtling back toward the ship with a continuous burn, keeping up the acceleration until his propellant ran out. He thumbed on the priority override and reached Letty.

"We're coming in at velocity," he said. "I'm out of fuel. Be ready to catch us."

"Aye, aye, captain."

Serendipity drew nearer with appalling inertia. Each instant cut

Jones like a razor. He held Beatrice in his arms, cursing her bravery, her God rotted courage, the very qualities that made him love her with such agonizing passion.

Thirty seconds.

"We have you in sight, captain."

Slowly, all too slowly, *Serendipity* swelled in bulk, fleshing out into the untidy convoluted structure that it was. A hundred-meter boom was maneuvering a wide-mouthed cargo net into place at their estimated point of impact.

"Don't get it wrong, Letty."

"We won't, captain. I swear it."

Then everything happened at once.

For a frightening moment Jones thought they would miss the net but they entered it cleanly and continued straight into the webbing, which lacerated their suits but had enough elasticity to kill their momentum without killing them.

Fifteen seconds.

Gas sprayed freely around them from a dozen cuts as the boom brought the net to the hull, where Letty and some other sailors were waiting with a medical tent.

Five seconds.

Jones wrestled Beatrice inside the transparent envelope and flooded it with a mixture of pure oxygen and helium. As the tent expanded with atmosphere, he plunged his arms into the flexible sleeves provided for them and clamped tubing to her femoral artery, drawing her blood through a scrubber chamber, which oxygenated and pressurized the fluid before pumping it back into her. Then he applied a defibrillator to her chest.

Her body jerked at the shock but failed to continue moving on its own.

Zero seconds.

Jones charged the device and shocked her again. Still Beatrice failed to breath. Nor did a third application of current cause her heart to beat.

It was then that Jones knew he had been too late. He had lost her.

"Captain—"

He refused to remove his eyes from Beatrice's face.

"What is it?"

"You're losing atmosphere."

He shrugged an emergency suit over his torn one and accepted a fresh set of tanks. Still Beatrice lay motionless.

"Status?" He heard his own voice as if from a distance.

"Twelve confirmed dead. Twenty-two injured. We're still estimating damage."

Jones allowed his gaze to drift from the unmoving form of his wife to the looming titan that was Saturn. Strangely his rage was directed not at the savages, not at Jasper, the hetman, but at the vast planet *Serendipity* was approaching, as if it were itself responsible for all this tragedy. If he could, he would have grabbed the world down from the sky and shattered it in his fist. But he was only human.

Jones let out a breath and turned away from Beatrice. He was also captain, by God, with responsibilities that outweighed his personal concerns.

"Well?" he roared to the assembly around him. "What are we waiting for? Let's get this damned vessel in shape. Letty—detail repair and salvage squads. You there, cousin, I want the bridge pressurized and operational within the hour. Leshawn? Where the hell is Leshawn?"

"D'Angelo . . ."

His name came to him so softly that at first he thought he was imagining she had spoken. Then she said his name again.

Monitor lights that had been dark were now flickering as they reported physiological activity. Beatrice's eyes were open, bloodshot and crimson. Her face was a single ugly bruise but beautiful to him. The swell of her breast as she breathed was the most wonderful thing he had ever seen.

He pressed his cheek against the transparent canopy separating them, unable to speak. Beatrice stretched up an arm and stroked the material with her fingertips as if it were his skin that she was caressing. In spite of her mask of pain, her smile was as mischievous as ever.

"Did I not tell you to take care," she whispered, referring to the gash across his forehead, her voice incongruously squeaky because of action of the helium. "D'Angelo, my love, why do you never listen to me."

Somehow she found the insouciant strength to wink. His heart breaking, Jones raised his head and regarded the crowd of sailors—of family—that was, despite orders, still gathered around them.

"God curse it, haven't any of you work to do?" he growled.

No one answered. No one moved, either. Then, suddenly, Jones just had to laugh, he couldn't help it, the laughter exploding from him. Soon everyone was laughing with him, in spite of everything, in spite of those they had lost forever, because at this moment they were alive and that was indeed very good. For now they would laugh.

"Get on with you," he muttered and took his wife, tent and tubing and life support equipment and all, into his arms and began heading for an airlock.

Now subtending fully two thirds of the sky, Saturn was immense beyond comprehension, her rings an ocean of so much panorama that it hurt to regard them.

Soon they would be on their way past her, assisted onward by the gravity of the gas giant toward the Kuiper Belt. By God, Jones marveled, it was good to be alive and to be a sailor!

ABOUT THE ANTHOLOGIST

Bascomb James (bascombjames.com) earned his Ph.D. degree from the University of Notre Dame and was a post-doctoral fellow in the NIH Laboratory of Persistent Virus Diseases. As a clinical virologist, he authored or edited four virology books, wrote a hat-full of scientific papers, and presented countless scientific lectures and workshops. A science-fiction fan since childhood, Bascomb credits his interest in science, engineering, and invention to the sci-fi stories he read as a child. Stories matter. They really do.

Coming Soon
from World Weaver Press

Alien Ways

a Darci Salazar SF mystery
David J. Rank

The trick to working with drug-addled aliens is not to lose your head…

2130: Great Lakes Metro polity amalgam, Chicago District. Aliens love to come vacay on Earth — where else in the glaxia can they find such a unique abundance of legal addictive compounds or as thriving a drug trade?

One ex-galactic-diplomat with the Bureau of Alien Affairs, Darci Salazar, eeks out a poco living as a freelance consultant for extra-terrestrials. These days she mostly finds ET's lost luggage and tries not to drink herself to sleep each noche, until fuzzy, blue alien royal hires her with a simple instruction: "Find my husbands…" and starts Darci on an investigation that will rapido lead her into Earth's sex slave trade, a string of brutal murders, interplanetary conspiracy, and serious attempts to remove Darci's head.

Full of quirky, colorful aliens and Darci's snarky wit, *Alien Ways* is a fast-pace, 22nd century take on the hardboiled detective story.

Coming Summer 2014

FAE

AN ANTHOLOGY OF FAIRIES

Edited by Rhonda Parrish

Meet Robin Goodfellow as you've never seen before, watch damsels in distress rescue themselves, get swept away with the selkies and enjoy tales of hobs, green men, pixies and phookas. One thing is for certain, these are not your grandmother's fairy tales.

Fairies have been both mischievous and malignant creatures throughout history. They've dwelt in forests, collected teeth or crafted shoes. *Fae* is full of stories that honor that rich history while exploring new and interesting takes on the fair folk from castles to computer technologies to modern midwifing, the Old World to Indianapolis.

Fae bridges traditional and modern styles, from the familiar feeling of a good old-fashioned fairy tale to urban fantasy and horror with a fae twist. This anthology covers a vast swath of the fairy story spectrum, making the old new and exploring lush settings with beautiful prose and complex characters.

Coming July 2014

SHARDS OF HISTORY

a fantasy novel by
Rebecca Roland

Malia fears the fierce, winged creatures known as Jeguduns who live in the cliffs surrounding her valley. But when she discovers an injured Jegudun, Malia's very existence—her status as clan mother in training, her marriage, her very life in the Taakwa village—is threatened by her choice to befriend the intelligent creature. But will anyone believe her when she learns the truth: the threat to her people is much bigger and much more malicious than the Jeguduns. Lurking on the edge of the valley is an Outsider army seeking to plunder and destroy her people, and it's only a matter of time before the Outsiders find a way through the magic shield that protects the valley—a magic that can only be created by Taakwa and Jeguduns working together.

"A must for any fantasy reader."
—*Plasma Frequency Magazine*

"Fast-paced, high-stakes drama in a fresh fantasy world. Rebecca Roland is a newcomer to watch!"
—James Maxey, author of *Greatshadow: The Dragon Apocalypse.*

"One of the most beautifully written novels I have ever read. Suspenseful, entrapping, and simply... well, let's just say that *Shards of History* reminds us of why we love books in the first place. *Five out of five stars!*"
—Good Choice Reading

Available in ebook and paperback now.

*White as snow, stained with blood,
her talons black as ebony...*

OPAL
a novella by
Kristina Wojtaszek

The daughter of an owl, forced into human shape...

"A fairy tale within a fairy tale within a fairy tale—the narratives fit together like interlocking pieces of a puzzle, beautifully told."
 —Zachary Petit, Editor *Writer's Digest*

In this retwisting of the classic Snow White tale, the daughter of an owl is forced into human shape by a wizard who's come to guide her from her wintry tundra home down to the colorful world of men and Fae, and the father she's never known. She struggles with her human shape and grieves for her dead mother—a mother whose past she must unravel if men and Fae are to live peacefully together.

"Twists and turns and surprises that kept me up well into the night. Fantasy and fairy tale lovers will eat this up and be left wanting more!"
 —Kate Wolford, Editor, *Enchanted Conversation Magazine*

Available in ebook and paperback now.

ALSO FROM WORLD WEAVER PRESS

Wolves and Witches
A Fairy Tale Collection
Amanda C. Davis and Megan Engelhardt

Beyond the Glass Slipper
Ten Neglected Fairy Tales to Fall In Love With
Some fairy tales everyone knows—these aren't those tales.
Edited by Kate Wolford

The King of Ash and Bones
Breathtaking four-story collection
Rebecca Roland

The Haunted Housewives of Allister, Alabama
Cleo Tidwell Paranormal Mystery, Book One
*Who knew one gaudy Velvet Elvis
could lead to such a heap of haunted trouble?*
Susan Abel Sullivan

The Weredog Whisperer
Cleo Tidwell Paranormal Mystery, Book Two
*The Tidwells are supposed to be on spring break on the Florida Gulf Coast,
not up to their eyeballs in paranormal hijinks… again.*
Susan Abel Sullivan

Heir to the Lamp
Genie Chronicles, Book One (YA)
*A family secret, a mysterious lamp, a dangerous Order with the mad desire
to possess both.*
Michelle Lowery combs

Specter Spectacular: 13 Ghostly Tales
Anthology
Once you cross the grave into this world of fantasy and fright, you may find there's no way back.
Edited by Eileen Wiedbrauk

Glamour
Stealing the life she's always wanted is as easy as casting a spell. (YA)
Andrea Janes

Forged by Fate
Fate of the Gods, Book One
After Adam Fell, God made Eve to Protect the World.
Amalia Dillin

Fate Forgotten
Fate of the Gods, Book Two
To win the world, Adam will defy the gods, but his fate rests in Eve's hands
Amalia Dillin

Beyond Fate
Fate of the Gods, Book Three
The stunning conclusion, coming September 2014
Amalia Dillin

Tempting Fate
Fate of the Gods Novella, #1.5
Mia's lived in her sister's shadow long enough
Amalia Dillin

The Devil in Midwinter
Paranormal romance (NA)
A handsome stranger, a terrifying monster, a boy who burns and burns...
Elise Forier Edie

Cursed: Wickedly Fun Stories
Collection
"Quirky, clever, and just a little savage." —Lane Robins, critically acclaimed author of MALEDICTE and KINGS AND ASSASSINS
Susan Abel Sullivan

A Winter's Enchantment
Three novellas of winter magic and loves lost and regained.
Experience the magic of the seson.
Elise Forier Edie, Amalia Dillin, Kristina Wojatszek

Legally Undead
Vampirachy, Book One—*Coming May 2014*
*A reluctant vampire hunter, stalking New York City
as only a scorned bride can.*
Margo Bond Collins

Blood Chimera
Blood Chimera, Book One—*Coming 2014*
Some ransoms aren't meant to be paid.
Jenn Lyons

Virgin
Paranormal/Urban Fantasy (YA)
Coming Fall 2014
Jenna Nelson

He Sees You When You're Sleeping
A Christmas Krampus anthology
Coming Holiday 2014
Edited by Kate Wolford

For more on these and other titles visit WorldWeaverPress.com

World Weaver Press
Publishing fantasy, paranormal, and science fiction.
We believe in great storytelling.

28722213R00158

Made in the USA
Charleston, SC
20 April 2014